P9-DOA-334

"Trust me."

Chloe laughed. "Did you ever play that game?"

"What game?"

" 'Trust me.' " The mattress flexed under him as she rolled onto her back, away from the edge. He inhaled her familiar almond-blossom smell; he felt her warmth filling the space between the bottom and top sheets. He commanded his body not to respond.

"The way it worked was, the boy would touch the girl somewhere—say her stomach—and say, 'Trust me?' And if she said yes, he'd inch his hand higher and say, 'Trust me?' And each time she said yes, he'd move his hand closer to her breasts."

Will took a moment to digest this. As games went, it wasn't much; but it sure sounded like great foreplay.

ABOUT THE AUTHOR

With twenty-five American Romance novels to her credit, Judith Arnold is one of the series's premier authors. Her versatility and uncanny ability to make us laugh and cry have become her hallmarks. In *Trust Me,* she takes us on a hilarious adventure that will have you reeling right along with Chloe Verona and Will Turner. Judith, her husband and two young sons make their home in Massachusetts.

Books by Judith Arnold

Don't miss any of our special offers. Write to us at the following address for information on our newest releases.

Harlequin Reader Service
P.O. Box 1397, Buffalo, NY 14240
Canadian address: P.O. Box 603,
Fort Erie, Ont. L2A 5X3

JUDITH ARNOLD

TRUST ME

Harlequin Books

TORONTO • NEW YORK • LONDON
AMSTERDAM • PARIS • SYDNEY • HAMBURG
STOCKHOLM • ATHENS • TOKYO • MILAN
MADRID • WARSAW • BUDAPEST • AUCKLAND

If you purchased this book without a cover you should be aware that this book is stolen property. It was reported as "unsold and destroyed" to the publisher, and neither the author nor the publisher has received any payment for this "stripped book."

D.M.—This one's for you

Published March 1992

ISBN 0-373-16431-9

TRUST ME

Copyright © 1992 by Barbara Keiler. All rights reserved. Except for use in any review, the reproduction or utilization of this work in whole or in part in any form by any electronic, mechanical or other means, now known or hereafter invented, including xerography, photocopying and recording, or in any information storage or retrieval system, is forbidden without the permission of the publisher, Harlequin Enterprises Limited, 225 Duncan Mill Road, Don Mills, Ontario, Canada M3B 3K9.

All the characters in this book have no existence outside the imagination of the author and have no relation whatsoever to anyone bearing the same name or names. They are not even distantly inspired by any individual known or unknown to the author, and all incidents are pure invention.

® are Trademarks registered in the United States Patent and Trademark Office and in other countries.

Printed in U.S.A.

Prologue

"Trust me, Chloe—you're going to love him."

"Yeah, sure," Chloe muttered. "I don't know why I said yes. I hate blind dates."

"But you're going to love Will Turner."

Chloe plucked her tortoiseshell hairbrush from the array of cosmetics and costume jewelry covering the surface of her vanity table, and plowed the bristles through her shoulder-length mop of brown curls. "What makes you so sure I'm going to love him?"

"He's smart and funny—"

"Funny?" Chloe snorted. "He invited me to go to the opera. Only serious people go to operas."

"You're going to the opera with him," Adrienne pointed out. "Does that make you serious?"

"It makes me stupid. I thought he was talking about going out for a beer. It wasn't until after I'd said yes and hung up the phone that I realized he'd said *Lohengrin,* not Lowenbrau." Chloe groaned, as annoyed by the prospect of her impending date as she was by her unruly hair. "The opera. I'm going to have to sit there for hours while a bunch of Vikings in helmets belt out songs in incomprehensible languages. Ugh. I'm going to hate him."

"No you aren't. He's a great guy."

"If he's so great, how come he has to resort to blind dates?"

"He only moved to Boston a few months ago. He doesn't know too many people in town yet." Noticing Chloe's haphazard groping as she searched her table, Adrienne located a matching tortoiseshell comb half-hidden by a paisley silk scarf and handed it over. "*You're* a wonderful person, and you're going on a blind date."

"With dire misgivings," Chloe reminded her. "With grave doubts about the sanity of the entire thing." Her comb was as ineffective as her brush. She tossed it down and raked through the curls with her fingertips.

"Don't be so negative. You're going to have fun tonight. Will is a nice guy. He's very handsome—"

"Looks aren't everything."

"Uh-huh. That's why you've just spent the last twenty minutes fixing your face in that three-way mirror."

Chastened, Chloe spun around on her stool. "Okay, so he's handsome. He's thirty years old and single. No handsome guy makes it to thirty without getting married, unless there's something wrong with him."

"You're twenty-eight, pretty and single," Adrienne pointed out.

"There's definitely something wrong with me. If there weren't, I wouldn't be going on this ridiculous date." She rose and padded in stocking feet to the closet, where she pulled out a black sheath. "This isn't too short, is it?"

"No, you always look fantastic in short skirts."

"Because I don't want him to think I'm easy or anything." Chloe pulled the dress over her head and poked her arms through the sleeves. "He's not an artist, is he?"

"No," Adrienne said. "He does something in publishing, I think."

"Because I've had it with artists." She stepped into her shoes and crossed the room to her dresser to fill her matching envelope purse. "What does he do in publishing?"

"Why didn't you ask him when he called you?"

"How could I ask him? He said, 'I got your number from my old school buddy. I understand you're a good friend of his wife's. You want to go to *Lohengrin* Friday night?' and I'm supposed to say, 'Yes, but only if you aren't an artist, because I'm sick to death of artists.'"

"You could have come up with a more discreet phrasing, but sure, why not?"

"He probably already thinks I'm a loser because I accepted his date. I don't want him thinking I'm a nut case, too."

"He doesn't think you're a nut case *or* a loser."

"What *does* he think I am?" It dawned on Chloe that Will Turner might have pumped Adrienne and her husband just as relentlessly about her as she was pumping her friend about him. "Did he ask about me? What did Scott tell him? What is he expecting?"

"A poised, attractive, self-confident woman."

"Great," Chloe moaned. "In other words, you lied through your teeth." She lifted a bottle from her vanity, uncapped it, inhaled and wrinkled her nose. "This perfume is too musky. If I wear it he'll think I'm hot to trot."

"Do you have a lighter scent?"

"All I have is what my Aunt Mathilda gave me for Christmas." She lifted the bottle again, sniffed, and put the stopper back in place. "Aunt Mathilda is very earthy. Unlike me."

Ordinarily, Chloe was supremely poised and self-confident, and while she wasn't fashion-model gorgeous, she was generally satisfied with her looks. But accepting a blind date was a major gamble. There was enough of a chance of winning to infuse her with hope, but the odds were stacked against her, and she couldn't help feeling like a ninny for having wagered her faith in a game she was bound to lose.

"This whole thing is a mistake," she grumbled, snapping her purse shut with a mournful click. "I've never had any luck with blind dates. Tonight's going to be a disaster."

"It's going to be fun," Adrienne insisted, rising and giving Chloe a hug to bolster her. "You're going to have a wonderful time. Trust me."

"TRUST ME, WILL—you're going to get her into bed."

Will's gaze traveled from the tickets in his hand to Scott, who was busy folding his squash clothes into his bag. Freshly showered and invigorated from the competition of their hour-long set, Will had hoped to head off for his date with Chloe Verona full of energy and optimism. But every time he thought about spending four hours listening to Wagner in the company of some unknown woman, his spirits plummeted.

"What makes you so sure I'm going to get her into bed?" he asked apprehensively.

Scott chuckled. "Hey, it's not like she's promiscuous or anything. She's a nice woman, really. But she hasn't dated anybody in a long time..."

Translation: She's a geek.

"...And she hasn't gotten any lately, if you know what I mean..."

A sex-starved geek.

"...And you're going to show up at her door, waving around these tenth-row-center orchestra tickets that you spent a fortune on—"

"I didn't spend a fortune on them. You gave them to me."

"Because a client of mine gave them to me, and I thought you could get more mileage out of them than I could. I'm telling you, Will, she's going to think you spent all that money on her and, presto! Putty in your hands."

A sex-starved, gold-digging geek. "Come on, Scott—I want to be prepared. What's wrong with her?"

"Nothing. Really."

"Is she neurotic?"

"Not that I've ever noticed. I haven't seen her medical records, so I can't say for sure."

"Is she one of those biological-clock maniacs, desperate to get married?"

"That's probably a couple of years off. She hasn't turned thirty yet."

"How come she happened to be free on a Friday night?"

"You were free on a Friday night."

"I'm new in town."

"And she broke up with her boyfriend last New Year's, and I guess she hasn't hooked up with anyone new yet."

A sex-starved, gold-digging, brokenhearted geek.

"Do you have her address?" Scott asked as they left the club.

Will nodded. "Some ritzy building overlooking the Charles River. I mean, what is she, a yuppie?"

"That's an outdated term. What she is is a successful professional woman."

"Whatever she is, if she makes one crack about my van—"

"She should," Scott remarked, eyeing Will's trusty old Dodge. "That thing is ugly."

"That's not the point," he said defensively. Scott's use of the word "ugly" triggered fresh misgivings. "What does she look like?"

"I've already described her a hundred times."

"I'm worried, Scott. Talk me down."

"She's very nice-looking. Dark brown hair—sort of frizzy, down past her shoulders. Brown eyes. A square jaw."

Will grimaced.

"Like Maria Shriver's."

Okay. I can live with that.

"About five-six, five-seven. Slim. Long legs."

Sounding better. "Exactly how long are her legs?"

"Long. The rest of her body isn't so bad, either."

"You've seen her body?"

"I'm a married man," Scott said indignantly. "On the other hand, I can use my imagination."

"You've used your imagination on her?"

"She's got that kind of body. She dresses like an accountant, but—well, she *is* an accountant, so what do you expect?"

Pinstripes. A necktie. Sensible shoes. "This is a mistake. I should never have let you talk me into this."

"Relax. You're going to have a great time."

"I don't even like opera."

"The hell with the opera. She's going to think you're cultured and extravagant, and she's going to fall at your feet. It's an easy score, Will. Trust me."

Chapter One

Will Turner was waiting for her. Six floors below, in the lobby of her building.

Chloe thanked the doorman, hung up the intercom phone and took a deep breath. She glided across the living room, directly to the carved mahogany humidor at the center of the mantel. Opening it, she pulled out a polished marble chip and rolled it between her fingers. Almost immediately the smooth, cool stone soothed her.

Some people had worry beads; Chloe had her humidor, the only asset her mother had bequeathed her. Yet she wouldn't have traded the box of marbles, pebbles, beach glass and shells for all the money her mother had left Orin.

After dropping the chip back into the humidor, she replaced the ornately carved lid and turned toward the door. She pulled on a peacock-blue blazer, gave her flyaway curls a final preening with her fingers and marched out of her apartment with all the gusto of a doomed prisoner heading for the gallows.

It was only one evening, she reminded herself, and she was going to spend it in the company of an allegedly handsome, smart, funny man who happened to be a friend of the husband of a friend. She had no reason to be anxious.

You have all the reason in the world, girl, she thought. *Blind dates are for the birds....*

Bad attitude. Clear your head. Slap on a smile. You can survive this.

With feigned self-assurance she rode the elevator to the ground floor. She took a deep breath and emerged from the car, as prepared as she would ever be to meet her fate.

Her fate stood near the doorman's desk, his posture relaxed, his hands shoved into the pockets of his pleated brown slacks, his perfectly horizontal shoulders shaping his jacket, his moccasin-stitched loafers well broken-in and his beige necktie knotted crookedly, with one end hanging a good two inches lower than the other. Gritting her teeth, she steered her focus higher, above his textured brown shirt and his lopsided tie, to his face.

Oh, God—he's cute!

Not quite handsome, not matinee-idol-magnificent, but...yes, indeed, this man was cute. His face was an ideal match for his lanky physique and his casually fashionable attire. He wore his glossy reddish brown hair parted on one side and swept across the crown of his head, with a few stick-straight strands flopping adorably over his brow. He had a high forehead, a long, narrow nose that wasn't quite as straight as the part in his hair, an equally long, narrow chin, thin lips that spread in a tentative smile, appealingly gaunt cheeks, and eyes as clear and sparkling as blue topaz.

He couldn't be thirty. He looked like a college kid. That must be it—he was there to visit someone else. Chloe's blind date was hiding behind the pillar, dressed in a tux—and a black cape lined in red satin, with a stand-up collar. He was lurking behind the pillar, sharpening his fangs with a steel rasp....

"Chloe Verona?" the blue-eyed man inquired, straightening up and pulling his hands from his pockets.

She fingered her pearls and nervously returned his smile. "Will Turner?"

He approached her as she approached him, their right hands extended before them like fencing foils. Will's fingers were long and thin, like the rest of him. He had a firm, friendly handshake.

He seemed much more confident than Chloe. His palm wasn't anywhere near as clammy as hers. Maybe he went on blind dates all the time. He probably attended the opera once a month; he didn't think it was worth dressing up for. Chloe wondered whether she was overdressed. Or underdressed, for that matter. She should have worn something longer. He was staring at her knees.

He lifted his gaze from her legs back to her face. A soft chuckle escaped him. "Well, I don't know about you, but I'm relieved."

She smiled through her anxiety. "What were you expecting?"

He chuckled again. "I'm not sure. You never know with these things."

"How true." How trite. If only she could send him some wit, some sparkling conversational gambits.

He gestured toward the double glass doors that led out to the circular driveway in front of her building. "Well, shall we?"

"Okay."

They exited, Will gallantly holding the door for her. "My car's over there," he said, indicating a maroon van with fake wood paneling on the sides, parked in one of the visitor spaces along the driveway. It looked like the sort of vehicle a suburban housewife in a car pool would drive.

A suburban housewife whose husband had recently done time on the unemployment line. The van was at least eight years old, mud-spattered and missing a hubcap. Chloe would have offered to drive, except that her Audi was currently in the shop, awaiting the arrival of a replacement alternator. The mechanic had informed her that there were no Audi alternators to be had in New England, so he'd arranged to import one from Germany. Given how long it was taking for the part to arrive, she presumed the mode of shipment was a rowboat.

She politely refrained from commenting on the van as Will unlocked the passenger door and helped her up into the high seat. She buckled the seat belt, then glanced behind her. The rear seats had been removed; the floor was covered with shaggy brown carpeting. The only cargo in the van was an athletic bag with a squash racket zippered into a specially designed side pocket.

She twisted to face forward as Will climbed into the driver's seat. "It must be quite a challenge parking this thing in the city," she remarked.

"If it conked out on me, I'd buy myself something smaller," he told her. "But it simply refuses to die. I haven't had to replace a single part in two years."

Chloe thought about the six-hundred-dollar bill she was facing on her broken alternator. There was a lot to be said for big, old vans.

"Do you know your way around the city yet?" she asked as he pulled away from the curb.

"More or less."

She folded her hands on top of her purse in her lap and stared ahead as he eased out of the driveway and into the flow of traffic. The sky was dark blue, beginning to reveal the first of the night's stars. Along the boulevard paralleling the Charles River, headlights and streetlights winked and glittered.

"I understand you only just moved to Boston a few weeks ago," she said.

"Three months, actually."

"What brought you here?"

"I lost custody of San Francisco."

She opened her mouth and then closed it. Two minutes, and he'd rendered her utterly speechless.

He laughed. His laughter was as soft and calm as the velvety baritone of his speaking voice. "I have an understanding with an old friend," he explained. "We can't live in the same city. When we do, things become homicidal between us. Anyway, circumstances brought her to San Francisco, so I decided to move."

Homicidal. Great. He was homicidal when it came to ex-girlfriends. Chloe had been so busy grilling Adrienne on what he looked like, she'd forgotten to ask whether he had any criminal tendencies. "I suppose Boston is lucky to have you," she said tautly.

He shot her another look, still grinning. "Don't worry," he said. "I'm basically harmless."

She swallowed and ordered herself to take it easy. He couldn't truly be homicidal. It was just that he had former lovers who inspired him to passionate depths.

And why not? Chloe had entertained murderous thoughts about Stephen on more than one occasion. If it weren't for the fact that Stephen was her brother's best friend... Then again, she'd entertained murderous thoughts about her brother, too.

"Do you like the opera?" she asked.

"Sure. Do you?"

"Sure." *Smart, Chloe. You're lying to a homicidal maniac.*

"So, how do you know the Logans?" he asked.

"Adrienne and I work in the same building. We got stuck in the elevator during a power outage one morning, and by the time the electricity came back on we were friends."

"You're an accountant, right?"

"Yes."

"You must be good with numbers."

"I'm good with calculators."

"And foreign languages."

"I beg your pardon?"

"Well," he drawled, "every time I read that 1040 book the IRS sends out on how to prepare your taxes, I can't make any sense of it. It sure as hell isn't written in English."

"I'm good at translating jargon," she said.

"That's a useful talent."

She shrugged. "It's simply a matter of knowing how to cut through the garbage. I happen to have an aptitude for cutting through garbage."

His eyebrows rose briefly. "I'll remember that."

She wished he weren't so cute. She really didn't think she liked him—except that his eyes were so amazingly blue, and he was so lean and lanky, and he smelled like wild mint. He had nice hands, too, she noticed—long, graceful fingers and clean, short fingernails. No telltale bloodstains.

Or ink stains, for that matter. "Adrienne told me you're in publishing."

Braking for a red light, he glanced at Chloe in surprise. "She did?"

"You're not?"

"Well, I am, sort of. It's just an odd way of putting it. I write the books—someone else publishes them."

"What kind of books?"

"Children's books. Ever hear of Rebecca the Witch?"

Chloe coughed. "I'm afraid not."

He shrugged and shifted into gear as the light turned green.

Rebecca the Witch. He wrote children's books about a witch. Maybe he had children. Maybe he was divorced. Maybe the friend who got custody of San Francisco was really his wife. Maybe he *wasn't* divorced—just separated. What on earth was Chloe doing in this van with him?

Going to the opera. *God,* she prayed, *get me through this and I promise I'll put in an extra hour volunteering at the hospice this week. An extra three hours. And I won't fight with my brother. And I won't chew out the mechanic when I phone him on Monday and he tells me the alternator still hasn't arrived from Europe. I promise. Just get me through this date in one piece.*

"How did you happen to become involved in writing children's books?" she asked, maintaining an impassive tone.

He sent her a crooked smile. "Strictly by accident. I had all these Rebecca the Witch stories I wanted to tell, and they just didn't cut it as adult literature. I mean, I got the first story on paper and realized that what I had was a kiddie book. It wasn't any deliberate choice on my part."

"I see," she said, although she didn't see at all. "Do you have any children of your own?"

"If I do, I've never met them." Another crooked smile.

They were spared from further attempts at conversation as he navigated through the congested streets of the theater district and steered into a municipal garage. She mentally added another fifteen dollars in parking costs to what he'd spent on the opera tickets and swallowed at the hefty estimate. Either his witch books sold phenomenally well or he was independently wealthy. A date like this was enough to bankrupt your average middle-class soul. She wondered why he'd spent so much on someone he'd never even met.

The least she could do was be scintillating. So far she had exhibited all the personality of a road kill.

On the other hand, given how often he'd gawked at her legs, he probably couldn't care less about her personality. He was probably hoping she'd turn out to be a brainless bimbo.

No, men didn't take brainless bimbos to the opera. Unless their only purpose was to throw money around, show off, make a big impression—and receive a bigger payoff in the end.

Forget it, buster, she silently warned him. She would give him as much personality as she could, but if he ogled her kneecaps one more time, she'd poke out his eyes.

"Are you familiar with Wagner?" he asked as they strolled down the sidewalk from the garage to the opera house.

"Wagner? You mean, the composer?"

"Yeah."

"Not really. I know he wrote a lot of operas, didn't he?"

"I recall reading somewhere that he was Adolf Hitler's favorite composer."

"Was he?" she said faintly.

Concertgoers swarmed outside the entry to the opera house. In order not to lose her in the crowd, Will took her elbow. She thought about how warm and strong his fingers had felt around hers when they'd shaken hands, how smooth and dry his palm had been. If he were less attractive she would enjoy this stupid outing more; she wouldn't be so self-critical, so irritated by everything she did wrong—and everything he did wrong, too. When a man with such enchanting eyes and such a sexy build talked about Hitler and witches, his strangeness seemed magnified in contrast to his more obvious charms.

He had mentioned that he had orchestra seats, but the reality of that didn't sink in until an usher led them down the aisle to what had to be just about the best seats in the entire theater. They had to cost fifty dollars apiece, minimum. Even without the parking fee, he'd spent more than a hundred dollars on this date so far—and he didn't even know Chloe. What would he do on a date with someone he actually knew and liked? Rent the Prudential Tower? Hire the Boston Pops for private entertainment? Charter the *QE II* and cruise down to Martha's Vineyard for dinner?

"Good seats, aren't they," he said once the usher had left them.

"Very good, yes."

"Where do you usually sit?"

"I beg your pardon?"

"When you come to the opera. Where do you usually sit?"

That's right, turkey—you told him you liked opera. "Well, I don't come here often. I listen on the radio."

"Oh." He waited for her to take her seat, then arranged his long body in the chair next to hers, angling one leg toward her and extending the other under the seat in front of him. He rolled his head back and gazed intently at the ceiling. "Want any popcorn?"

A startled laugh escaped her and he shot her a playful grin. Even in the muted lighting of the opera house his eyes seemed unsettlingly bright and blue. Her cheeks warmed; she felt as if he'd somehow trapped her, as if her acknowledgment of his joke drew them closer together.

Unconsciously, she crossed her legs away from him. Realizing how much of her thigh that position exposed, she uncrossed them and tugged down the hem of her dress.

"So, have you lived in Boston long?" he asked.

"Six years. I came here for my MBA and never left."

"Ah." He nodded, his gaze narrowing slightly. She wondered what she'd said wrong. "I guess last month must have been pretty busy for you."

"Yes. April is always a hectic time at the office. But a lot of our corporate clients don't file their tax returns in April—they operate on different fiscal calendars."

"That's interesting."

Sure, she thought. *About as interesting as bread mold.*

The overhead lights dimmed, and the audience hastened to their seats. A row of lights came up on the stage and an unseen orchestra began its slow, soft overture.

Not soft enough. And much too slow.

She sent one more prayer skyward: *God, make this opera end quickly, and I'll advance Orin a loan the next time he's broke—without even lecturing him first. I swear. Just help me get through this thing, and I'll be a generous little sister.*

But if you don't come through, God—if this evening continues to drag, if I continue to make a fool of myself in front of Will Turner, if he continues to trip me up with bizarre comments—then all deals are off. Hear me? All deals are off.

HER LEGS WERE, INDEED, terrific. Long and slim, but with enough muscle tone to convey that she didn't live a pampered life. And those two-and-a-half-inch heels, while undoubtedly bad for her posture, beckoned his appreciative gaze to her delicate insteps again and again.

But she had an MBA. Great legs notwithstanding, she was a standard-model yupster. Fashion togs, eye shadow the color of a fresh bruise, wafer-thin wristwatch, one of those impractical little purses that couldn't possibly hold more than a house key and a comb...

Still, a guy could imagine. It was hard to tell, with that bulky blue jacket hiding her upper half, but his guess was that her torso was as superlative as her legs.

Her face wasn't bad, either. As a matter of fact, it was extremely good. Her chin wasn't really square; angular, but not overly so. And her hair wasn't so much frizzy as frothy, a cascade of round, rippling, bubbly curls in a shade halfway between brown and black. And under the purple-mauve-bluish-black smudges staining her lids, her eyes were mighty pretty—as dark as her hair, with long, spidery lashes. Really. Things could have been a whole lot worse.

And so they would be, if this date kept lurching and stumbling along the way it had begun. Chloe Verona was great to look at, but Will wasn't sure he could talk to her. Every time he said something, she sprang a look of grave alarm. She was too literal. Try to kid around, try to loosen her up, and she started scouting out the exits.

Okay, things could have been worse. He could have actually paid out of his own pocket for this gig, and she could have turned out looking like a brussels sprout. Not that looks were all that important, but if you haven't got anything else going for you...

That wasn't really fair. Chloe Verona was a personable young woman. She obviously practiced good hygiene. She

used good grammar. Things could have been a whole lot
worse.

As the orchestra plodded through the overture, he
conceded that things were getting worse. The music was
boring. It wasn't just innocuously dull—it was painfully
tedious. Beside him, Chloe rested her elbow on the arm of
the chair and propped her head up. He could relate to
that: he felt as if the sonorous harmonies were pressing
down on his skull, straining his neck.

Worse and getting worser. The lights came up on the
stage and someone began to sing, loudly and in German.
Visions of Hitler goose-stepped through Will's brain.

He flipped through the program the usher had handed
him, but the theater was too dark to allow for reading.
Onstage a woman—Elsa, he gathered from what little he
was able to decipher in the program—was warbling with
a vibrato as thick as cottage cheese. All around him people in the audience gazed raptly at her, nodding, sighing,
enthralled by her lush, shivery voice. Everyone except
Chloe.

There, Will thought. They had something in common:
they were not enthralled. He was thinking about Nazis
and she was probably thinking about tax shelters, but
neither of them was appreciating the performance.

By the time some fellow—Lohengrin himself—made his
entrance in a boat pulled by a swan, Will's mind had
traveled far from the spectacle on the stage. *Maybe in my
next book, Rebecca could exorcise the ghost of an opera
singer. The ghost has inhabited the body of one of the kids
in school. . . .*

Forget it. If he didn't want to sit through an opera, kids
weren't going to want to sit through a book about an
opera. He was dried up, damn it. He was tapped out. He
was never going to get another good idea. . . .

Thunderous applause jolted him—and Chloe, too. She actually flinched in her seat, then propped her head up with her other arm and let out a weary sigh. Maybe the applause meant the first act was over.

No such luck. The performers embarked on a fresh round of singing. Will studied the pasty makeup of the singer portraying Lohengrin. He pondered the visible vibrations in the man's throat. He checked his watch. He eyed Chloe's legs. He contemplated various forms of torture for Scott, who'd pressed these stupid tickets on him and promised that they would unlock the secrets of Chloe's body. At this point, Will supposed he'd be fortunate if she didn't hate his guts for making her sit through this.

More loud German singing, accompanied by wooden choreography. Will squinted at his watch once more and prayed for intermission.

At last—it felt like hours later—the stage went dark and house lights came up. He glanced at Chloe.

"I think I've developed a migraine," she muttered.

"I understand those can be murder," he commiserated. "Have you got any medicine you can take?"

"No—I mean—I think maybe I should just go home."

"All right," he said, perhaps a bit too eagerly.

"No," she corrected him, touching his wrist as he started to his feet. "I can catch a cab home. There's no need for you to miss the rest of the opera."

"Don't be silly," he said nobly. "I'll take you home." He captured her hand in his, then helped her to her feet. For someone allegedly in the throes of a dire headache, Chloe seemed remarkably spry and energetic as she hurried up the aisle to the theater lobby. Will could have sworn he detected a smile on her lips.

Outside, she slowed her pace and adopted a grim countenance. "I'm really sorry, Will."

"No problem. If you'd like to wait here, I can drive the car over."

"You don't have to do that. Getting out into the fresh air—I already feel a little better."

He gave her a skeptical look. When his gaze met hers she smiled sheepishly, and he realized at once that she didn't have a migraine.

He almost called her on it, almost pointed a finger at her and demanded a confession. He almost wrapped her in a bear hug. They were allies in this, two refugees fleeing from the Teutonic plague. They were both guilty. He considered suggesting that they take in a Walt Disney movie or the laser show at the Planetarium, to celebrate their daring escape.

But she broke her gaze from his before he could say anything, and the moment of tacit understanding ended. With a slight shrug, he shoved his hands into his pockets and strolled with her down the block to the garage.

When the van pulled into the street, she spoke. "I've really ruined this evening."

She sounded awfully solemn. "Forget it," he said.

"I just . . . I should have known . . ."

"Known what? Can you predict when a migraine's going to happen?"

She shot him a quick, penitent look, then turned away. "Well, it's just the whole thing. You spent so much money on the tickets, and I've spoiled everything. . . ."

Now it was his turn to feel penitent. "Don't worry about it."

"And Scott probably told you I'd be so appreciative—and I *am,* Will, but—I mean, I'm not showing my appreciation well at all."

*Scott told me you'd show your appreciation by giving
me the royal tour of your bedroom. And you still have the
chance to do that, Chloe, dear. I could be talked into it
without too much effort.*

"I'm just not very good at this, I guess," she concluded.

"Good at what?"

"Blind dates."

"I'd hate to think what sort of person *would* be good
at them."

She cast him another tentative smile. "Well, thank you
for being so understanding."

"That's one of my greatest shortcomings."

Neither of them said anything more for the remainder
of the drive back to her apartment. He pulled up to the
curb on the circular driveway and shut off the engine. He
noticed Chloe reaching for the door handle and he hurried out of the van to help her out. His chivalry earned
him another of her shy, hesitant smiles.

They ambled through the elegant lobby, ignored by the
uniformed doorman, who was talking to someone on his
intercom phone. Will pressed the elevator button, and
Chloe glanced suspiciously at him. She looked as if she
were girding herself for battle.

Battle, or maybe something else. Maybe she *wanted*
him to make a pass at her. He was a well-bred man, up on
his manners, but hell, if she was going to keep looking at
him that way...

She averted her eyes. Out of coyness, he wondered, or
resentment? He hated these games, he really did—but he
wasn't going to throw away an opportunity. He might play
just one more round and see what developed.

"You don't have to see me upstairs," she said.

So much for something developing. "If I didn't see you to your door," he said, "my mother would slap my face for showing such bad manners." If his mother knew what he really wanted to happen after he and Chloe got upstairs, she'd slap his face even harder. So would Chloe, probably.

She jabbed the elevator button impatiently. "Really, Will," she said without looking at him. "It isn't necessary."

Apparently she wanted to get away from him as quickly as possible. And he almost, almost gave her her wish. But certain habits were too deeply ingrained. He couldn't leave her punching an elevator button. It just wasn't right.

Before he could think of a way to explain that she didn't have a chance against a lifetime of brainwashing by his mother, the elevator arrived. Foregoing an explanation, he stepped inside right behind her. She shot him another distrustful look, then lowered her gaze to her feet. He stared at her feet, too.

The elevator reached her floor. As she headed down the hall she opened her microscopic purse and withdrew a key ring. At her apartment she inserted the key and turned the doorknob.

"Well . . . thanks again," she said to the brass-trimmed peephole.

"I won't bite."

Startled, she spun around to look at him.

"I took you to the opera. I took you home. You don't have to be afraid of me."

"I'm not afraid of you," she said, her dark eyes courageously steady on his.

Oh, man, if she keeps looking at me like that, she might have grounds to be afraid. This is one sexy-looking woman.

And I'm going home alone tonight.

"Well," he said, "I know how it is when a woman has a headache."

Her cheeks darkened slightly. She scowled and broke her gaze from him. "Good night, Will," she said tersely, yanking open the door and stepping inside.

"Good night." He watched her close the door and heard her bolt the lock. The finality of the sound should have prompted him to leave, but he lingered at the door for a moment longer, picturing what her short dress had revealed. And what her eyes had revealed: that she was beautiful, and utterly uninterested. That whatever designs Will had on her, whatever favors he had hoped to purchase with those two blasted opera tickets, he was doomed to disappointment.

Sighing, he glanced at his watch one last time. Not much past nine o'clock. If he drove straight home he would be able to catch most of the Celtics' play-off game. Not as exciting as accepting an invitation into her apartment might have been, but it was a vast improvement over *Lohengrin.*

He started back down the hall to the elevator. He had gone only a couple of paces, however, when the air was split by a shrill, anguished scream. A woman's scream. Chloe's scream.

Chapter Two

"Chloe?" He rattled the doorknob, then rang the bell. "Are you okay?"

Through the thickness of the door he heard a muffled wail. He rang the bell again. "Chloe? Open up."

After several long seconds, she did. She seemed smaller to him—and then he noticed that she had removed her high-heeled shoes, thereby sacrificing a good two inches in height. Her cheeks were mottled; her lips were pressed together so tightly the tendons in her neck stuck out. A few tears trembled along her eyelashes, but she wasn't crying.

He peered past her into the apartment, expecting to see the place ransacked. Quite the contrary, it looked as if it were all set for a photographic layout in *Architectural Digest*. Everything in the room was perfectly coordinated with everything else, from the floral upholstery of the sofa and chairs that matched the drapes to the symmetrically hung paintings on the walls. The only items out of place were her shoes, lying on the floor near the coffee table, and her purse, tossed casually onto the sofa.

He returned his focus to her. The spots of color in her cheeks were fading to a waxy white, and her hands fisted at her sides as she spun away from him. She stared at the fireplace, then shut her eyes and moaned.

"What is it?"

"The humidor."

"Huh?"

"It's missing." She jabbed a finger toward the mantel shelf. "Somebody stole my humidor."

"Your humidor." He scowled. "Isn't that one of those things that you spit into?"

"You're thinking of a cuspidor. This was a humidor. A special canister for holding pipe tobacco."

Oh. Of course. If someone stole my special tobacco canister I'd be screaming bloody hell, too. "Do you smoke a pipe?" he asked cautiously.

"No," she said, sounding exasperated. A shudder gripped her and she sighed, her rage dissolving into grief. "It didn't have tobacco in it."

"What did it have in it?"

"Pebbles."

"Ah." *Why didn't Scott warn me she was a few cards shy?* "There were a lot of pebbles in the driveway," he said with mock solicitousness. "If you'd like, we could go downstairs and gather some."

"Don't make fun of me," she retorted. "These were not just any old pebbles. They were my mother's pebbles."

He took a minute to review everything she'd said so far, and decided she wasn't merely a few cards shy—she was missing an entire suit. "Forgive me if I'm having a little trouble with this, Chloe—but why on earth would someone break into your apartment and steal a box of your mother's pebbles?"

She didn't answer. Setting her jaw, she marched over to the fireplace and stared at the empty space between two arty brass candlesticks. A frown darkened her brow as she discovered a folded sheet of paper on the mantel. She pulled it down, unfolded it, read it and cursed. "It's my brother," she told Will. "Idiot that I am, I once gave him a copy of my key so he would have a place to stay if he was in Boston. He let himself in and stole the humidor."

"Why?"

"God only knows." She thrust the note at Will.

He read:

Dear Chloe,
I need to have the rocks with me at the colony for a little while. I promise I'll return them when I'm done. Stay cool.

                                        Orin

"They're mine," she asserted fervently. "He had no right to do this."

"Granted, no one has the right to let himself into someone else's apartment and help himself to whatever he wants," Will conceded. "But really, Chloe—a box of pebbles?"

"They were my mother's," she repeated, sinking onto the sofa and rubbing her eyes. "She died two years ago. She left her entire estate to Orin, because he's always broke and she figured he needed the money more than I ever would. The only thing she left me was her pebbles. And now he's stolen them."

Okay. The pebbles had sentimental value. Chloe's histrionics made sense, sort of. "Why would he steal the pebbles? I mean, what does he need them for?"

"How should I know? Because he's greedy and selfish and immature, and he's a taker and a user and an artist."

"Well, that certainly sums it up," Will remarked dryly. "All those things, and an artist, too. Sounds like he's beyond redemption."

"He is," she declared grandly. "I used to think there was hope for him—but now this. He's robbed me of the only thing my mother left me. How could he do that?"

"Well, like you said—he's got some major character flaws."

"I've got to get those pebbles back. I swear—if I do nothing else, I'm going to get them back."

"Um...Chloe, just to inject a little perspective here...they *are* pebbles. I can see you're attached to them—your mother, the emotional ties—but they're pebbles."

"I don't expect you to understand," she snapped.

"Well, that's downright decent of you."

"I'm sorry," she said in a quieter tone. "I shouldn't be taking this out on you. You're just an innocent bystander. You can't possibly understand the dynamics of the Verona family, or what's left of us." She let out a weary breath, then proceeded to explain. "My father died nine years ago. He was an artist, too, and a user and a taker and all those other things. Orin takes after him. Both of them go through life, helping themselves to whatever they want and justifying it by saying they're artists, so everyone has to cut them some slack." She leaped to her feet, her mood undergoing another transformation, this time from grief to steely resolve. "I've cut Orin more than enough slack over the years, him and his dingbat artist-colony comrades. This time he's pushed me too far. I'm going after him. I'm going to get those pebbles back from him."

"I can't say that I blame you."

She was pacing around the living room, ranting to herself about all the slack she had cut her brother in the past. "He asks me to fill out his tax return for him," she grumbled, "and then, after crabbing because I can't get him a refund without breaking a dozen federal laws, he asks me to loan him enough to cover his tax bill. He calls me collect to wish me a happy birthday...."

Will concentrated on her feet, which looked just as sexy out of her shoes as in them. Through her stockings he could see that her toenails were polished the same peach shade as her fingernails. He should have found the idea of a pedicure frivolous, but it struck him as incredibly sexy.

Trust me, Will—it's an easy score....

No. He couldn't take advantage of her in her weakened emotional state. She was the victim of a crime—and the victim of an apparently loony family. Much as he would like to, he couldn't put the moves on her now.

"Damn," she muttered, running her fingers through the lush tumble of curls crowning her head. "How am I going to get there?"

"Where?"

"To my brother's place. My car is in the shop."

"Why don't you phone your brother—"

"He hasn't got a telephone."

Of course not. Why should he? To own a phone would be normal. "If you want to go to his place now," Will said, "I could give you a lift."

Her eyes grew round, and she let out a startled laugh. "Oh, no. I mean, it's nice of you to offer, Will, but you don't have to do that."

"I don't mind. Really."

"Don't you want to go back and see the rest of the opera?"

"That's all right, Chloe," he said magnanimously. "I'd rather help you out."

"But you spent all that money on the tickets."

"Uh..." *Don't disillusion her. The night still has possibilities—although heaven only knows what they are.* "Your pebbles are obviously more important. Let me drive you to your brother's. Okay?"

"No, Will—you're very kind, but—"

"I insist."

She angled her head and appraised him thoughtfully. "I think I ought to warn you," she said slowly, "that my brother lives in Minnesota."

Minnesota.

One hour ago he was living a lucid, logical existence. Somewhere along the way he'd made a wrong turn. Chloe Verona had lured him into the twilight zone.

And with a figure like hers, and those dark, sultry eyes, he couldn't say he minded.

"How could your brother have come here and taken your pebbles if he's in Minnesota?" he asked.

"He flies into Boston all the time. My Aunt Mathilda's son works for an airline, and Orin applied what little artistic talent he has to faking an ID that says he's our cousin's brother, and as the brother of an employee he qualifies for eight free airplane tickets a year. He's probably at the airport right now, boarding a plane back to Minneapolis."

"Well, then, perhaps you ought to consider boarding a plane yourself."

"Oh, no," she said swiftly. "No. I don't believe in airplanes."

"What do you mean, you don't believe in them?"

"I don't believe they really fly. I mean, I've seen them in the sky, but—I just know it isn't possible that those huge, heavy contraptions can actually stay up there. It defies the law of gravity. It doesn't make sense.''

"None of this makes sense," Will muttered.

"You don't have to be a part of it, Will," she declared. "I'll get myself out to Minnesota, thank you. I'll rent a car and drive there myself." Her eyes betrayed her, though. They were profoundly dark, shimmering with desperation—with need. She needed Will.

He wanted to save her. He wanted to be her hero. And afterward, in reward for his heroism, he wanted . . . well, lots of things, he thought, using his imagination until his body threatened to betray him.

"I'll take you," he said decisively. The ringing certainty in his voice surprised him—and then it didn't. It was springtime, the season of magic, of rising sap and chances just waiting to be taken. Why not drive out to Minnesota with Chloe?

"You aren't serious," she half asked.

"Dead serious."

"But—it's a long trip."

"We can take turns behind the wheel."

"No, I mean—what about your work?"

"I'm self-employed. What about *your* work?"

"I can take personal days if I have to. But, Will—"

A few days alone in his van with her. A few days with her totally dependent on him. He liked it. "End of discussion," he said. "Go pack what you need, and we'll hit the road."

She gaped at him, confusion battling with gratitude in her magnificent brown eyes. "You're crazy," she said.

"Sounds like a case of the pot calling the kettle black," he countered with a smile. "Go pack."

She stared at him for a moment longer, then shook her head and mirrored his grin. "You'll let me pay for the gasoline, at least."

"We'll negotiate my fee later. Go pack, or you're going to get stuck wearing that black silk dress all the way to the banks of the Mississippi River. Not that I'd complain if you did."

She favored him with one final, dubious look, then vanished into the bedroom without a word.

HE'S CRAZY, Chloe thought. Pots and kettles notwithstanding, Will Turner was non compos mentis.

Preferring not to dwell on his lunacy, she simultaneously tugged down the zipper at the back of her dress, pulled her suitcase out of her closet, and prepared a mental list of the toiletries she'd need. "Toothbrush," she murmured, slipping her dress over its hanger and shimmying out of her panty hose. "Address book, nightgown, Swiss Army knife, diaphragm—"

What was she going to need her diaphragm for? She hardly even knew Will. She couldn't imagine spending the next three days in that godawful van of his, let alone... Well, he did have a terrific build, and those gorgeous blue eyes, and that low, throaty laugh and those strong hands...

Be prepared, her mother used to say. Better safe than sorry. Of course, Chloe was hardly the femme fatale her mother had been. She spent most of her nights safe *and* sorry....

She tossed the round plastic case back into the drawer of her night table. If she could trust Will to drive her to Orin's place, she could trust him not to turn the trip into an orgy.

A big if. Two big ifs, actually.

And, then the third: if she could trust herself.

Of course she could trust herself. Just because Will Turner was incredibly appealing didn't mean she had to succumb to his appeal. The man was obviously insane, to want to drive her to Minnesota. One thing Chloe didn't need in her life was a crazy man.

By the time her bag was packed and she was dressed in jeans and a loose-knit cotton sweater, twenty minutes had elapsed. In all that time she hadn't heard a sound from the living room. She wondered whether he had come to his senses and beaten a retreat. If he had, she wouldn't blame him.

Emerging from her bedroom, she spotted Will lounging in one of the armchairs, his long legs stretched out in front of him, his cockeyed tie loosened at his throat and his collar button undone. His head rested deep in the cushions and his eyes were closed. He appeared to be asleep.

He looked disconcertingly at home in her chair. His comfort increased her discomfort. She made a faint sound at the back of her throat. His eyes popped open and he rose to his feet. After inspecting her in her informal attire, he smiled. "You got rid of that stuff on your eyes," he observed.

"What stuff? My makeup, you mean?"

"Yeah. You've got gorgeous eyes, Chloe. You shouldn't put all that stuff on them."

She sent him an edgy look, not the least bit placated by his compliment. Tension rippled along her nerve endings, causing the muscles in her thighs and abdomen to clench. What she needed was something smooth and hard, something she could close her hand around and rub until everything felt better.

A pebble from the humidor. Damn Orin for stealing her pebbles when she was in dire need of the solace they provided.

"Let's go," she said quietly, crossing to the door.

He took her suitcase from her so she could lock her apartment, and he continued to carry the bag as they walked down the hall to the elevator. Waiting for it to arrive, she glanced at him and found him studying her, his eyes surprisingly clear and alert. "Are you tired?" she asked.

"Not particularly."

"You probably would rather wait until the morning to leave, wouldn't you."

"I don't mind driving at night. It's kind of fun when you have the road to yourself."

"It's just that I want to get a prompt start. The sooner I can get to Orin, the sooner I can get my pebbles and come home."

"No problem."

"You looked like you were dozing in the living room."

The elevator door slid open, and he gestured her into the car ahead of him. "I was psyching myself."

"Oh." He didn't really want to do this, she realized. He'd gotten himself roped into a blind date with her, and he couldn't get himself out of it. He wasn't crazy so much as softhearted. "You don't have to do this, you know," she reminded him gently.

He grinned. "I know."

"You're under no obligation—"

"I know." He sent her a smile which he probably meant to be reassuring, but which was anything but. His eyes sparkled with amusement and something else, something she might have interpreted as desire, if she dared.

She didn't dare. The instant the elevator door opened, she bolted onto the lobby. The doorman raced toward her: "Oh, Miss Verona? Your brother was by earlier."

"No kidding," she grumbled.

The doorman looked concerned. "You told me he has his own key to your place, so I let him upstairs."

"I know," she said wearily. "Don't sweat it." Will was holding the door open for her, and she left before the doorman could detain her further.

She climbed into the passenger seat of the van as Will tossed her suitcase into the back, beside his athletic bag. Then he got in behind the wheel and started the engine. "I should have packed some food," she said, disgusted with herself for having neglected to think of that. "Some snacks or something."

"That's all right. We'll throw some food together at my place, while I pack."

She couldn't believe he was so enthusiastic about trekking halfway across the continent to help her rescue her humidor. But she had given him more than enough opportunities to change his mind, and he hadn't changed it.

She scrutinized him in the dimly lit cab of the van. He was smiling, his chiseled cheeks hinting at dimples, his blue eyes still sparkling with amusement and other, more dangerous, emotions as he concentrated on the traffic. It dawned on her that he was more gung ho about this trip than she was. To her, it was something that simply had to be done. To Will, it was a grand adventure.

Why was it her fate to be surrounded by adventurous, impractical men? Why was she stuck with a brother who acted on all his dreams, and then cajoled her into paying for them? Why had she gotten herself into a long, rocky love affair with her brother's best friend? Stephen Borisovich was handsome, talented, smart and romantic. But he was another artist, another flake, dreaming his big, expensive dreams, and never letting his feet touch the ground.

She'd truly loved Stephen. But then, when it came time to start talking about commitments, he'd explained that to marry him would mean moving with him here and there, so he could sculpt at this studio and that school, in East Coast sunrise and West Coast dusk, and she had seen her mother's life all over again in her own future, a life where Chloe herself wouldn't exist. She'd pulled her favorite onyx chip out of the humidor, squeezed it and caressed it and searched for the right solution in its amber-and-black surface. The solidity of the stone had imparted its strength to her, and she'd found the courage to say no to Stephen.

So here she was, driving through the night with another man who showed definite signs of flakiness.

"You have the soul of an accountant," Stephen had accused her more than once, and it was the truth. Why couldn't she find a soul mate? Why couldn't she find herself a nice, stable businessman to fall in love with?

It didn't take long for Will to reach a quiet neighborhood of apartments down in the South End, brownstones, storefront galleries and dingy shops. He parked, led Chloe to a nondescript brick building and unlocked the front door. "This won't take long," he promised, holding the door open and ushering her inside.

They rode the elevator up to the fourth floor and Will led her down a hall to his door. The door swung in, and he reached inside to flick a light switch before stepping back to let her precede him into the apartment.

The room she entered was surprisingly large and bright, with high ceilings, freshly painted white walls and a polished hardwood floor. It seemed even bigger than it was due to the sparseness of the furnishings—an old camel-back couch, a portable television on a wheeled chrome cart, a pole lamp, a few potted plants, a couple of folding chairs...and a drafting table.

Chloe moved directly to the broad table with its hinged clip-on lamp, its sloping, easel-like surface, its adjustable swivel stool and its shelves to hold supplies. She stared at the large sheet of white paper spread across the surface, containing a rudimentary pencil sketch of a young girl in overalls. She studied the drawing, the professional tools, the markers and fine-tipped brushes.

Oh, my God. He's an artist.

She swallowed hard and turned away from the table. "You're an artist," she said, half an accusation and half an apology for the sweeping condemnation of artists she had made earlier.

"Uh—no, not really. Not the greedy kind," he said with an affable smile.

She turned back to the drafting table. The drawing was obviously in a preliminary stage, yet Chloe could already sense the proportions of it and the mood. The child was gazing off, her features not yet drawn but the angle of her head expressing a certain wistfulness.

"I illustrate the books I write," he told her. "They're children's books, so they need a few illustrations, and I do them. I design the covers, too."

"You're an artist," she muttered.

"But I don't steal pebbles."

"I'm sorry," she said, forcing herself to face him. "I'm sure there are plenty of decent artists in the world. I shouldn't have said all those nasty things about them."

"Forgiven."

She didn't want him to exonerate her so easily. She felt horrible. "You seem like such a good, kind person—"

"But it's always possible that I'm a jerk," he said with a wicked smile. "I'm going to go throw some things into a suitcase. The kitchen's in there." He waved toward an open doorway, then vanished down a short hall.

She gaped after him. Maybe he was a jerk. Maybe he was a typical artist, full of himself and his genius.

And here she was, fated to spend the next several days in his van with him. All right, so this trip was going to be a disaster. But she wanted her pebbles back, and catching a ride out west with Will seemed like her best chance for getting them.

And with eyes like his, and thick, glossy hair, and a lanky, supremely masculine build, and a smile that for all its wickedness was unbelievably sexy...well, if he did turn out to be a jerk, at least she could enjoy the scenery.

Chapter Three

"If you want to know the truth," said Chloe, "I'm not exactly crazy about adventures." She scooped some cheddar-flavored crackers from their foil-lined sack and placed them in Will's outstretched palm, then helped herself to some.

He tossed the crackers into his mouth one at a time, chewed and swallowed. "What's wrong with adventures?"

"They're too...I don't know, whimsical," she said, groping for the right word. "I think I overdosed on whimsy when I was a kid."

"Whimsy isn't my thing, either," Will agreed. "But adventure isn't the same thing as whimsy. Adventure is mystery and challenge. It's marching boldly into the great unknown."

Swell, she thought. Here she was, stuck in a van on I-84 in western Connecticut at midnight with a philosopher.

Actually, philosophy was almost palatable coming from Will Turner. He seemed to exude vigor, his eyes sparkling and his posture alert, his lean physique well suited to the faded blue jeans and the casually tailored plaid shirt he was wearing. He had opened his window a crack, and the mild breeze that slipped in playfully tangled his hair.

Chloe's fingers itched to join the breeze, winding through the long auburn locks, teasing the skin behind his ears, stroking the nape of his neck. She didn't know why she was so attracted to him—other than the fact that he was an extremely attractive man. And it was night, and they were alone, and this was supposed to be a date, although it certainly couldn't be considered a date anymore.

She watched him chew a cracker, watched the rhythm of his jaw and the motion in his neck as he swallowed. Even when he wasn't smiling his mouth was expressive, his lips strong and seductive.

It was really too dark in the van for her to see his mouth clearly. But her imagination filled in what she couldn't see—and it told her that kissing him would be a devastating experience.

Which was a very good argument for not kissing him, she resolved. She did not care to be devastated, by Will Turner or anyone else.

"Tell me about it," he said, rousing Chloe from her dangerous reverie.

"About what?"

"About your whimsical childhood."

"Maybe whimsy is the wrong word," she reflected, staring ahead at the broken white lines sprinting past the van, dividing the highway lanes. She wasn't sure she wanted to discuss her childhood with Will. Bad enough that she was thinking rather obsessively about his hair and his lips; talking about her private life with him in a dark van late at night would be perilously intimate.

They were going to be in each other's company for the next several days, though, and she supposed they would have to talk about something.

"My childhood was unpredictable," she said. "Unstable. Chaotic."

"It sounds like fun."

"It wasn't." She sighed, shifted the tote bag filled with goodies to give herself more room, and stretched her legs under the dashboard. "My father figured that since he was an artist he was absolved from being organized or rational or anything like that. Inspiration struck, and—" she snapped her fingers "—we were off."

"Off where?"

"Anywhere. Everywhere. Sometimes he'd get a guest professorship at a university, so we'd ship off to some campus for the school term. Or a colleague would write and say, 'You've got to come to Prince Edward Island this summer—the evening light is unbelievable,' and off we'd go to Prince Edward Island."

"I've always wanted to go to Prince Edward Island," Will commented.

"And I've always wanted to spend twelve months at the same address."

"Was your father famous?" Will asked, shooting her a swift glance and then turning back to the road.

She shrugged. "You tell me. His name was Aldo Verona. Ever hear of him?"

Will frowned as he thought. "As a matter of fact, yeah, that name does ring a bell."

"Then I guess he was famous." Sighing again, she felt her anger slip away. "By the time I was sixteen he had developed a decent reputation as an abstract expressionist. Of course, he was sixty-eight, by then. My mother was his third wife."

"Your childhood sounds wonderfully exotic to me," he said. "My parents have been living in the same house since they first got married—which was almost forty years ago."

Chloe eyed him enviously. "Wow. The same house."

"And the same spouse. We're less than an hour away from them right now. They live in Rowayton, down on the shoreline."

"I would love that sort of permanence," Chloe said. "I've been living in the same apartment for three years— that's a record in my family—and working for the same firm since I finished school. It's very comforting to know where I belong."

He appeared to be on the verge of disputing her, but he fought off the impulse with a shrug. "Could you open a soda for me?" he asked, gesturing toward the tote.

"Sure." She dug through the junk food to the chilled cans at the bottom of the canvas bag.

"Thanks." He took a drink and handed the can back to her to hold. She felt the warm spots where his palm had curved around the can, wiping the condensation away.

His hands were as intriguing as his hair and his mouth. And his eyes, of course—but they were in a class by themselves. She rarely revealed much about her own strange version of Life with Father, certainly not to strangers. But Will...Will was too intriguing, damn him.

She didn't want to be intrigued. She wanted her pebbles. In fact, the more she thought about the warmth in his hands and his smile and his dazzling blue eyes, the more she wanted her pebbles. There were times she needed to hold on to something firm and familiar, something with no rough edges and no surprises inherent in it.

"So, your father was married three times," Will said.

"With occasional love affairs mixed in for variety," she elaborated, then bit her lip. Would Will think that because her father had been a roué, Chloe might also be morally lax? She tried to think of a polite way to say she hadn't inherited her father's gene for fooling around, but she couldn't come up with anything that wouldn't plant ideas in Will's mind.

"Is this thief we're going to visit your full brother or your half brother?" he asked.

"Full. My mother was the only one of my father's wives who had kids. My mother told my father Orin and I would provide inspiration for his art."

"Did you?"

Chloe snorted. "I guess so. My father would do anything—even go to his studio and paint a canvas—to avoid having to change a diaper."

"You were close with your mother, I take it."

"Look, Will, I don't really want to talk about it," she said abruptly. She was tired of baring her soul to him, and annoyed that he had gotten her to bare it with so little effort. She didn't like the fact that he could have his emotional way with her so easily.

Leaning back in her seat, she squinted at the cars sporadically passing them in the eastbound lanes, their headlights glinting along her eyelashes. She preferred the van wrapped in blackness, when Will remained facing forward, his sharply defined profile pointed toward Minnesota and his features obscured by shadow.

"Men tend to be real suckers when it comes to devoted women," he said.

"I beg your pardon?"

"Like the way your mother was devoted to your father, picking up and moving with him, and having children to inspire him. That kind of devotion. Men eat it up."

She did not want to think about men eating anything up—especially not in the context of male-female relationships. "Some men do, maybe," she said testily.

"It's because, deep down inside, we're terribly insecure."

"Are you looking for sympathy?"

He chuckled and reached for the soda can. "If you're offering some, I'll take it."

"Why on earth should I give you sympathy? You don't need any." She knew she sounded unreasonably cross, but it was her only defense against his phony vulnerability. Will Turner was about as insecure as the Rock of Gibraltar.

God, but she could use a rock right now. Onyx, quartz, even a chip of beach glass—anything would do. She often wondered about people who patted rabbits' feet or took comfort in liquor. Chloe believed the most effective comforters had to be hard and strong and...well, secure.

Like Will.

Don't even think about it, she warned herself. As if she'd spoken the caution out loud, he turned and glanced at her. His eyes were much too bright, given the darkness, the late hour and the fact that he'd been subjected to the soporific experience of *Lohengrin*'s first act just a few hours ago.

"I do need sympathy," he said in a cajoling tone. "Here I am, stranded with a beautiful woman—"

"You're hardly stranded!" she cut him off.

"With a beautiful woman," he repeated, "who obviously is the descendent of a pair of maniacs."

"They weren't maniacs," she retorted. "My father was talented but selfish, that's all."

"And your mother collected pebbles."

"The pebbles..." Chloe took a deep breath. "As I said, we moved around a lot, and wherever we went my mother accumulated pretty stones. They were her mementos, souvenirs of all the places we'd lived. When I was a child I loved playing with them, spreading them out on the floor and arranging them in different patterns, organizing them into families and stuff."

"Families?" He hooted a laugh. "Like, Daddy and Mommy Granite and all the baby Granites? I've heard of chips off the old block, but that's taking it pretty far." He laughed heartily.

Chloe didn't see the humor in it. She steadied herself with a deep breath, not wanting Will to realize how easily he could rile her. "Some kids play with buttons, or pots and pans. I played with my mother's collection of pebbles. There's really nothing so strange about it."

"No," Will said, stretching out the word and giving it a skeptical quality.

"All right. What's strange about it?"

"You made families with them, and then, years later, your brother breaks into your apartment and steals them. Really, Chloe, you can't exactly call that normal."

"It's perfectly normal for children to play with things. And as for my brother, he's a creep."

"Lots of people are creeps. Most of them, if they had access to someone's apartment and wanted to steal something, would head for the jewelry box."

"Yes, well...my mother left everything but her pebbles to Orin. By the time my father died, his paintings were worth a lot, and when my mother died she was fairly well off. She spent most of what she inherited from my father on herself, but she had a nice little estate, and she left the money to my brother because he's always broke and he needed it more than me."

"And you needed the pebbles more," Will said, then continued before she could speak in her own defense. "Look, Chloe, if I thought you were wrong, I wouldn't be making this trip with you. I know how it can be with items of sentimental value. I'm only trying to figure out why your brother would take them. Do you think the pebbles have sentimental value to him?"

"Not a chance. He doesn't know what sentiment is. Or value, for that matter. I can't begin to guess why he took them."

"Is there a chance that some of the stones were actually, I don't know, semiprecious?"

"If they were, my mother wouldn't have let me play with them."

"Maybe she thought there was something to this family business. You know, put a mommy and daddy geode together, and nine months later you've got a pair of amethyst earrings."

His statement was ridiculous, and the blush it brought to her cheeks was even more ridiculous. Thank God for the darkness. She couldn't stand the thought that Will might learn he could rattle her simply by joking about procreation. "Don't make fun of my mother, all right?" she said quietly.

He apparently sensed the solemnity in her request. He nodded. "I didn't mean to make fun of her. I'm only trying to learn more about you."

"Why? So you can make fun of me?"

"So I can get a handle on this thing. Like . . . I'm trying to picture your mother."

"She was drop-dead gorgeous."

"You obviously take after her."

She scowled. "Don't flatter me."

"Oh. Excuse me. You're ugly, Chloe. Is that what you want to hear?"

She wanted to hear that she was safe. And she knew that if Will told her she was safe he'd be lying even more than he was when he'd implied that she was gorgeous.

Either he was trying to boost her spirits or he was trying to butter her up. Driving her to Minnesota was butter enough; she didn't need compliments, too. She just wished she felt a little more certain about what, besides gas money, he expected from her in return.

She peeked at the down-filled sleeping bags he'd tossed into the rear of the van. Two separate bags, each with its own zipper. Still, zippers were meant to be opened. . . .

Stop thinking about it, she cautioned herself. *You didn't pack your diaphragm. That has to mean something.*

It meant she was an idiot.

No. It meant she was being careful and cautious and self-protective. The darker it got, the less she could see of Will, and the less she could see of him, the less susceptible she was to his allure.

Anyway, this was a business trip. A misery trip. She was going to have it out with Orin and get her humidor back. Love had nothing to do with it.

Sex had nothing to do with it, either.

"Are you planning to drive straight through the night?" she asked, eager to clear her head of troubling thoughts about how pretty Will considered her and how many different ways those two sleeping bags could be arranged.

"I'm not particularly tired, so. . ." He shrugged. "If you're drowsy, go ahead and get some shut-eye. That way you'll be able to take over the wheel in the morning."

"I don't think I'll be able to sleep. I've never been good at sleeping in cars."

"Meaning, you want to stop for the night?"

"No. Whatever you want to do is fine with me. I'm completely at your disposal." *Jeez, did that come out wrong!* Completely at his disposal? Not a chance. She would pay for his gasoline and even his meals, if he wanted, but those sleeping bags were going to remain separate, and she was going to remain safe and sorry.

Not sorry. Just safe. Whatever Will wanted from her, she didn't want anything more from him than this trip. He thought her childhood sounded exotic, a former female friend of his made him homicidal, and he earned his living writing children's books about a witch named Rebecca—and illustrating them, which made him an artist. This was not the kind of man with whom she wanted to share a sleeping bag.

"Well, then, I'll keep going for a while. This road takes me straight through to Pennsylvania, right?"

"Do you want me to check the map?" she asked, twisting in her seat to reach the road atlas on the floor behind her.

"Nah. We're headed west—that's all I need to know."

She glanced dubiously at him. Didn't he care about reaching their destination?

Probably not. This was simply an adventure to him, a bold spur-of-the-moment jaunt into the great unknown.

What the hell was she doing in this van? She hardly knew him. She was his prisoner, his hostage. She shouldn't have trusted him. She would have been safer in an airplane, even if the pilots were relying on voodoo chants to keep the thing aloft.

But ... He *seemed* trustworthy. And he was a friend of Adrienne's—well, technically, a friend of Adrienne's husband. Whose sole contact with Will since college had been their yearly exchange of Christmas cards until a few months ago, when Will moved to Boston. How well did Adrienne and Scott actually know Will Turner? And here Chloe was, all alone with him, traveling sixty miles an hour on an interstate in the middle of the night.

She was a goner. Accepting this ride was the stupidest thing she'd ever done. She might as well have been hitch-hiking, catching a ride with a total stranger. At least then she might have wound up with someone who shared her opinion of opera.

This was it; she was really meeting her fate now. A state trooper was going to find her lifeless body lying on the shoulder of the highway in western Pennsylvania during the Monday-morning rush hour, and Will Turner was going to turn up next July in Mexico with a crew cut and a new name. And Orin would get to keep the humidor, damn him.

"Go ahead, close your eyes," said Will, his voice low and placating. "Even if you don't sleep, you ought to get some rest."

She did close her eyes—and her mind conjured that image of Will on a beach in Mexico. He didn't look as good in a crew cut as he did with his long, glossy hair...but he looked too good for her comfort. She hastily opened her eyes. "I'll stay awake...so I can pass you your snacks."

"I'm all snacked out for the time being," he said. "Just prop the soda by the emergency brake. I can reach it."

"Yes, but then you'll have to look away from the windshield."

He laughed. "I promise I won't drive off the road."

"Well...it's just..."

"Close your eyes, Chloe."

"Well...just for a little while," she mumbled, too tired to argue—or to fight off the mental pictures of him bare-chested and sun-bronzed on an Acapulco beach . . . with her blood on his hands. If he was going to kill her, she might as well be asleep when he did it. And she wasn't going to sleep, anyway—just rest. Just try to unwind a little. So she'd have enough strength to fight him off if he did turn out to be a murderer.

She nestled her head into the backrest and shut her eyes. He started to hum. After a minute she recognized the tune: the overture of *Lohengrin*.

In spite of herself, she smiled.

BY THE TIME THEY HAD crossed the Hudson River she was asleep. He could tell by the depth and rhythm of her respiration, by the limpness of her hands in her lap, by the way her head swayed in tandem with the bumps and swerves in the road. Her complexion was a mystery of silver highlights and lush shadow, emphasizing the hollows of her cheeks and the notch in her upper lip.

Relieved of the obligation to make conversation, he sank into thought. First thought: how was he going to keep his hands off her?

Why should he? They were adults. If she gave any indication that his advances would be welcome . . .

She hadn't, of course. He was just a chauffeur, a means to an end. He'd known that going in.

So why the hell had he agreed to drive her to Minnesota? It might have had something to do with his love of adventure, but it also had something to do with the writer's block that had gripped him for over a month. He had a contract hanging over his head, an agent sitting on his back, and a big void in his brain where story ideas were supposed to be. What better way to deal with the problem than to run away from it?

There was that, and then...there was Chloe. He couldn't run away from that truth, even if he wanted to. There were her dark eyes and her fading perfume, her inviting curves, her delicate lips—lips she kept pursing in disapproval, he reminded himself.

She was obviously a space cadet; half of what she said made no sense, and the other half didn't relate to any reality Will had ever known. But that plush, dark mane of curls crowning her head, and those sultry eyes, and that angular chin, and those legs, which exceeded Scott's assessment of them in every aspect...

Scratch the thought. Forget about starting anything with her. She was distraught, torn apart by her brother's thievery, grieving over her mother's final bequest, nursing a ten-ton grudge against her famous father. Chloe Verona was one screwed-up lady.

The last screwed-up lady Will had been involved with had caused him so much heartburn, they couldn't even reside in the same city.

"Derek is being transferred," Peggy had told him over the telephone last October. "He's been assigned to head up the San Francisco office. We'll be moving shortly after the new year, Will. I hope you'll be able to clear out by then."

Two years earlier, he'd cleared out of Denver. Five years before that he'd cleared out of Manhattan. He'd been content in San Francisco—he wasn't ready to clear out again. "Peggy, be reasonable," he had protested. "I don't want to move."

"We have an agreement, Will," she'd snapped. "Written by a lawyer and signed by you."

"I know, I know—but we drew up that agreement before you married some guy who gets transferred every two minutes."

"Every two years. And you didn't have to move when he got transferred to Chicago or Phoenix. Those transfers didn't affect you at all. It's just a coincidence that he got transferred to Denver and now San Francisco."

"All right. So you'll move here. I live in the Sunset district. You can have Nob Hill, Russian Hill, Pacific Heights, the Marina, South of Market.... I cede the entire rest of the city to you. The odds that you and I might bump into each other on the BART are negligible—and if we do, so what?"

"So what? We have a legal agreement, Will. You got custody of Rebecca. Just take her and move, okay? I don't want to bump into you on a cable car or on the planet Earth. That's the way we worked it out, remember?"

Loco ladies. Will didn't need them. Not that Chloe Verona was necessarily in the same class as Peggy, when it came to insanity. *Nobody* was as bad as Peggy.

Come on, Rebecca. It's pushing one-thirty in the morning, and we're getting close to the Delaware Water Gap. Give me a story idea. Distract me from Chloe.

Nothing. Nothing but the silhouettes of trees lining the highway, black against midnight blue. Nothing but a sliver of moon, an expanse of empty road, the tangy aroma of the May breeze, the scratchy broadcast of a New York City new-wave rock station pumping tunes into the wee-hour air. Even though the music faded in and out, it sounded infinitely better than what he'd had to listen to in the fine acoustics of the opera house.

Now there was proof of Chloe's mental health: she'd been bored silly by the opera. More than that, she'd come up with a grand excuse to flee from the theater. Pebbles or no pebbles, she had a fine strategic mind.

And what the hell—driving to Minnesota was more fun than sitting home, watching the NBA play-offs.

He tried to picture Chloe's brother: tall, thin, with an abundance of curly brown hair. He tried to picture her father: bearded and barrel-chested, dressed in a clichéd smock and beret, smelling of cognac and turpentine. He tried to picture her mother: drop-dead gorgeous.

He pictured Chloe, her drop-dead gorgeous cheekbones and lips, her drop-dead gorgeous figure, her drop-dead gorgeous eyes—and her feet, with their drop-dead gorgeous pedicure. He wasn't a fetishist, but, man, those sweet little peach-tipped toes...

She let out a soft, breathy sigh. Wondering whether she was about to wake up, he glanced briefly at her. Her eyes were still closed, but her lips were parted. In the shape of a kiss.

Reaching for his soda, he directed his attention back to the road and emptied the can in three long swallows. The caffeine wasn't kicking in fast enough; the cola left a film of cloying stickiness on his tongue. In front of him the road continued endlessly, drearily. He really didn't want to be driving anymore. He'd rather be looking at Chloe.

And reminding himself, with every ounce of self-preservation he possessed, that her only interest in him was to get Ma and Pa Gravel back again.

The white lines blurred in front of him. He yawned. Minnesota was a long way off—and Chloe had never specified *where* in Minnesota her telephone-less brother lived. Heaven only knew how much farther they'd have to drive once they entered the state.

They had time, but only one life apiece. He wasn't going to risk their lives by trying to reach Pittsburgh before sunrise.

Another yawn. The van's headlights illuminated a sign up ahead: *Rest Stop, Two Miles*.

The radio had dissolved into full-fledged static and he turned it off. An eighteen-wheeler barreled past him at seventy miles per hour, its axles rattling and its engine wheezing. Will welcomed the silence the truck left in its wake.

Rest Stop, One Mile. Next to him Chloe had turned in her seat, contorting her body so she was sitting almost sideways. Her head drooped forward and she let out another hushed sigh that was half a moan.

The exit loomed ahead, neared them, veered off to the right. Will took the ramp, downshifting and coasting along a ceiling-less corridor of ancient evergreens to a parking area with a few picnic benches alongside it, as well as a small, squat building marked with the international symbols for men's and women's rest rooms. He parked away from the building, so its lights wouldn't glare into the van, then killed the engine and switched off the headlights.

Climbing out of the van, he stretched, rubbed a crick out of his neck and filled his lungs with the refreshing night air. Then he slid open the side door and climbed into the back. It took less than a minute to unroll both sleeping bags and smooth them out on top of the shaggy carpeting.

He exited the van and opened Chloe's door. Reaching across her lap to unfasten her seat belt, he caught a faint whiff of her shampoo, a subtle almond-blossom fragrance that reminded him of California. Smiling, he wedged one arm under her knees and arched the other around her back.

With a cautious heave, he eased her out of the seat and into his arms. He staggered slightly, then regained his balance. She was actually rather light, more fine-boned than he realized. He was no muscle man, but carrying her didn't strain him at all.

Not his arms, anyway. The strain on his libido was sudden and nearly crippling. Maybe it was the gentle weight of her head against his shoulder, or the silky fluff of her curls against his chin, or the pressure of her hip against the buckle of his belt, but he found himself aching for Scott's most torrid predictions to come true. He wished Chloe had been dazzled by his expensive tickets and transported by the opera, and afterward had invited him back to her place. He wished that they had stripped naked and dived into her bed and had made wild, sweaty love. That they scarcely knew each other didn't matter. In fact, that they scarcely knew each other might have heightened the experience.

He grinned at the thought. Chloe Verona was an accountant, not a vamp. At the moment, she was also the victim of a cockamamy theft. Will wasn't her lover; he was her savior.

Which might bring him compensation of a physical sort sometime in the future.

He lifted her through the sliding door and lowered her gently onto one of the sleeping bags. She made a soft, unintelligible sound, rolled onto her side and cushioned her head awkwardly with her arm. He climbed in behind her, slid the door shut and locked it. Reclining on his own sleeping bag, he studied her for a moment and frowned. She didn't look much more comfortable now than she had in the front seat.

He crawled down to the rear of the van and tugged off her shoes. Through her socks he saw her wiggle her toes reflexively. With a sigh, he pulled off his sneakers, then rotated and stretched out beside her once more, ignoring the unyielding hardness of the van's floor beneath the layers of carpet and down and concentrating instead on her scent, her warmth, the peaceful tempo of her breathing.

He bunched the top of his sleeping bag beneath his head to create a pillow, then closed his eyes and felt the final traces of stiffness wane in his neck and shoulders. As the last lingering strain of the drive melted away, he heard Scott's voice echoing softly in his skull: *Trust me, Will— you're going to get her into bed....*

Well, he thought, there were beds and there were beds.

Chloe unconsciously nestled closer to him, shifting her head until it came to rest on his arm. Her fingertips brushed against his jaw and he smiled.

Trust me, Chloe, he thought. *I'm going to get you somewhere, all right. Into bed, into Minnesota... One way or another, I'm going to get you.*

Chapter Four

So comfortable... warm and safe, such a strong shoulder, such a long, limber body... So cozy. So warm. So male...

His arm arched snugly around her and his chest rose and fell under her hand. Her lungs filled again and again with his mint-soap scent, and her pulse beat in time with his slow, rhythmic respiration.

Yes.... Oh, Will, I'll say yes to anything. Hold me tight, Will. Tighter. You drain me of will, Will....

His aura was everywhere around her. He was in the air, against her skin, enveloping her body. He felt so good, so strong and secure. Like a rock, except that he was alive, and very, very masculine. *Put a mommy and daddy geode together...* Her abdomen clenched, then relaxed, sending sweet ripples of promise through her flesh.

She could be happy to dream this dream for a long, long time.

Only it wasn't a dream. Her eyelids fluttered open and her vision filled with the beard-stubbled edge of Will's jaw. He lay on his side facing her; her head was actually cushioned by his upper arm, not his shoulder. Her hand rested flat against his chest. One of his arms curved under and around her and the other draped over her waist. His knees brushed against hers, denim to denim.

How had she gotten here? The last thing she remembered was dozing off in the front seat while Will cruised down the highway through the night. It wasn't night anymore. Pale morning sunshine spilled into the van. She lay nestled in the shelter of his arms, his breath ruffling the matted waves of her hair, her palm molded to the muscular wall of his chest.

He must have brought her here. While she was asleep, he'd carried here here and laid her down and... Oh, God. If she could sleep through that, what else had she slept through? Why did he move her from the front seat? What had he done to her?

She lowered her hand to the waistband of her jeans and found, to her great relief, that the button and fly were closed. The ribbed edge of her sweater had ridden up to her belly and she quickly yanked it back down, not wanting to think about whether he might have touched her skin there. He'd removed her shoes—what else had he done?

If he had attacked her, she would not be dressed so neatly. And she certainly would not have slept through it. She would have been enraged, instead of drifting in and out of the most erotic dream she had ever had.

Face it, Chloe: he's virtue personified, she told herself. Either that, or he considered her a loser, unworthy of even a halfhearted seduction attempt.

She should have been consoled by the possibility that he wasn't romantically interested in her. This trip would be a whole lot easier for both of them if there were no sexual complications tossed in. She would be able to trust him—whether or not she was awake—and she wouldn't have to worry about dazzling him, or fighting him off, or analyzing the implications of his every word and deed.

Yet she *wanted* him to desire her. Not act on that desire, of course, but ... *You want to play with fire, girl—and that's stupid.*

Fine. She was stupid. She went on a blind date—surely that proved how stupid she was.

She studied his face, just inches from hers. A strand of his hair, glinting with coppery highlights, fell on the wrong side of his part. She longed to fix it, to put it back where it belonged. She longed to find out if his hair felt as silky as it looked.

If he could lug her from the front seat to the back of the van without waking her, she could touch his hair without waking him. Slowly, tentatively, she raised her hand to the errant lock and lifted it across the part. It was even softer than she'd imagined, immeasurably softer than her own Bozo-the-Clown curls. She indulged herself for a moment more, twirling her fingertips through the auburn strands, savoring their sleek texture.

Suddenly she was staring into a pair of uncannily blue, startlingly astute eyes. Embarrassed, she jerked her hand away. He didn't react, didn't recoil. He only mirrored her stare.

"Good morning," he murmured after a minute.

"Good morning." Her voice emerged in a toneless rasp.

He directed his attention from her eyes to her lips. The arm he had tucked underneath her came to life, his hand drifting lazily across her upper back. "How did you sleep?" he asked.

She continued to study his eyes while he continued to study her mouth. "Okay, I guess," she said, still sounding oddly congested.

He inhaled deeply. His knee bumped hers and he left it where it was, pressing gently into her leg until the entire limb felt numb from her effort not to move it away—or closer to him. His gaze remained on her lips; his fingers inched upward toward her neck, twisting through the dark curls that drizzled down past her shoulders.

"Were you comfortable?"

"Yes." No. Unless comfortable meant tingling all over and feeling feverish and achy, and wanting things she shouldn't want....

His fingertips played over the skin at the nape of her neck, making her tingle and ache and want even more. "It's kind of stiff, don't you think?"

Her immediate impulse was to glance down below his belt. Then she realized he might not be referring to his anatomy—or at least not the part of it she had in mind. Maybe he meant his neck was stiff, or his back, or his arm was stiff from bearing her weight all night.

Maybe she shouldn't be thinking about his anatomy.

"The floor of the van," he clarified, sliding his fingers deep into her hair and cupping his palm against the curve of her skull. "The rug doesn't provide much of a cushion."

"Oh." But she hadn't needed the rug to cushion her. She had been cushioned by Will's arm and her own billowing, surging fantasies.

His knee shifted upward to nudge her thigh. His hand tightened at the back of her head.

He was going to kiss her. She knew he was, and the objection she ought to have voiced failed to materialize. Her heart began to race; she stopped breathing. His mouth was close to hers, moving closer as he angled his head. She skimmed the tip of her tongue anxiously over her lips, and the gesture provoked an audible sigh from him.

God, he was sexy. And she wanted this. She wanted him. She shouldn't, but she did. She hardly knew him, last night she was figuring him for a murderer, he was obviously nuts for having offered to drive her to Orin's art colony, he loved the opera... but she wanted him. She wanted his blue eyes and his manly shadow of beard and his tall, lean body. She wanted him to gather her to himself and cover her mouth with his....

"Will." It was a protest, a capitulation, a helpless groan. She had no idea whether she'd spoken his name in encouragement or panic or equal parts of each.

He drew back, his eyes once again coming into focus on her. She tried to decipher the emotion in them, but when it came to reading his expression she was functionally illiterate.

Whatever had been about to happen was not going to happen, and she should have been grateful that some tiny shred of self-preservation had reared up and stopped her in the nick of time. For some reason, however, now that she was back to her usual safe-and-sorry state, her heart was beating even faster and harder, and her nerves were crackling with the spiritual equivalent of static electricity.

He smiled enigmatically. His eyes remained inscrutable. His hand once again stirred at the back of her head. His fingers wove through the curls, setting off more sparks that twinged and flickered down her spine, through her body.

"We have to be rational," she mumbled.

His smile evolved into a chuckle. "You may be many things, Chloe, but rational isn't one of them."

She bristled. "What makes you say that?"

"You don't believe in airplanes."

"And you do?"

"Of course I do. I've even flown in them, on occasion."

"You're lucky you survived."

"We could fly right now, if you wanted. We could soar, Chloe."

His smoldering gaze left no question in her mind about what he meant. Chloe suspected she might not survive the sort of flight Will had in mind. "I'd rather keep my feet on the ground," she said.

"That's hard to do when you're lying down." He still had his arm looped around her; his fingers continued to wander through the dense tangle of her hair. His knee remained against her thigh, exerting subtle but devastating pressure, and her toes curled and uncurled along the rigid surface of his shin. She and Will still faced each other, their noses scarcely a centimeter apart, their lips easily within kissing range.

She found it impossible to do anything but react, respond, feel herself being tugged back into the dream world she had found in his arms. As long as she was lying down, her survival remained in grave doubt. But the thought of breaking from him and sitting up was so unbearable, not surviving seemed almost preferable in comparison.

"It looks like it's going to be sunny today," he commented mildly. His thumb plowed deep enough into her hair to reach the nape of her neck, and he sketched an abstract design across the sensitive skin. Chloe stifled the urge to arch her back and purr with pleasure.

She arched her foot instead, sliding her toes down to his ankle and smiling internally as he tilted his foot to offer her access to his instep.

"How far do you think we'll go today?" she asked, then bit her lip and blushed at her ill-chosen words.

He grinned rakishly. "As far as we can."

"Ohio."

He laughed. "Where's your sense of adventure?"

"Ohio is as adventurous as I get."

"You know we're going to get past Ohio sooner or later."

"Not today," she muttered, a vague warning.

He accepted her limit with a reluctant nod, but his eyes still glittered with challenge. "Are you going to do some of the driving?"

"If you want me to."

"I want you to." His thumbs traced the edge of her sweater's neckline, teasing, threatening, making her shiver. "Taking turns might ease the strain."

"The strain of driving, you mean?" If she'd sounded hoarse before, she sounded downright laryngitic now. So help her, if Will let his thumb venture below the sweater's edge, she'd die—of frustration, delight, embarrassment, or all of the above. She needed to shove his hand away and sit up and get her feet on the ground, both literally and figuratively, before it was too late. "I've got to stretch my legs," she said.

"I'll stretch them for you."

"Will." She smiled in spite of herself.

"Okay, then, stretch them yourself. Whatever feels right."

The tantalizing motion of his thumb felt right—and very wrong. "Is it safe to get out here?" she asked.

He opened his mouth, then thought better of his first answer and said, "We're in a rest stop."

"Are we?" She'd been so dazed by Will's caresses, by his nearness and the humor dancing in his eyes, it hadn't even occurred to her to look out the window and see where they were.

"We can wash up in the rest rooms," he suggested.

"What a marvelous idea."

He abandoned her sweater, sliding his hand upward and running his thumb along the crevice behind her ear. She swallowed a sigh, rolled onto her back and pushed away to sit up. A chill swept through her when he let his hand drop. Swallowing again, she busied herself with her suitcase, opening it and pulling out her quilted satin toiletries bag. By the time she had closed the suitcase again Will was sitting up as well, observing her. He looked guilty but utterly without remorse, his smile defiant and his eyes still glowing.

"Can you open the door, please?" she asked briskly, gesturing toward the side door of the van.

"Your wish is my command," he said, pushing the lever and sliding it back.

I wish you'd stop looking so enticing, she thought, but even if she'd spoken the command out loud she knew he wouldn't obey. Sending him a distrustful scowl, she climbed out of the van and dashed across the parking lot, eager to put some distance between him and herself.

The rest rooms were located in a squat cinder-block building abutting the parking lot. She hurried inside, passing the vending machines and the racks of brochures describing the Pocono region's numerous tourist attractions, and entered the ladies' room.

A quick glance in the mirror above the sinks appalled her. Her eyes were unnaturally bright, her cheeks flushed. Her hair seemed even more hopelessly frizzy than usual and her clothing was, not surprisingly, rumpled and wrinkled.

Even though she'd had on the outfit for less than half a day, she longed for a shower and a change of clothes. Tonight, wherever in Ohio they ended up, she would insist on proper accommodations: separate beds—separate *rooms*—and modern plumbing. Specifically, cold showers.

She moved to one of the sinks, twisted the cold-water faucet, and splashed the chilly water repeatedly onto her overheated cheeks. It seemed ridiculous and rather unfair to her that Will could get her so steamed up without even kissing her. Just the possibility of a kiss, and she was jittery and inflamed.

How was she going to get back into the van with him? Even Ohio seemed much too far to travel in his company. She empathized with the early pioneers, forging west into the wilderness, not knowing what perils lurked ahead on the trail.

The trouble was, Chloe could guess exactly what the peril might be on the trail she and Will were following.

And the other trouble was, one part of her was looking forward to it.

She hastily doused her face with another double handful of icy water.

All done washing up, she hovered inside the lavatory for a moment, regrouping her strength. It was too late to revert to the stilted good manners of her ill-fated opera date with Will. But she couldn't just march out and slap him on the cheek for getting fresh—but not fresh enough. She needed to be poised and in control; familiar, but not *too* familiar. She had to stick to some variation on the theme of "Let's be friends." She required some way to keep Will at arm's length—which, of course, she could never accomplish, given the close quarters of the van.

She waited for inspiration to strike. When none was forthcoming, she sighed, grabbed her bag and shoved the swinging door open.

She spotted Will loitering near a rack of brochures, unfolding a glossy advertisement that described one of the honeymoon hotels for which the Pocono region was famous. On the back of the brochure Chloe saw a photograph of an amorous young couple lounging amid mounds of foamy white soap bubbles in a heart-shaped red bathtub.

All her cold-water washing had been a waste, she realized with dismay. The mere juxtaposition of Will Turner and a photograph of two naked honeymooners was enough to scorch her nervous system all over again. How the hell was she going to be friends with him?

Steeling herself, she strode across the room. Will glanced up and grinned. "Interesting reading," he said, waving the brochure in front of her eyes.

She stared at the sudsy couple in the valentine-shaped tub because it seemed less dangerous than staring at Will. "My taste in reading material differs from yours," she grunted.

"We're only ten minutes from this hotel," he remarked, thumbing ostentatiously through the brochure. "It says here they've got circular beds. With built-in vibrators."

"I don't think I want to hear this," she said, irked by her overreaction, but unable to prevent it.

"Personally, I've never been a big fan of mechanical devices. How about you?"

Personally, she'd never been a big fan of anyone who could fluster her so effortlessly. Gritting her teeth, she stalked toward the door leading outside.

He tossed the brochure aside, grabbed his brown leather toiletries bag and chased her to the door, positioning himself in front of her so she couldn't leave. Unable to avoid him, she lifted her gaze to his face. His cheeks were now clean-shaven, his hair combed and his eyes sparkling. His teeth gleamed from their recent brushing.

"Are you hungry?" he asked.

If he was talking about food, she was too edgy to have much of an appetite. If he was talking about something else...that was a hunger she didn't even want to acknowledge. "Breakfast," she mumbled.

He nodded. "I've checked out the vending machines here, and there's nothing worth buying. Unless you're into greeting the day with a fistful of taco chips."

"Not particularly."

"They haven't got a coffee machine, either. I think we're going to have to stop somewhere down the road."

"Fine."

He held the door open for her and she bolted into the pink-hued morning light. A recreational vehicle cruised slowly past them, lumbering to the parking area for trucks and buses. A half-dozen cars shared the smaller parking area with Will's van. The air was pleasantly cool, aromatic with the fragrance of pine and newly cut grass.

Before they reached the curb Will took her elbow and turned her toward him. Even without looking at him she knew what he was going to do. His hand closed snugly around her arm, his fingers gentle but firm as he urged her around to face him. She opened her mouth to warn him off, and then her eyes met his and the words stuck in her throat.

His kiss was swift and decisive, the sexual equivalent of a surgical strike. Drawing back, he smiled and whispered, "We really need to get this out of the way."

She wanted to question him on exactly what he believed was in the way. But his mouth was zeroing in on hers again, and the question dissolved into a wisp of vapor in her suddenly steamy brain. Without letting go of his toiletries case, he wrapped his arm around her. He cupped his other hand beneath her chin, tilting her face so his lips could merge fully with hers. The last semicoherent thought she had before succumbing was that his breath was deliciously sweet.

And then sensation took over. The sensation of his fingertips stroking her cheek, of his tongue probing the edge of her lower lip, the surface of her teeth and then deeper. The sensation of his chest pressed against hers, igniting a shimmering warmth in her breasts as her nipples swelled in arousal, and an even greater warmth in her hips as her abdomen tensed with expectation.

His tongue moved skillfully, deliberately, circling hers and sliding against it, luring it to his lips and then into his own mouth. His fingers explored her face, gliding delicately over her cheekbones and along her hairline. The arm he'd wrapped around her waist remained motionless, neither denying her escape nor hauling her unceremoniously against him. It was simply there, staking a quiet but pervasive claim on her.

Indeed, his kiss, while incredibly arousing, didn't force any issue. It didn't make demands or intimidate her in any way. Whatever Will wanted to get out of the way, he was succeeding with a minimum of coercion and a maximum of effectiveness.

Chloe continued to clutch her toiletries bag in front of her like a shield. She had no true defense against his nearness, though, and she knew it. She knew, from the way her body responded to him, the way her tongue parried the thrusts of his and her eyelids grew heavy, the way her heart continued to pound and her breasts to throb, that a quilted bag filled with lip gloss and dental floss wasn't going to prevent anything from happening between her and Will Turner.

To her chagrin, Will was the one who finally brought the kiss to an end. He loosened his embrace and she shrank back a step, alarmed that he'd been able to regain his self-control before she regained hers. Then again, perhaps he'd never lost his self-control in the first place.

"There," he said calmly.

"What do you mean, *there?*" Her bewilderment expressed itself in a flare of rage. "What kind of thing is that to say? *There?* Where the hell is *there?*"

He frowned slightly. *"There,"* he repeated, as if to an imbecile. *"There,* I've kissed you. *There,* you've kissed me. Now we've been through it and found out it's not as risky as flying in an airplane."

"I'm glad you think this is funny," she grumbled.

His frown vanished. He cast her an amused look. "Do you think it's sad?"

"I don't know what I think it is!"

"Look, Chloe—if we hadn't kissed we would have spent the whole morning thinking about it, right? We would have had to tread on eggshells with each other. We would have been all keyed up about it."

"Speak for yourself," she muttered, even though she allowed privately that he had pretty well summed up her sentiments, too. The trouble was, kissing him keyed her up just as much.

"All things considered," he went on, taking her arm and ushering across the parking lot to the van, "I'd say it was a success, wouldn't you?"

"If by success you mean we're both still standing, sure. If you mean we've gained some great insight into the meaning of life, no, it wasn't."

"Are you this stubborn about everything, or is it just that you can't bring yourself to admit you enjoyed kissing me?"

"You know damned well I enjoyed it," she fumed. "So get off my case."

With a smug smile, he opened the passenger door and helped her into the seat. When he got in on the driver's side he was humming again.

"Is that *Lohengrin?*" she asked grumpily.

"No." He started the engine and backed out of the space.

She struggled to reel in her temper. Will truly didn't deserve her wrath. All he'd done was knock her nervous system out of alignment and make her incredibly uneasy about spending any more time in his company.

"What song is it?" she asked.

"You wouldn't believe *Götterdämmerung,* would you?"

"What's *Götterdämmerung?*"

"Aha!" He let out a triumphant hoot. "You don't like opera, do you?"

"Is *Götter*—whatever—an opera?"

"By none other than Wagner himself."

"Oh." All right. What terrible thing was he going to do now that he knew she was ignorant about opera? Would he leave her on the shoulder of the highway and drive off? Turn around and head back to Boston?

He let her stew for a minute before informing her, "The only reason I happen to know about *Götterdämmerung* was that my father used to say that instead of 'God damn' when he was upset. He'd howl, '*Götterdämmerung!*'" He paused, then added, "The truth is, I'm not all that excited about opera myself."

Chloe gaped at him. "You don't think much of opera?"

"The less I think of it the happier I am."

"But—but you took me to see *Lohengrin.* You bought tickets to the best seats in the house."

He mulled over his response for a moment. "Maybe I wanted to impress you."

"Well, you did. You impressed a headache into me."

"Do you really get migraines?"

"Don't change the subject." She pinned him with a stony gaze. "Why did you spend so much money on those tickets? Why was it worth a hundred dollars to impress me?"

"I'm a big spender?" he posed, then shook his head. "Scott Logan gave me the tickets."

"Scott? Adrienne's husband?"

"The Machiavellis behind our date."

"He gave you the tickets? For free?"

"For free."

"But..." She shook her head in disbelief. "I've met Scott a few times, and he's a nice guy, but he doesn't seem like the sort who'd pay a hundred dollars for opera tickets and then give them away."

"I told him I thought he was being too generous, but he insisted. He begged me to take them before Adrienne got it into her head that she and Scott should use them themselves. He didn't pay for the tickets, either, by the way. A client gave them to him."

"Why didn't the client use them himself?"

"How should I know? Maybe the client has the same opinion of Wagner as you and I do."

"So, if you hate Wagner so much, why were you humming *Götterdam*—et cetera?"

He chuckled. "I was humming 'Me and Bobby McGee.'"

"Oh."

"Which is not an opera."

"I know the song."

"You didn't recognize it when I hummed it."

"Because you were humming off-key." *Calm down,* she ordered herself. Will had her unglued, and she was letting it show. She had to ignore his head games—and she had to avoid kissing him again; it turned her into a cranky, defensive shrew. She had to concentrate on what really mattered: the stolen pebbles. If she kept her mind on that, she'd be fine.

He continued to hum—on-key, she reluctantly granted. He had a pleasant voice, and she could easily recognize the tune now that she knew what to listen for. Although he didn't sing the lyrics, she sang them to herself, meditating on their soulful tale of a man and a woman traveling the highway, loving each other and losing each other.

She wished he would hum something else, something a little less evocative. "A Hundred Bottles of Beer on the Wall" would suit her just fine.

"Where are you going?" she asked. He had switched on the right directional signal and slowed at the approach of the exit ramp.

He stopped humming. "Breakfast. Remember?"

"Yes, but—why are you leaving the highway?"

Once again he adopted his forced-patience, I'm-talking-to-a-moron voice: "We're going to breakfast."

"I assumed," she said with as much composure as she could muster, "that when we discussed breakfast we were referring to a quick meal on the highway."

"If we were going to have a quick meal on the highway I would have asked you to open the bag of cookies at your feet," he remarked, indicating the tote full of snacks with a wave of his hand. "My idea of breakfast is something recognizably organic, nutritious, tasty and served at the proper temperature. In all my life, Chloe, I have yet to find a highway eatery where the food meets those four basic requirements."

She conceded the point. "So where are we going?" she asked again, too vexed to appreciate the picturesque mountain scenery, as the road twisted, rose and dipped in its serpentine passage north.

He shrugged. "There was a sign on the highway that said we'd be able to find food at this exit. I assume we'll come upon a restaurant sooner or later."

Later, no doubt. They were losing valuable time searching for a restaurant that met Lord Turner's gourmet standards. If he'd been willing to settle for a doughnut and coffee at a roadside joint, they would have been that much further along toward their destination—and that much closer to the end of this nerve-racking journey. Chloe didn't want to spend a minute more than she had to with him. If she did, she might start thinking about his eyes, and his arms, and his mouth. She might start thinking about the power of his kiss, and about the "this" which he'd intended to get out of the way, but which in fact loomed even larger between them now that she knew what kissing him was like.

"There," she said, pointing to a diner with a log-cabin facade and a faded sign protruding from the roof, identifying the place as the Alpine View Café. A neon advertisement for Rolling Rock beer glowed a bit too cheerfully in the window, but Chloe didn't care. She had to get out of the van. Being enclosed in the vehicle with him was making her crazy. Her voice was edged with desperation when she said, "Let's try that place."

"Okay," Will agreed. He pulled into the lot in front of the cabin, the van's tires spitting loose gravel as he maneuvered into a narrow space between a tow truck and a pickup. As soon as he turned off the engine, Chloe leaped out.

She had intended to race into the diner, a public place where Will couldn't entertain any more notions about getting things out of the way. But one bracing whiff of the menthol mountain air stopped her. The sky was a crisp, cloudless blue; the winding two-lane blacktop was lined with majestic spire-tipped fir trees growing in dense forests along the rustic slopes. Chloe took another deep breath, transfixed by the pastoral beauty of her surroundings.

The unexpected heat of Will's fingers closing around hers untransfixed her fast enough. She eased her hand from his and hurried into the café.

"Isn't this great?" Will proclaimed grandly, surveying the Formica-topped tables, the ladder-back chairs, the stubby steel napkin dispensers and scallop-edged paper place mats. "This is an adventure, Chloe."

"Oh, sure," she snapped, refusing to let him know how charmed she was by the diner. "And you're so wonderful for finding it."

He smiled. "Thank you."

She resented him for ignoring her sarcasm. Grinding her teeth, she followed the bouncy waitress to a table and slumped into a chair, doing her best to avoid glimpsing Will's dimpled smile. In an unexpected show of sympathy, Will didn't try to draw her into a conversation. He perused the menu, recited his order and occupied himself surveying the restaurant.

By the time her scrambled eggs and bran muffin arrived at their table some fifteen minutes later, she had drunk two cups of the rich, strong coffee and was feeling less rancorous. She tasted the muffin, then offered Will a grudging smile. "This is delicious," she admitted.

"So, you don't hate me anymore?"

"I never said I hated you."

"You adore me, then?"

"All I said," she emphasized, "was that the food was good."

"Are you going to worship the ground I walk on, for insisting that we leave the highway to eat?"

"No. But if you behave yourself I'll pick up the check."

"I'm not so sure I want to sell my behavior for $3.79."

"Go ahead, then—name your price."

Still smiling, he let his gaze meet hers. His eyes were a darker blue than the morning sky but just as crystal-clear. Staring directly into them caused Chloe to suffer a flash of heat, an echo of the way she'd felt in his arms, under the spell of his kiss.

On second thought, she probably did hate him for being able to affect her so strongly.

"My price," he drawled, lifting his coffee mug, "is—"

"Don't say it," she cut him off. She couldn't bear hearing him suggest anything carnal.

"—is that you trust me. You admitted I was right about leaving the highway. You may as well admit that I'm always right," he declared, drenching his pancakes in maple syrup before he sliced through the stack.

Relieved that he hadn't steered them back to the subject of passion, she snorted at his boast. "Last night you told me you were terribly insecure."

"I was speaking of men as a species, then," he reminded her. "And of course, since I'm always right, I was right about that, too."

She smiled reluctantly. "You're impossible!"

"No, I'm very possible."

As she reached for her juice glass, her gaze met his. Although she was looking at his eyes, it was his mouth she thought of—strong and demanding, in contrast with the feather-light gentleness of his fingertips against her cheek.

Will Turner was possible, all right. And those possibilities frightened her.

He must have read her mind. "Trust me, Chloe," he said. "I won't kiss you again unless you want me to."

She wanted him to. Damn it, but she did.

As she lifted her glass with a slightly trembling hand, she wondered whom she trusted less—Will or herself.

Chapter Five

"Trust me—we're going the right way."

Chloe pursed her lips and tightened her grip on the steering wheel. "We're lost," she muttered. "You and your adventures. You had to eat in a restaurant off the highway, and now we're lost."

"We're not lost." They had been driving on the back road for less than ten minutes. Will saw no cause for alarm. "We can't miss the highway," he assured her. "After we exited, we got onto this road and stayed on it. So if we just stay on it now, we'll get back."

"We didn't drive this far before we found the restaurant."

"Sure we did."

"There was a fork in the road back there," she said, pointing her thumb over her shoulder. "We should have taken it."

"There wasn't a fork when we were going to the restaurant."

"No. *Going,* it was a merge. *Coming,* it was a fork."

She might be right—but so what? Going just a bit astray was one of life's great pleasures.

"Listen, Will, if we don't find the highway soon—"

"We'll find it," he said. "Trust me."

Her nose twitched. "That does it. Whenever you say 'trust me,' I start to worry."

"All right, so maybe we missed the highway," he conceded. "It's no big deal. This road is sure to meet up with the highway a little further along."

"This road runs perpendicular to the highway. The next highway it's going to meet up with is probably in Philadelphia."

"Okay, then, take the next right turn. That'll run us back to the highway."

"Check the map."

"There." He pointed to a road up ahead. "There's a right turn. Take it."

"Check the map," she repeated sternly, although she took the turn.

"Okay. We're heading west. Are you happy?"

"No, I'm not happy," she snapped, swooping down a decline in the road. "Look at the map and find out where the hell we are."

He opened the atlas to the Pennsylvania page. "We're here," he said, circling the northeastern corner of the state with his index finger.

"Would you mind narrowing it down a bit?"

"Actually, this works out well," he said, examining the map more conscientiously. "If we take the next left—"

"Where are we?"

"If we take the next left, we'll be heading south again, and then we'll end up on I-80, right where we want to be."

"We would have been on I-80 if we'd stayed north."

"Wrong. I-84. For an accountant, you're lousy with numbers."

"Where are we?" This time she sounded exasperated.

"Somewhere near the Promised Land, if you want to know the truth."

"The Promised Land?"

"It's a state park."

"Good Lord—"

"Exactly."

"Where are we?"

"Here," he said, thrusting the atlas toward her and poking the map with his finger. "You want to know where we are? We're here."

She glanced toward the page. The road took a sharp left. By the time she lifted her eyes from the map the van was halfway off the road, bouncing noisily over rocks and parched underbrush and down into a ravine. Her sunglasses lurched off her nose into her lap and the atlas slid onto the floor at his feet.

Chloe screamed, then buried her face in her hands.

Will let out a slow breath and gazed through the windshield. The ravine was shallow; the van was intact. He felt fine and Chloe, except for her muffled wailing, appeared undamaged, as well.

"Chloe," he murmured.

She moaned and buried her face deeper into her hands.

He reached for her shoulder and cupped his hand over it. He could feel the tremors racking her. "Chloe, it's all right," he said. "No harm done."

"Oh, God." She peeked between her fingers and shuddered. "We could have been killed."

"And so close to the Promised Land," he observed pleasantly. When she bowed her head and sobbed, he urged her around to face him. "Chloe, it's all right. We could have been killed, but we weren't."

She lifted her face. Her eyes were watery with tears. "It's your car, Will. I've never even been in an accident in my own car."

"There's always a first time."

"Why? Why should there be a first time for this? I had planned to live my entire life without ever being in an accident."

"So your luck didn't hold. It's not the end of the world. Hey," he added with a teasing smile, "I think we left the ground there for a few seconds. You were flying without an airplane."

She shuddered again, more dramatically. "That's not funny."

"Oh, come on. If you don't laugh about this you're going to cry."

"I am crying," she said, wiping her hands across her tear-streaked cheeks. She sniffled a bit, and then her gaze tightened on him. "This is all your fault," she charged.

"*My* fault? You were the driver."

"And you shoved that map in front of my face while I was driving. How do you expect me to drive when you're shoving maps in front of my face?"

"You asked where we were. I showed you where we were. If you've got a problem with that—"

"We *both* have a problem with that, Will. Look at us!" She swung her arm in a wide circle, displaying their predicament. "We're in a ditch and it's all your fault."

"Fine," he concurred wryly. "It's my fault. You can't drive, and it's my fault."

"We could have died."

"We didn't. But if you don't stop bitching at me, one of us might."

"Oh. Right. I forgot about your homicidal tendencies." Pressing her lips shut, she stared out the window.

So did Will. By his estimation, the van was resting at a thirty-degree angle, the rear wheels perched on the crumbling shoulder of the road and the front wheels balanced on a cushion of dead vegetation near the bottom of the ditch. A tree stood less than an inch from the right front fender, another a couple of inches from the left side and another directly ahead of them.

"Good aim," he grunted.

She exhaled, then lowered her eyes to her hands. "I'm trembling," she whispered, her fury apparently spent. She glanced out the windshield once more, then peered over her shoulder at the back of the van. "Oh, God, Will. I'm so sorry."

Yes! She's sorry! An auspicious sign. It was just a tiny step from "I'm sorry" to "How can I make it up to you?" Will could think of a whole lot of ways she could make it up to him.

"Forget it," he said in his most indulgent voice. "Nothing happened here. You drove off the road, that's all."

"I'm glad you think it's nothing. It's your van, and..." She let out another long sigh. "What if I've damaged it?"

"Your insurance will cover it."

"My insurance." She groaned, in the throes of a new tragedy. "They'll raise my rates."

"Only if I file a claim against you."

She shot him a leery look. "And if you don't?"

"I'm sure we can settle this thing amicably, just the two of us."

Her suspicion increased perceptibly. "I think I'd rather deal with my insurance company."

"Look—I'm not going to file a claim, okay? I'm not going to bill you for repairs. The van is fine."

She sniffed back a tear. Eyeing the slant of the earth below them, she grimaced. "How are we going to get back onto the road?"

He glanced behind him at the van's upraised rear. "Maybe we aren't stuck. I'm going to go out and have a look."

He marched slowly around the van, assessing the position of the tires and searching for damage to the chassis. He noticed no fresh dents, and the finish had already had plenty of dings and nicks before this minor disaster. One or two more wouldn't make any difference.

He was able to clear most of the broken branches and loose rocks away from the tires. But the steep angle didn't bode well. He opened the driver's door. "Let me see if I can back it out," he said, offering Chloe his hand to help her down from the seat.

She pointedly refused his assistance and climbed out herself. The ground was lower than she'd expected, though, and she stumbled, nearly losing her balance. He grabbed her elbow and held her upright.

Her expression was filled, not with gratitude, but with venom. "This is all your fault, you know."

He rolled his eyes. "Oh, yes, of course. I think, therefore I'm guilty."

"It's your fault for making us leave the highway in the first place. If we'd stayed on the highway for breakfast, this wouldn't have happened."

Will liked to think of himself as a patient man. He could be infinitely patient if he knew it would lead to something as magnificent as another kiss from Chloe, another night spent with her in his arms—preferably with fewer layers of clothing between them. For the promise of that, he could be the most patient man in the world.

But given her undisguised animosity toward him, he didn't see much hope for what Scott had so optimistically called an easy score. And if Will was going to strike out, he sure as hell was going to strike back. "If you hadn't been so obsessive about locating our position on the map," he argued, "you wouldn't have driven off the road. It's *your* fault for having to know exactly where you are every minute of every day."

"Which is better than not knowing."

"You have no sense of adventure."

"And you obviously don't give a damn where you're going. You're aimless and purposeless."

"Don't forget useless," he prompted her, his tone caustic. "And feckless, and witless, and maybe brainless."

She shook off his hand. "Go ahead, get in," she dared him, gesturing belligerently at the door. "Work a miracle, why don't you?"

He revved the engine and shifted into reverse. The van rocked an inch or two, then rolled forward. He tried again, playing the clutch and the gas with as much precision as he could. The van rocked back a little farther, but gravity defeated his efforts and pulled the van back into the gully.

"Okay," he said, getting out. "You back it up and I'll push."

"Push?" She eyed him nervously. "You're going to push the van? From the front?"

"It's worth a try."

"Will..." Her resentment of him seemed to fade, replaced by a glimmer of fear. "You can't stand at the front of the van. If you push it up the slope and then it comes back down, it could roll right over you. You could get hurt."

"Don't tell me you care," he said with exaggerated disbelief.

She pursed her lips again. "I don't," she said. "I'm just concerned about what they would do to my insurance premiums."

"Glad to see you've got your priorities straight. Get in."

With a dubious scowl, she took her place behind the wheel. He planted his feet at the base of the gully and his hands on the front edge of the hood. She drove backward while he pushed forward, an inch, another inch, an entire foot—and then the tires began to spit twigs and chips of stone at him, losing traction, slipping. The van lunged forward. With a yelp, Will jumped, tripping over a log and sprawling out backward upon a cushion of dead leaves and pine needles.

Chloe screamed again. Will took some satisfaction in the knowledge that her scream this time was not for his van but for him. She raced over to him. "Oh, my God! Will! Oh, my God! Are you all right? Oh, God, please don't be hurt!" Dropping to her knees, she cradled his upper body in her arms, clung to him, hugged him tight. "Oh, God! Talk to me, Will! Tell me you're all right."

He could have told her he'd never felt better. How much better could it be than this: his head resting on the sleek thighs of a beautiful woman, the gentle swell of her breast brushing against his temple, her fingers stroking anxiously over his other temple, pushing back his hair and trailing warmth down his cheek. Her breath rapid in sheer distress over his well-being, her fingers skimming over his jaw to the hollow of his neck in search of a pulse. Her breast curving closer, practically pressing into his mouth.

He *was* a sucker when it came to devoted women, and right now Chloe was offering a mighty convincing show of devotion. All her bickering and crabbing meant nothing. The truth was out now: she cared about him.

He felt fantastic. But just for effect, he closed his eyes and groaned a little.

"Where?" she whispered. "Where does it hurt? Don't move, Will—something could be broken." She ran one hand lightly over his ribs, searching for signs of injury.

He groaned again, curious to see what would happen.

She slid her other hand further around his neck, behind his ear. "Talk to me," she pleaded. "Say something. I know you're alive, Will—say something." She lifted his shoulders a bit higher, so his lips were truly pressed into the soft swell of her bosom, and the groan that escaped him was genuine.

She lifted his head higher. Unable to stop himself, he arched his hands around her, twining his fingers into her hair, and grazed the silky hollow of her throat with his lips.

She flinched and let go of him. His head bounced off her lap before landing on a pile of crunchy leaves. Opening his eyes, he saw her glowering down at him, her hands curled into fists.

"You're a miracle worker," he said with a hopeful smile. "You've brought me back from the dead."

"My mistake," she grumbled, springing to her feet and dusting off her slacks. "I should have left you there."

"Hey, really—it was a close call. I'm horribly traumatized. A little hug would go a long way."

"Don't even ask."

"You're cruel," he said, sitting up and pulling a few scraps of Mother Nature out of his hair. "I really could have been hurt, you know."

"This just isn't my lucky day." She stalked toward the van, not even offering him a hand. He heaved himself to his feet, moving slowly, making a big production of shrugging his shoulders, rolling his head and shaking the cricks out of his legs.

His performance earned him nothing but a scornful, grossly unsympathetic glare. "So, what do we do now?" she asked. "Walk to Minnesota?"

"No. We walk to a service station and arrange for a tow."

"Wonderful. We're in the middle of the mountains, miles from the highway. Where the hell are we going to find a service station?"

"Wanna bet we'll come across a service station before we come across Minnesota?"

She made a huffy noise at the back of her throat, sent him a final, lethal frown, and tramped through the mulchy ground cover to the passenger door. Behind the seat was her purse. She pulled it out, slung the strap over her shoulder and scaled the slope to the road. Will locked the van and joined her.

"Which way, O Wise One?"

He gazed up and down the twisting road, pretending to deliberate. Eventually he pointed to the right. "This way."

She started hiking along the road, Will a step behind her. "Are we going south?" she asked.

"Southwest."

"How can you tell?"

"Moss always grows on the north side of trees."

She glanced at the towering trees that bordered the road. "The moss is growing all around these tree trunks."

"Uh-oh. The Boy Scout manual lied."

She kept her gaze firmly on the road ahead. "I'm glad you're enjoying this, Will. I'm glad you're having so much fun."

"You've got to admit it's a nice morning for a walk," he said, waving toward the cloudless sky.

"I'm not in the mood for a walk," she said unnecessarily. "I'm in shock, Will. I've never been in an accident before. I've never driven off the road. I've never even gotten a speeding ticket. I've never run a red light."

"You live a tame existence."

"I like it that way."

He shoved his hands in his pockets and ambled along the road, wishing she could take as much pleasure in this invigorating country stroll as he did. "You've never even scraped a fender?" he asked.

"Never."

"Have you ever kissed bumpers while trying to park in a tight spot?"

"No."

"Ever parked and gotten into a tight spot by kissing something warmer than a bumper?"

"You're disgusting."

"Hey, the way I figure it, I can either listen to you complain all the way to a service station, or I can tune out your sulking and think about how sexy you are. What would you do if you were me?"

Another huffy sound.

"Come on, Chloe," he said, increasing his stride until he was beside her. She kept her eyes resolutely forward, even when he looped his arm around her and gave her a friendly squeeze. "Things could be worse."

"How?"

"You could have driven your own car into that ditch. Imagine how upset you'd be then."

She bit her lip and sighed. "I respect other people's property. I don't like it when someone enters my home and absconds with something of mine, and I certainly don't think it's right for me to go around ruining other people's things. I feel terrible about what happened."

His arm still around her, he murmured, "I could make you feel better."

She shot him a distrustful look. "Try it and I'll scream."

He had already heard her scream twice that morning, and he considered that quite enough. "You know," he said, keeping his voice low and his arm snugly around her shoulders, "It's not a crime to want a little comforting."

"No, but it's probably a crime to want what you want."

"I want you happy," he said ingenuously.

"Then take your hand off me."

He chuckled. "I don't want you *that* happy," he clarified, although he relaxed his hold on her slightly. She did nothing to escape from him. Whether she was after comfort or something more criminal, she seemed almost content snuggled within the curve of his arm.

He discerned the tension leaving her as they trekked along the road, the muscles in her back unclenching, her movements resembling less a forced march than a shambling gait. After a few minutes a car passed them traveling in the opposite direction. Will tried to flag it down so he could ask the driver about a service station in the vicinity. But the driver sped up as soon as Will waved his hand, roaring past them as if they were contaminated.

"Real friendly guy," Will muttered.

"He had a smelly exhaust, too."

He caught her eye, and she tendered a faint smile, one that made him particularly glad that he had his arm around her. Maybe her chin was a bit too square, her hair a bit too unruly, but at a moment like this, with her eyes large and luminous, with birds trilling through the forest and the road edged with new ferns that floated above the ground like a green mist...

"It's pretty here, isn't it," he said.

"Yes."

"I think there's a river nearby. Can you hear it?"

She strained to listen. The sound of rushing water murmured through the trees.

"Let's see if we can find it," he suggested, grabbing her hand and urging her into the woods.

She resisted. "What about finding a service station?"

"Checking out this river won't make it any harder to find a service station."

"Maybe not, but—"

"You know the old saying about how you've got to stop and smell the roses?"

"I can smell the roses while we're walking. And anyway, there aren't any roses here."

"No, but there's a river, and I say we go and look for it." He smiled, beckoning her to follow him away from the road.

Her expression was transparent—skepticism warring with curiosity. "What if we get lost?" she hedged.

"We already are lost." He reached out and took her hand. "Trust me, Chloe—I know my way around forests."

"How? From studying that faulty Boy Scout manual?" But her fingers twined through his, and she let him lead her away from the road and into the forest.

"I'll have you know," he boasted, "that I won more merit badges than any other boy in my troop."

"Did you?" she grunted, apparently unimpressed. "Tying knots—I bet you got that one."

"I've always been very creative in the use of ropes," he teased, delighted when she responded with a short, dry laugh. "I also had a merit badge for lighting fires—"

"Rubbing two sticks together?"

"Rubbing anything that generated heat. Then there was the badge for helping ladies in distress—"

"Right. You probably dragged them across the street against their will."

"Whatever I did with ladies, they were always willing." He grinned. "My favorite merit badge was for nature studies—what we used to call 'letting nature take its course.'"

"I should have guessed."

"And last but not least, the merit badge for finding rivers in forests." He held back a springy branch to help Chloe through the heavy underbrush, and they reached the banks of a shallow brook, effervescent with the runoff of the previous winter's snow. The gurgling sound seemed louder toward their left, and Will headed in that direction, dodging the trees, stepping over downed logs and avoiding the swampy spots along the creek's bank. He no longer sensed any reluctance in Chloe, as she picked her way along the river's edge behind him, her fingers laced through his. She seemed as eager as he was to find the source of the sound.

Around a bend in the brook they came upon a small, beautiful waterfall. The water cascaded unevenly over a ragged granite formation, no more than a ten-foot drop, splattering and splashing in a playful tumble down to a tiny pool which narrowed back into a brook at the lowest point.

"Wow," Chloe whispered.

"Exactly what I was thinking."

Letting go of his hand, she scrambled ahead of him down to the edge of the pool, stepping selectively on the smoother rocks and avoiding the muddy patches. Clover sprouted among the moss-covered stones; ferns rose up around a rotting log that formed a dam on one side of the pond.

Will followed her down to the pond's edge, delighted by the turn her spirits had taken. Her eyes widened, glowing with rapture at the scenery, at the secluded magnificence of this glade. All her distress about the mishap with the van vanished. She simply stood before the waterfall, her face bright with pleasure and her hair a wild, dark tumble of curls.

He approached her quietly. When he was balanced on a rock behind her, he cupped his hand gently over her shoulder. She didn't flinch, so he took the liberty of sliding it down her arm until his fingers wove through hers once more. "Worth a detour?" he asked.

She apparently was too transported to argue. "Yes."

"You look like you belong here."

She glanced at him in bemusement. "Meaning, you're going to leave me here?"

"Meaning, you're as beautiful as the scenery. More beautiful."

"You're laying it on pretty thick, Will," she reproached, although he could tell by the dark radiance in her eyes and the delight in her smile that she adored his compliments.

They weren't empty, either. She *was* more beautiful than the scenery. His fingers tightened slightly around hers, and the pinch of her manicured nails against the back of his hand sent an electrical charge through his body. "Just think," he whispered, gazing around the glade before he let his eyes come back to hers. "If we hadn't gone to the opera, we never would have found this place."

"It's almost enough to make one appreciate Wagner."

"It's certainly worth a migraine."

"Or getting your van stuck in a ditch."

"To stand here with you is worth just about anything I can think of," he murmured. So he was laying it on *very* thick—but he meant every word of it. And the intensifying darkness of her eyes implied that she believed him.

He wanted to kiss her, slowly this time, without her pushing him away or standing rigid and frantic. He wanted to kiss her deeply, savagely, thoroughly. He wanted to strip off her clothes and his own, and plunge into the water, and climb up the rocks to stand beneath the waterfall. He wanted to see her naked body streaked with moisture, her nipples beaded tight from the clash of cold water and warm air, her skin golden in the narrow shafts of sunlight filtering through the leaves. He wanted to weave ferns into her hair and cup his hands around her hips and earn a million merit badges letting nature take its course. He wanted to make love to her all over the place— and the waterfall seemed like a good starting point.

"Let's go behind the waterfall," he said in a deceptively casual tone.

She gazed toward the splashing cascade and laughed. "What are you, crazy?"

"Look at it." He pointed to the rock formation. "The water falls beyond that overhang. There's a dry rock ledge underneath it. We can stand on it."

"We'll fall in." She sounded ominously like the pragmatic accountant she was supposed to be.

"No we won't," he said. "Trust me—it's a wide ledge. Let's just try, all right?"

Before she could object, he began to work his way along the rocks bordering the pond, urging her along after him. No matter how apprehensive she was, she didn't let go of his hand. They hopped from rock to rock, Chloe a little more cautiously than Will, tracing his footsteps as he avoided the slick surfaces where the water washed and splashed, until they reached the uneven wall of granite. The ledge Will had noticed was about ten inches wide.

"We can do this, if we're very careful," he said.

"Or we can not do it at all."

"I'm afraid that's not an option." He edged onto the narrow shelf of rock, guiding her along behind him. Cool droplets of water sprayed onto his cheeks. The babbling current sang in his ears.

Chloe's steps became mincing, and her nervous gaze remained on the silvery water that showered down in front of them. Her fingers stiffened within his clasp. As soon as she had both feet fully on the ledge she pressed her back into the rocks, closed her eyes and took a deep, tremulous breath. "There. I did it."

"Not as scary as flying, is it?"

"Not as scary as driving off the road, either. But that doesn't mean I'm enjoying this."

He rested his shoulders against the damp, mossy rocks next to her and rubbed his thumb along hers, trying to thaw the iciness in her hand. "How can you not enjoy it? It's beautiful."

She opened her eyes. "Yes, it's beautiful. I just don't want to fall in."

"Do you know how to swim?"

"Yes."

"And that pond can't be more than three feet deep at its deepest."

"I know, Will—you don't have to explain it to me. I know it's not dangerous." But her voice was taut and muted, her fingers still locked around his, her eyes wide and vigilant and her cheeks pale.

Turning toward her, ignoring the water that spattered onto his shoulder, he slid his free hand under her jaw and rotated her face to his. Given how frightened she was, kissing would either ease her tension or else heighten her terror. But he needed to kiss her as much as he'd needed to find the waterfall once he'd heard it. This kiss seemed as inexorable as the gravity that caused the water to plunge over the rocks and into the pool below.

He touched his lips lightly to hers.

Easing back, he studied her face. She didn't exactly look terrified. "I'd push you into the pond," she said softly, "but if I did I'd probably fall in, too."

"Then you'd better not do it." He leaned forward and grazed her lips with his again, lingering for a luscious moment. "I've always wanted to do this."

"Do what?" she mumbled, her gaze darting between the waterfall and Will as if trying to gauge which posed the greater hazard.

"Kiss a woman under a waterfall. I think I saw it in a movie once."

"I saw that movie, too. Doesn't the heroine poison the hero in the last reel?"

"Different movie." He skimmed his lips across hers again. "Come on, Chloe—kiss me back. You practically totaled my van. I need some cheering up."

"Will..."

If she pulled back, he would stop. If she pushed him away, turned her head, said no—he would stop in an instant.

Her eyelids slid lower and her hand stopped squeezing the blood out of his. Her breath seemed shallow through her parted lips.

"Admit it," he urged her. "This is romantic."

"Maybe a little."

"A lot." He peered into her dark, enchanting eyes. "Kiss me, Chloe."

With a sigh of surrender, she pivoted away from the rocks, moving toward him enough for her mouth to meet his fully. He coiled his arms around her and she leaned into him. His sleeve became drenched and his hair began to drip with water, but he didn't care.

All he cared about was her mouth on his, hot and eager, her lips molded to his, her tongue meeting his. The kiss they'd shared outside the rest stop had been business, but this kiss was pure pleasure.

Around them the water clattered and splashed, churning the air, magnifying the musky perfume of damp soil and spring foliage. Chloe pressed against him, clung to him—no doubt to keep from plunging into the pool, although he chose to believe there was also desire in her embrace. Given the way her tongue danced with his and her fingers fisted against his back... Oh, yes. She wanted him as much as he wanted her.

He lifted one hand to the back of her head and angled it slightly, allowing him to slide deeper. He didn't hear her moan above the loud rush of the water, but he felt it in the vibrations of her lips and her chest, in the eager motions of her mouth on his. He felt it in the way she rose on tiptoe, aligning her hips with his.

His other hand slid down to her waist, then below it to her bottom, holding her to himself. His body hurt in a glorious way for her, and he wanted her to know it. He arched his hips, pulling her higher, seeking the warmth between her thighs. Her gasp filled him the way he wanted to fill her, with passion and lust and the splendor that lay waiting for them at the end of nature's course.

He arched again. She moaned again, and tore her lips from his. "Will," she murmured, hiding her face in the hollow of his neck.

He kissed her hair, which sparkled with droplets of water. He ran his hand down her back to her waist and up under her sweater, caressing the warm, smooth skin of her back. She mouthed his name, her lips skimming the underside of his jaw.

He wanted to lie down with her—or remain standing. He didn't care. Right here, right now, against the rocks, in the water, on the fern-covered earth. He wanted her as he had never wanted anyone before.

A delicate shiver rippled through her. "I'm getting wet," she said.

"And I'm getting hard."

She jerked back and gave him an indignant look. "Let go of me!" Her voice sounded husky, but her eyes blazed with animosity.

"I can't," he said, grinning beguilingly. "If I do you might fall in."

She flattened her hands against his chest and gave him a gentle shove. "I'll take my chances."

He let go. She teetered slightly, glanced toward the water and leaned breathlessly against the rocks at her back, closing her eyes and swallowing. Her face glistened; her lips were dark, inflamed by his kiss. Her jaw jutted forward, advertising her anger. She didn't move.

"Chloe," he said. "Let me help you."

"I'd rather stay here for the rest of my life."

"Fine, but I can't get around you. And I don't feel like staying here for the rest of your life."

"Then push me into the water. What do you care? Go ahead, push me out of your way."

He smiled. If she knew how arousing he found her stubbornness, maybe she'd be more accommodating.

Nah. If she weren't stubborn she wouldn't be who she was. "Come on, Chloe." He planted his hands on her waist from behind, turned her in the right direction, and propelled her out from under the waterfall. "There you go," he said, once they were back on solid ground. "That wasn't so bad, was it?"

"It was horrible."

"You enjoyed every minute of it."

"Don't flatter yourself." She took several long steps away from him, then plunged her fingers into her hair and jiggled her hands, trying to shake the water from her curls.

Will slicked his own equally wet hair back from his face. He peeled his soggy shirt away from his chest and swabbed his face with his sleeve.

"Don't ever kiss me that way again," she muttered, not looking at him.

"What way should I kiss you?"

She glared at him. "I hardly even know you, Will. This is just a blind date, and it's never going to be anything more than that."

"Dream on," he muttered under his breath, just loud enough for her to hear.

She hugged her arms around herself to ward off the chill of her damp clothing. "Just get me out of this forest, Will. Get me to the nearest bus depot and we can pretend we never met. Okay?"

He chuckled and cupped his hand over her shoulder, ignoring her reflexive attempt to pull away. "I'll get you to Minnesota," he promised. "You don't have to take a bus. I'll get you there, safe and sound. Trust me."

Chapter Six

Trust him?

Not in a million years.

Chloe sank wearily against the passenger seat, her eyes closed behind the protective shield of her sunglasses, her hands deceptively still in her lap and her lips pressed lightly together to disguise her teeth-gnashing. Her hair and clothes were still damp, but she tried to pretend the moisture didn't bother her. She tried to pretend that all the other calamities of the morning didn't bother her, either.

Her very first car accident. That ridiculous hike along the mountain road and into the woods. The waterfall... The kiss.

It was all Will's fault.

Like hell. Chloe deserved her share of the credit. After all, she'd been the one to drive off the road. They had ultimately found a resort hotel from which they could call the auto club and arrange for a tow, but were it not for her lousy driving, they would never have had to take that trek to the hotel in the first place. They would never have tramped through the woods and discovered the waterfall. They would never have climbed onto the ledge behind the water. Will would never have kissed her.

Yes, he would have. The circumstances might have been different, she might not have been so emotionally raw and vulnerable to him, but . . . if Chloe could trust anything about Will, it was that he would have kept coming on to her again and again until she'd thrown up her hands in surrender.

The worst part was, she'd wanted to surrender. She'd felt as drawn to him as he was to her. There was only so much blame she could ascribe to the lovely scenery and the stream's lulling song. The rest was all her own doing—hers and Will's.

She was mortified to think of how aroused she'd been in his arms, clinging to him as if her only alternative were to plunge headfirst into the pond and drown. Instead, she'd drowned in his kiss, erotic pleasure cascading through her as the water cascaded around them, only warmer, hotter, making her forget about the van and her stolen humidor and everything else in her life but that one stunning moment with one stunning man.

Not stunning—dangerous. He was going to do a number on her, and then she was going to spend the rest of her life ordering him to steer clear of her, even if it meant he had to move out of her city. He was going to make her homicidal, like that other ex-girlfriend of his. He was going to wind up banned in Boston, as well as San Francisco.

They were back on the highway now, Will driving. The mere thought of taking the wheel made Chloe queasy; she didn't trust her driving skills at the moment.

As shaky as she was, he was in an offensively buoyant mood. He cruised along with his left elbow propped on the open window and a pretzel stick wedged jauntily between his teeth. He did not look like a man who had not one but two women craving his head on a pike. No wonder he wrote books about a witch, Chloe thought wryly. Any woman who spent enough time in his company wound up raining curses and hexes down upon him.

"Tell me about Rebecca," she said.

He glanced curiously at her, then turned forward again and bit into the pretzel. He chewed, switched lanes to pass a car and swallowed. "What about her?"

"She's a witch?"

"Is she ever."

Chloe furtively studied his profile from behind her sunglasses. "She's based on your old girlfriend, isn't she?"

He threw back his head and laughed. "No. She's based on my great-great-great—eleven times or so—grandmother."

"Really? You're the descendent of a witch?"

"I can trace my genealogy back to the *Mayflower*," he told her. "Among the first few American generations of Turners was one Roger Turner, who married a sweet young thing named Rebecca Francis of Salem, Massachusetts. Rebecca was the seventh daughter of a seventh daughter. She was an herbalist, and a bit too independent and freethinking than was considered acceptable at the time, so she was hanged as a witch."

"How interesting." It didn't sound like such a great idea for a series of children's stories, but who was Chloe to question success?

"My old girlfriend—whose name was Peggy, not Rebecca—was my collaborator on the first two books."

"And now she wants to kill you? That must have been some collaboration."

"It certainly was."

Chloe waited for him to elaborate. She wanted to know how this exile business worked, just in case she decided to banish Will from the Hub. When he didn't speak, she asked, "How come she wants to kill you?"

"I don't think she really wants to kill me."

"But she doesn't want you around."

"Well, she was kind of high-strung. *Very* high-strung, in fact. When we broke up, she freaked out."

"Why?"

He meditated. "I don't know. We were young. We lacked grace. Peggy was too intense." He considered what he'd said and shrugged. "I don't know."

"You met her through your writing?"

He shook his head. "We were both fresh out of college, working for a greeting card company in New York. I was in the birthday card department—she was in the calendar department. We met at an office party. It was one of those things."

"Love at first sight?"

"Something like that."

"She was drop-dead gorgeous," Chloe guessed.

"Your term, not mine. But…yeah, she had the sort of looks that can freeze a guy in his tracks. She was incredibly sexy. A half hour after our eyes met we were at her place, tearing off our clothes."

"That's not love. It's lust."

"Don't knock it, Chloe. Whatever it was, it lasted two years."

Chloe swore to herself that she wasn't jealous. Just because this other woman was flawlessly beautiful and sexually uninhibited didn't mean Chloe had anything to envy her about. After all, the poor woman had spent two years in a relationship with Will.

Maybe Chloe should pity her.

"So, she worked in the calendar department," Chloe said blandly. "Does that make her a calendar girl?"

He acknowledged her joke with a polite smile. "She composed inspirational messages. She had a message for every day of the year. In February, she'd come up with things like: 'As clear ice covers the mountain pond, may your soul lie peacefully within the crystal of life.' Or, say, in August: 'Sizzle, don't fizzle!' Or in October: 'As the grape ripens on the vine, let love flow like sweet wine.'"

"I hate sweet wine," Chloe muttered.

He shrugged again. "It was her job to come up with stuff like that. It certainly wasn't a credo she lived by. I don't think her soul ever knew a peaceful moment."

"She sounds weird."

He shook his head. "She was wild. I was young. It was an adventure."

And she was gorgeous, Chloe reminded herself, *and she and Will were great in bed together.* "So, it took two years for the sweet wine to start flowing like vinegar."

"We had our ups and downs right from the start. *Major* ups and downs—Mount Everest and Death Valley. I was inexperienced enough to think it was exciting for a while. After a couple of years, though, the novelty wore off. I kept trying to get her to calm down, not to work herself into a lather over everything, not to swear that she hated me and storm off in a rage whenever we disagreed on some issue. If she could have leveled off a little, we might have made it work. But she was given to melodrama. I'd ask her not to leave her earrings on the bathroom counter, and she'd tell me she hoped I'd burn in hell."

"She sounds weird," Chloe repeated.

"Not weird," he insisted. "Just...she had a difficult disposition. The trouble was, we'd done two successful collaborations on Rebecca books and there were publishing contracts to fulfill, and I wasn't sure I could keep writing the books without her input. The whole thing got pretty messy.''

''Kind of like a divorce, huh.''

''Yeah. Lawyers and everything. She finally agreed to give me custody of Rebecca—I had the blood connection, after all. But then she said she could no longer live in the same city as me. Her lawyer drew up the papers, my lawyer told me she was a crackpot and I wouldn't want to be living too close to her anyway, and I moved to Denver.''

''Just like that?''

''Just like that. Rebecca and I hit the road.''

Chloe pondered what he'd said. It didn't quite compute. ''You must have broken the woman's heart.''

''If you're asking whether I was rotten to her, the answer is no. I have my faults, Chloe—but nastiness isn't one of them.''

''What are your faults?'' Chloe asked with a cool, quiet smile.

He eyed her speculatively. His grin fading, he provided an unexpectedly sober self-analysis. ''According to Peggy, I wasn't serious enough. If I feel like picking up and going someplace, I pick up and go. I don't sweat the details. I like watching Godzilla movies on TV and eating take-out Chinese food straight out of the container. I laugh during sex.''

He'd said it so nonchalantly, she forgot to put up her defenses. Her mind suddenly filled with the warm, throaty sound of his laughter. She heard it, felt it breezing along her nerve endings, gusting over her skin and vibrating deep inside her. She imagined him stretched out, as he'd been when she'd awakened beside him that morning, touching and kissing her and laughing as ecstasy ran rampant through her. She imagined his strong, expres-

sive hands gliding over her, his sun-bronzed skin pressed
to hers, his lips parting hers and his laughter rising up,
soundless but palpable, filling her...

"Do you?" she blurted out before she could stop herself.

"Do I what?"

"Laugh during sex."

He tossed her a mischievous grin. "Wanna find out?"

"No!"

"You sound awfully sure of that."

"I'm positive."

His smile expanded. "Sometimes," he said.

"Sometimes what?"

"Sometimes it's funny and I laugh. Sometimes it isn't,
and I don't."

Chloe found herself recalling his kiss yet again—both
his kisses. The resolute kiss outside the rest stop and the
deep, demoralizing kiss under the waterfall. Remember-
ing his taste, his powerful arms around her, his lean, hard
body pressed to hers, she experienced a quivering heat in
her abdomen. It wasn't the least bit funny.

"This all must have occurred years ago," she said in a
curiously dry voice.

"You mean, me and Peggy? We broke up seven years
ago."

"And yet just this past winter you had to evacuate San
Francisco because of her."

Will sighed. "Less than a year after we broke up, she
married a guy whose job requires him to relocate every
couple of years. Most of the time that hasn't affected me,
but when he got reassigned to Denver, she whipped out
the contract and demanded that I leave the city. The same
thing happened last winter in San Francisco."

"Isn't there a statute of limitations?"

"It's never really bothered me. I like moving around. I was ready to leave Denver anyway—it was too smoggy. And San Francisco...who knows when the next earthquake is going to hit?"

"Yes, but—but what if *you* got married, and your wife had a job where she couldn't pick up and move every time this old girlfriend of yours snapped her fingers? What would you do?"

"If it came to that, I'd jump through the loophole in the contract."

"There's a loophole?"

"Of course there is. Given how much I paid my attorney, I made sure he'd leave me a way to get out of the thing if I had to."

"Oh."

Will polished off the pretzel rod and extended his empty hand toward her for another. She passed one to him, holding it by an end so she could avoid touching him. If she touched him, she suspected she would start reliving his kisses once more, and thinking about his laughter, and wondering whether his idea of funny was anything at all like hers.

"What does the loophole say?" she asked.

"In very tiny print, in very legal jargon that only someone with a talent for cutting through the garbage would understand, it says that if I have a compelling reason to stay where I am, I don't have to move. I think a wife who can't move would qualify as a compelling reason."

"So you drew up this contract with the expectation of getting married someday."

His pointed glance made her regret her words. Bad enough she had inadvertently wandered into a discussion of sex with him. To ask him about his marital prospects was even worse.

But her questions had just slipped out—as if she cared one way or the other about whether he planned to get married. As if she gave a hoot whether he someday decided to make that kind of commitment to a woman. As if anything about his love life or sex life mattered at all.

"Maybe we ought to think about stopping for lunch," she remarked, grimacing at how weak and scratchy her voice sounded.

His easy laughter made her want to crawl under the seat and hide. "My appetite's under control," he said. "How's yours?"

"Under control," she grunted, searching frantically for a new topic. "So. You've figured out how to write your Rebecca books without a collaborator?"

He was obviously considering whether to prolong the torture. In a burst of good-heartedness, he chose instead to follow her lead and discuss something safe. "I've gotten the hang of it," he said with a nod.

"What's the book you're working on now about?"

"Who's working? I'm blocked."

"Blocked?"

"Stymied. Stalled. Blank. Barren."

"And what do you do when that happens?"

"I drive to Minnesota."

Ah, so that was what it was all about. Chloe was merely an excuse for him to abandon his work. An excuse, an adventure and someone to scratch his itches for him. Certainly she had never thought this trip meant anything more than that.

"The one thing I really miss about collaborating with Peggy," he went on, "is that Rebecca is supposed to be ten years old, and Peggy knew better than I did what's going on inside a ten-year-old girl's head. I've never been a ten-year-old girl."

"Barbie," Chloe told him.

"Huh?"

"Barbie is what's going on inside a ten-year-old girl's head."

"You mean, a Barbie doll?"

"That's right."

"Not in Rebecca's head. She isn't into Barbie dolls. She's a witch."

"It doesn't matter. If she's ten years old in America, she dreams of being Barbie."

"No kidding?" He regarded Chloe with astonishment.

"No kidding. Your Rebecca is obsessed with having a dream house and a Corvette and five hundred different outfits. And a Ken."

"Really? Don't you think ten years old is a little young for a Ken?"

"She doesn't want him now," Chloe explained. "She thinks she'll want him someday, though. Of course, once she grows up she'll know better."

"Oh?" Laugh lines crinkled the corners of his eyes as he smiled. "What will she know?"

"That a dream house and a Corvette and five hundred different outfits will make her a lot happier than Ken ever could."

He clearly didn't take the insult personally. "Tell me—do ten-year-old girls fantasize about having Barbie's figure?"

"The eighteen-inch waist and the forty-inch bust? That's Ken's fantasy, not Barbie's."

"In Ken's fantasy, Barbie would be anatomically correct."

Chloe felt her cheeks warming up. She adjusted her sunglasses a little lower on her nose and hoped they would cast a shadow over her face, camouflaging her blush. "If you want to focus on Ken's fantasy," she said crisply, "write a book about Rebecca's brother."

"Let's skip that," he agreed. "Tell me more about Rebecca's fantasy."

Chloe shifted in her seat. She felt her blush descending down past her chin to her throat, way beyond the reach of her sunglasses' shadow. Rebecca was no longer the issue. Will was asking about Chloe's fantasies, and they had nothing to do with dream houses and dream cars or anatomically incorrect creatures named Ken. To her utter shock, her most prominent fantasy at the moment was of hearing a tall, auburn-haired, blue-eyed man above her, kissing her, caressing her . . . and laughing.

The blush crept down below the neckline of her sweater. She gazed resolutely out the side window.

He took a moment to contemplate her edgy mood. "You want to know my fantasy?"

"Not at all."

"A waterfall," he forged ahead. "A passionate woman with long legs."

"I don't want to hear this, Will."

"A swell of Wagnerian harmony as the sky opens up and a chorus of angels sings . . ." He paused.

She resisted. She fought against the reflex—and lost. "Sings what?" she asked.

"'Ah, Sweet Mystery of Life.'"

"Yuck!" She burst into laughter.

"What would you have them sing?"

"Something less soppy than that. How about, oh, 'Something in the Way She Moves.'"

"Old Beatles. Sure. Or 'Light My Fire.'"

"Too obvious."

"You want subtle? Okay. 'Something in the Way She Moves.' Slow, with a heavy, bluesy bass. And we're dancing on that little rock ledge, rocking and rolling the way it's meant to be, and you're unbuttoning my shirt—"

She sat up straighter and folded her arms primly across her chest. "I thought you were talking about some fantasy woman," she scolded, fighting the quaver in her voice.

"Hey, you take your fantasies where you can find them."

"In other words, I'm in this fantasy only because no one else is available."

"Are you available?"

"No. Stop it, Will, okay? Please. Just stop it."

He appeared on the verge of speaking, but he tactfully fell silent. He was apparently satisfied just to goad her into losing her temper. His posture in his seat relaxed and his smile grew quietly triumphant.

His fantasy wasn't about a waterfall or anything else. It was about rattling her, and it was coming true in a big way. She wished he couldn't fluster her so easily. She wished she were immune to his mocking, his innuendo. His eyes. His hands. His long, strong body. His lips.

Damn him. She wanted out of his fantasy. And she wanted him out of hers—even though she wasn't yet ready to admit he was in it. She wanted him out.

She gave him a malevolent look. Refusing to acknowledge her discomfort, he focused on the highway ahead, his lips curved in a smug grin, his eyes sparkling with fiendish delight. He was probably fantasizing right now, and if he chose to cast her in a starring role, there wasn't a hell of a lot she could do about it.

There didn't seem to be a hell of a lot she could do about her own fantasy, either. Minnesota was a long way off, and Will was already taking over her imagination, and she couldn't seem to stop him.

She forced herself to admit an even more disturbing possibility: she *could* stop him, but she didn't want to. Maybe she wanted him right where he was, center stage in her dreams, with "Light My Fire" in the background and a waterfall descending from above, and his eyes working their magic on her.

Maybe she was enjoying the fantasy too much to end it. And that was a disturbing possibility indeed.

Chapter Seven

"I've never been in Ohio before," Will remarked.

"I have," Chloe said. "When I was eleven, this woman my father once had an affair with invited the whole family to come and stay at her farm down near Cincinnati. We lived in a barn."

"A barn?"

"She'd converted it into a house of sorts. Orin never passed up the opportunity to point out that my bedroom was where the sow's pen used to be." She drifted off for a moment, lost in a memory. "My father was in his 'land' period, then—he was working on a series of paintings revolving around the theme of land."

"Land."

"The series was eighteen enormous canvases, with huge squares on them in various shades of brown and green. They were incredibly depressing, if you ask me, but they brought a ton of money at auction, when my mother finally sold them off. I guess there's a certain class of people who like having ugly green-and-brown paintings hanging in their living rooms."

Silence. Boring scenery passed outside the van's windows, green and brown and free for the looking. Will yawned.

He wished she would remove her sunglasses. He was the one driving—and given her performance behind the wheel this morning, he had the feeling he was going to be doing the rest of the driving all the way to her brother's. Even if the sun was in front of them, she didn't really need to wear the shades if she wasn't driving.

He wished she would take them off, and he wished she would wear a dress. She looked good in jeans, but that skimpy little black dress she'd had on when they'd started this date... He wanted another look at her legs, a long, appreciative, hands-on look.

All right, so he was indulging in a greater degree of lustfulness than usual. He was a healthy red-blooded male. She wasn't exactly anemic, herself.

Too bad she couldn't forgive herself for kissing him—and enjoying it. Too bad she couldn't forgive him. Too bad they hadn't said, "Screw the pebbles!" and checked into that resort hotel for a few days of bliss.

He wondered whether she had any shorts packed inside her suitcase. Any miniskirts. Any lingerie. He wondered what she wore in bed.

He wondered what it was about her that made him want her so much. Besides her beauty, of course. Besides her passion—when she let him catch a whiff of it. Besides her intelligence and her ambivalence and her intriguing background, her superficial cool and her deep-down heat...

"Do you want anything?" she asked.

He flinched, his hands jerking the steering wheel so they swerved into the fortunately empty adjacent lane. Did he want anything? Oh, yes, indeed. Her legs, her unsunglassed eyes, her mouth on his, her clothing wet—or altogether removed.

Did he want anything? He wanted *everything*.

"A snack, I mean," she said, rummaging through the tote bag at her feet.

He smothered a groan.

"Or, if you'd rather, we could stop for dinner. It's getting on toward that time."

Stop for dinner. New possibilities loomed before him: stop for dinner and then spend the night somewhere. Not in the back of his van but in a room. With a bed. "We could find a motel for the night," he said with spurious nonchalance.

Her head twitched around; he could feel the glare of her eyes right through those damnably dark lenses.

"I think we've spent too much time cooped up in this van today," he rationalized.

She contemplated his statement for a minute, then nodded. Hope surged inside him until she said, "I'll pay for your room, of course."

Separate rooms. He got the picture. "Forget it," he grunted. "I'll pay for my own room."

"No, Will. You're driving, you're sacrificing your work time for me—even if you're barren and blocked and wouldn't have been getting any writing done anyway, you're giving me your time. You've even supplied the snacks. The least you could do is let me pay for your room."

"Fine. You want to waste your money? Be my guest."

She folded her hands primly in her lap. "In what way is it a waste of money?"

Don't make me spell it out, he almost retorted, then went right ahead and did just that. "We could share a room." Another killing stare from her, and he added, "For the sake of economy."

"Right."

"Look, Chloe—I'm not a beast. I mean, yes, let's be honest, I want to sleep with you—"

"Let's *not* be honest," she said, holding up a hand to silence him.

Undeterred, he went on. "I want to make love with you. But if you don't want that, fine. I think you're a world-class hypocrite, but fine. I won't touch you. We can still take a double room, two beds, and save some bucks. If you're going to insist on footing the bill...I'm only thinking of you," he concluded, pouring on the sincerity.

She looked highly skeptical.

She isn't worth it, he tried to convince himself. There were plenty of other women in Boston. He would return to the city in a few days and meet someone else.

Someone he would be willing to drive halfway across the country with? Someone who could kiss the way Chloe could? Someone who could turn those big brown eyes on him and reduce him to his animal essence?

He wanted her. Only her. And she didn't trust him.

And to be honest, he really couldn't blame her.

THIS WAS RIDICULOUS. They were miles from civilization. Did Will truly believe they were going to find a restaurant, let alone a motel, in the wilds of north-central Ohio? If they were lucky, maybe they'd find a lemonade stand. Now that they were off the highway, Chloe sensed a deep foreboding in her bones.

"We're not going to find anything here," she muttered, staring sullenly at the flat blacktop that stretched through the cultivated fields before them.

"Check the map again," he suggested. "There's got to be a town somewhere."

"I'm sure there is, *somewhere,*" she said, leafing through the atlas's pages. "If we go south, eventually we'll hit Columbus."

"How far south?"

"About a hundred fifty miles."

Will grinned, his devious blue eyes glowing with excitement.

How on earth was she going to survive the rest of this trip if she couldn't even resist his smile, his eyes, his tawny hair and his lanky body and her own troubling knowledge of what his kisses could be like?

Never let a man kiss you on the first date. As Will drove further and further into the countryside, Chloe understood the wisdom behind that old precaution.

If only she had her pebbles, she would feel stronger against Will Turner's allure. A little fondling of some polished stones would go a long way toward restoring her mental balance.

"What, ho!" Will announced. "I see a building."

She saw it, too: a bunkerlike structure with concrete walls and a corrugated-metal roof. "Is it a restaurant?"

"If it is, I don't think I'm going to be impressed by their wine list." He slowed the van slightly as they neared the building, which looked like a warehouse. After a fleeting inspection of the place, he sped past it.

A car cruised by in the opposite direction. "Do you suppose they know something we don't know?" Chloe asked.

When Will grinned this time, she reluctantly smiled, too. "There's another building," he said. "We must be getting somewhere."

Sure enough, more buildings appeared—a few that resembled the concrete bunker they had just passed, a huge double silo, a scattering of clapboard farm houses set back from the country road and reachable by long dirt drive-ways. One house had an elaborate multipronged TV an-tenna rising above its roof; another had a gigantic satellite dish planted amid the gardenias in its front yard.

"This must be civilization," Will declared. "They've got electricity."

"They've got television," Chloe countered. "That's the antithesis of civilization."

Will laughed. Chloe tried not to, but a tiny chuckle slipped past her lips. *Dangerous, Chloe,* she chided her-self. *Very dangerous.* Laugh with him, and the next thing she knew, he would have her agreeing to go skinny-dipping in a lake with him, or running through a sprin-kler with him, or taking a bubble bath with him in one of those heart-shaped honeymoon tubs...

She stopped laughing, real fast.

A small cluster of mobile homes appeared on the right, an auto repair shop on the left. Then a row of houses closer to the road, surrounded by newly planted vegeta-ble gardens and white picket fences. "A sidewalk!" Will exclaimed with exaggerated enthusiasm. "Look, Chloe! Sidewalks. And a fire hydrant! What do you want to bet we're going to come to a traffic light soon?"

As it was, they drove past a few more blocks of houses before reaching a traffic light. No doubt about it, they were definitely in a town.

"This is Main Street," Chloe said, reading the sign on the pole at the corner.

"Main Street. What an amazing name. I bet we're go-ing to find a restaurant within the next mile."

"How about within the next block?" Just past the in-tersection the village's commercial district began: a drug-store, a liquor store, a hardware store, a clothing store, a barber shop and, at the corner, a cozy glass-walled café with a fifties-era neon sign reading Jasper's above the door.

"I'm in love," Will announced, his eyes radiating adoration as he pulled into a metered parking space at the curb not far from the restaurant.

Chloe gazed at Jasper's, feeling less love than resignation over Will's choice of eatery. Through the glass panes that formed the upper half of the front wall, she could see a cashier's counter with an old-fashioned cash register and a spike upon which were impaled the day's receipts. "I don't think this place is going to have a great wine list, either," she muttered as she climbed out of the van.

Will locked the van and inserted a quarter into the meter. "This place," he predicted, "is going to have vintage coffee. I can tell just by looking at it."

"You've got some imagination," she retorted. The confusion that had buffeted her for much of the afternoon was augmented by an edginess akin to panic. As long as they were driving, she felt reasonably safe with Will. Dinner—even at a greasy spoon such as Jasper's—would deprive them of any distractions. Chloe would be forced to deal directly with him.

But what was she going to do? Go on a hunger strike?

She managed a weak smile as he opened the door for her. Entering the diner, she was immediately wrapped within Randy Travis's molasses-smooth baritone, which poured from the depths of the jukebox in one corner of the room.

Chloe considered suggesting to Will that they sit at the counter. If they did, they could sit side by side and she wouldn't have to gaze into his eyes.

But then she would have to contend with his elbow brushing hers, his body much too close to hers, his leg rubbing hers as he pivoted on his stool....

A waitress carrying two plastic-coated menus greeted her and Will with a smile and ushered them to a table against the left wall. "There you go," she said cheerfully, setting the menus on the table between them. "Today's soup is split-pea, and the special is turkey potpie."

"Turkey potpie," Will echoed reverently. "Tell me, Chloe, when was the last time you had turkey potpie?"

"In a former life, probably." She didn't think as highly of potpies as Will apparently did. But the menu offered other equally hearty selections. Nothing exotic. Nothing Cajun-style, *cuisine minceur,* Thai, Dijon, *en croûte* or finished with capers.

She settled on roast chicken; Will ordered the potpie for himself. The waitress filled their glasses with water, then delivered a plastic basket of dinner rolls.

Will beamed and helped himself to a roll. "Isn't this great?"

"It's a diner, Will."

His smile changed from euphoric to impatient at her prickly mood. "Trust me, Chloe. It's not against the law to have fun."

"I'm having all the fun I can handle," she argued.

"Oh, yeah, I can tell. Any more fun and your face might crack."

"I'm sorry if my face doesn't meet your exalted standards."

"There are only two things wrong with your face. You don't smile enough, and you're wearing sunglasses. In case you hadn't noticed, we're indoors."

"I noticed." She removed her sunglasses and slipped them into her purse. Then she spent several long minutes arranging her napkin smoothly across her lap.

He exhaled, as if to blow away any dust their squabble might have kicked up. "When do you think we'll get to your brother's place?" he asked.

In other words, how much longer were they going to be stuck with each other? "We should get there the day after tomorrow, I guess. Probably early in the day."

"Where exactly are we going?"

"It's a small town called Hackett, a bit south of Minneapolis. About as nowhere as this town we're in right now."

"It must be even more nowhere. You told me they haven't got telephone service."

"Oh, there's telephone service in Hackett. Orin doesn't have a working telephone because he neglected to pay some bills and the phone company cut him off. He's got a neighbor with a phone, in case of emergency, and there's a general store with a pay phone about a mile up the road."

"What's this art colony like?"

"I've never been there," Chloe admitted.

"What do you mean, you've never been there?"

"It's not an easy drive, and I don't fly," she reminded him. "Besides, Orin is always coming to Boston with his freebie airline tickets. I see plenty enough of him." She'd seen more than enough of him during the previous two years, when he'd been visiting Stephen as well as Chloe.

Stephen had been living in Somerville, then, doing construction work so he could learn metal working techniques—and spending most of his evenings with Chloe, romancing her with his intensity and his virile good looks, and making her understand, in her less lucid moments, how a woman like her mother could have fallen for a man like her father. Stephen would describe to her the magnificent sculptures he planned to create someday, and like a fool—or a woman in love, which was probably the same thing—Chloe would nod and sigh and share his dreams with him, never questioning his utter indifference to her dreams.

She hadn't had a reason to travel to the colony, then—and she had even less of a reason to travel there now, knowing that Stephen was currently residing there. She saw no benefit in driving all the way to Minnesota to listen to Stephen berate her for possessing the soul of an accountant, and for breaking up with him before she lost sight of her own goals and hopes. If it weren't for her humidor she wouldn't be making this trip.

Will appeared puzzled. "So we're driving all this way, and you've never even been there before?"

"I'm not going to get us lost, Will. Unlike some people I can name, I know how to read a map."

He looked askance at her, weighing his words. "Forgive me if I think your family is bizarre."

"You're forgiven." Leaning back in her seat, she listened to Randy Travis croon about lost love and heartbreak. She recollected everything Will had told her about his tumultuous love affair with Peggy. Given that he'd confessed his romantic past to her, she owed it to him at least to inform him of what might lie ahead. "One of the people who lives at the colony," she told him, "is a man named Stephen Borisovich. He's Orin's best friend. He's also a former boyfriend of mine."

The waitress arrived at their table with two overflowing bowls of salad. Will waited until they were alone before speaking. "*A* former boyfriend, or *the* former boyfriend?"

"What do you mean, *the* former boyfriend?"

"Scott Logan told me you just broke up with some guy."

"We didn't *just* break up," Chloe said brittlely, unnerved by the fact that Scott would have revealed such details about her—even though she had pumped Adrienne for the same sort of details about Will. "We broke up last New Year's Eve."

"What a way to start the new year," Will commented. "He broke your heart?"

She scowled. "Did Scott tell you that?"

"Uh...no, actually. I just sort of figured you must have been recovering from something serious, because he did tell me you hadn't been dating for a while."

"Scott Logan is a creep!"

"In other words, you *have* been dating."

"Whether or not I've been dating is irrelevant. Scott had no right to talk about it. I can't believe he told you that!" She stabbed a chunk of cucumber and bit down on it with vicious force.

Will clearly sensed the need to make amends. "Whoever this guy is," he said, "you seem to have recovered just fine."

"Believe me, I have."

Crystal Gayle's mellifluous voice replaced Randy Travis's on the jukebox. Chloe listened long enough to identify the song, the one about her brown eyes being blue. Gazing into Will's riveting blue eyes gave the lyrics an added dimension. She almost wished his eyes would turn brown. Maybe she'd find him less formidable if they did.

"Why are you telling me this?" he asked before digging into his own salad. "Does Boris get homicidal when you're in town?"

"His name is Stephen. And, no, he doesn't get homicidal—at least, not that I know of. We haven't seen each other since we broke up."

"So you're expecting some awkwardness when you see him, is that it?"

"Perhaps."

"You're afraid you might suffer pangs of regret?"

"No," she said firmly.

"Do you want me to run interference?"

"No, thank you. I can handle the situation."

"You're just a little strung out about it."

"I'm not the least bit strung out, Will. I only thought I ought to give you some warning."

"So, this guy's your brother's best friend?"

"Yes." She sighed. "If there *is* any awkwardness, Orin will be just as much to blame as Stephen. Orin always wanted us to be together forever. His sister and his best buddy—it made everything nice and symmetrical for him."

"Hey, give the guy a break. Maybe he wanted you to love each other because he loves you both."

Chloe snorted. "It's amazing that I was able to talk myself into loving Stephen at all. He and Orin met in art school."

"He's another artist?"

She nodded.

"Another user and taker and all those things," Will summed up.

"I thought he was different, but it turned out he wasn't. At first I was caught up in the excitement of his work. He's very talented, and he said I was his inspiration and I felt honored. But after a while, I realized his art came first, and he wanted to be with me because I contributed in some way to his art. I needed more than that."

"So he dumped you."

"I dumped him. He was the dumpee."

"Do you think he's one of the walking wounded?"

"I doubt it," she muttered, busying herself with her salad.

"Why do you doubt it?" he asked. "I'm sure you could wound a man pretty severely if you put your mind to it."

She snorted again.

"Don't underestimate yourself, Chloe. Maybe the guy's holed up in Minnesota, drowning in tears and attacking his canvases with a bowie knife because you told him to take a hike."

"You're confusing him with your Peggy. I only date sane people."

He laughed. "Well, I guess I should thank you for preparing me. Who knows? He might think there's something going on between you and me and use the bowie knife on me."

Chloe coughed into her napkin. Did Will think there was something going on between them? A couple of kisses wasn't the same as *something*. But, then, when she thought of the sensations he'd aroused in her under the waterfall, when she'd clung to him as if her life depended on it, and believed in that instant that it did, and she'd wanted never to let go...

All right, so *something* was going on. She just didn't want to think too deeply about what it might be.

The waitress arrived with their food. Will's eyes glowed with rapture as he gazed upon his potpie. Evidently, he was done discussing Chloe's previous love life. Frankly, so was she.

The Crystal Gayle ballad ended. A sturdy middle-aged man in jeans and a duck-bill cap dropped a coin into the jukebox, and the diner filled with a throbbing orchestral introduction and then a classically trained tenor warbling in Italian.

Will dropped his fork in astonishment. Then he erupted in laughter. "It's opera!"

"Obviously."

"Here in the middle of nowhere, they're got an aria in the jukebox! This is fantastic," he said, twisting in his seat to survey the room. None of the other customers appeared startled by the musical selection. "It must be a sign."

Chloe eyed him warily. "A sign of what?"

"A sign of destiny. Opera is our fate."

Chloe too felt a sense of destiny. Destiny, or maybe doom. He called it fate; she called it fatalism. But whatever it was, she could not bring herself to deny its spell.

Their waitress was ambling past. Will waved her over. "Excuse me, miss—what is that song?"

"It's from *Pagliacci,*" she said. "'Vesti la giubba.' Al Racey has a thing for it. He donated the record, and he plays it whenever he's here."

"I see."

"If it's bothering you—"

"Oh, no, not at all. We love it. Don't we, Chloe?"

Chloe smiled faintly. "We love it."

"Okay. How are your dinners?"

"Wonderful," Will declared.

"By the way," Chloe interjected, "you wouldn't happen to know if there's a motel in the area, would you?"

"A motel? Like a Holiday Inn? Not in town. We're kind of off the beaten track. But I'm sure you could find something down in Norwalk. That's less than an hour from here."

"Norwalk," Chloe echoed.

"Or if you want to head up north to Sandusky..."

"Sandusky."

The waitress smiled good-naturedly. "Forty-five minutes, maybe. I tell you what, let me ask around. Someone else might know of a place closer by."

Chloe had thought the waitress would vanish into the kitchen and question her coworkers. Instead, she turned and, drowning out the overwrought tenor on the jukebox, bellowed, "Hey, folks, where's the nearest motel? These nice young out-of-towners need a place to spend the night."

Pagliacci went forgotten as Jasper's patrons all turned to Chloe and Will. Chloe found their attention discomfitting. Will, quite the contrary, seemed greatly amused by it.

"You the folks from Massachusetts?" asked a balding middle-aged man in a Cleveland Browns shirt three tables away. "I saw the license plates on that van outside."

"Yes, we're from Boston," Will told him.

"Boston? No kidding," a wiry woman with bleached red hair exclaimed. "My brother's boy goes to Boston College. Is that anywhere near you?"

"Actually, Boston College isn't even in Boston," Will informed her. "It's across the city line, in Chestnut Hill." This stirred up a bit of comment.

"So, what are you, honeymooners?" someone else asked, and before Chloe could correct him, he stood up, raised his mug of coffee high into the air and said, "Let's drink a toast to the honeymooners from Boston!"

Everyone smiled. A few people applauded. The waitress eyed Will and Chloe benevolently and said, "We don't get too many out-of-towners around here."

"I could have guessed," Chloe muttered through thin lips.

The counter man set a glass coffee decanter down and said, "How about the Luden place?"

"That's more a rooming house, Jay," the waitress called back across the room.

"So? It's right here, just outside town."

"They keep a clean place," a grandmotherly woman chimed in. "Nicer than any of those chain motels."

"I understand they've got a real nice bridal suite there," her silver-haired companion added with a wink.

"Oh, go on with you," someone hooted, and most of the patrons laughed.

"No, seriously," the silver-haired man persevered, "they run the nicest establishment around—ask anyone. Bridal suite and all. Anna Luden puts out a great spread for breakfast, too."

"Better'n mine?" the counterman growled, though he was obviously joking.

"Wait a minute," Chloe said, though her voice came out choked. She was abruptly afflicted by stage fright. "Will," she whispered, "say something."

He gave her a compassionate nod, then turned to the waitress. "What's the bridal suite like?" he asked.

Chloe tried to kick him under the table, but she hit the table leg instead. Will's brash smile caused her cheeks to burn. "Excuse me," she mumbled to the waitress, "but we aren't—"

The waitress ignored her, choosing instead to follow the debate raging throughout the restaurant. It was decided that Anna Luden's breakfast *was* better than the counterman's, and that the bridal suite was absolutely charming, and that the Harrises would continue to spend every anniversary there because it was just so romantic, and certainly these two lovebirds were bound to have a grand old time tonight.

Will sat across from Chloe, grinning and nodding while the lush, romantic strains of *Pagliacci* swelled around them.

We're going to be staying at Anna Luden's tonight, Chloe thought morosely. *We're going to be the newlyweds from Boston, staying at the nicest establishment around.*

Call it destiny or call it doom—it was Chloe's, and it was inescapable.

Chapter Eight

"They think we're married," Chloe groaned.

Will grinned and helped her into her seat. "That's not the worst thing anyone's ever thought about me," he said, glancing behind him at the band of well-wishers crowding into the doorway of Jasper's to wave them off. Will played up to the audience by bowing gallantly and touching his lips to her knuckles before he released her hand. His kiss should have made her even more jittery, but for some reason it calmed her down.

She presented the crowd with a tenuous smile as Will loped around the front of the van to the driver's side. "Have a good life!" one of the women shouted.

"Have a good night!" one of the men added, a comment that was greeted by a lot of clucking from the women and hooting from the men. Chloe shielded her face with her hand, unsure whether to wince or laugh.

The laugh won out, but as soon as Will was behind the wheel she grew sober again. "Will," she said urgently. "I'm worried. We're going to have to spend the night in the bridal suite."

His grin took on a Groucho Marx lecherousness. "I wonder how it'll compare to those honeymoon hotels in the Poconos."

"Will, this is serious."

"No it's not. It's hilarious."

He's going to be laughing all night, she thought, then sucked in a sharp breath as she recalled Will's comment about laughing during sex. She'd damned well make sure he had nothing to laugh about tonight.

As he pulled away from the curb, they both heard the noise—a metallic clanking sound. He frowned. "What the heck . . . ?"

"Is something broken?"

"I don't know." He shifted into idle, yanked on the parking brake and listened to the healthy purr of the engine. "It sounded like it was coming from outside. I'll go and have a look."

He pushed open his door and jumped out. Chloe closed her eyes, wondering if it was damage from when she drove off the road. Then she heard Will's familiar chuckle. "Cans," he said.

She opened her eyes again and found him leaning through the open door with his elbows propped on the driver's seat. "What do you mean, cans?"

"I mean, someone must have left the diner and tied a few empty tin cans to the bumper. And a Just Married sign."

"Oh, God." She spun around to look out her side window at the diner. In the doorway the jovial patrons of Jasper's were nudging each other in the ribs, slapping their knees and waving jubilantly at her.

She fluttered her fingers feebly in a responding wave, then hid her face again. Will resumed his place behind the wheel and steered down the road, trailing the rattling cans behind him.

"Why didn't you untie them?"

"In front of all those people?" He grinned playfully. "That would have hurt their feelings."

"So instead, we're going to drive up to the Luden place, where that idiot counterman phoned ahead to reserve the bridal suite for us, and the Ludens are going to see the cans and the sign before we have a chance to explain the situation to them."

"Explain what situation?" Will asked, intentionally obtuse.

"We can't pretend to be newlyweds."

"Why not?"

Why not? Because if they did, she wanted to scream, they'd wind up in some damned matrimonial bed together, that was why not. Yet his smile, with its intriguing blend of innocence and charisma, rendered her mute.

How could she argue with someone who had sworn he wasn't going to touch her? On the other hand, how could she share a room with someone who'd come right out and declared that he wanted to make love with her?

Of all the men in the world, how had she wound up masquerading as a newlywed with Will Turner?

Apparently unconcerned about the thoughts stampeding through her head, Will drove down Main Street toward the western edge of town. The helpful diners at Jasper's had described the Luden place as a small spread less than a mile beyond the town's limits. At one time the Ludens had farmed, but when they'd grown older and their seven children had moved out, Frank and Anna Luden had retired from farming and converted their oversized, underused house into a bed-and-breakfast establishment. The counterman at Jasper's had telephoned them to make arrangements, and had reported back to Will and Chloe that the Ludens had promised to have their best room ready for the nice couple from Boston.

The best room. Chloe listened to the clatter of cans chasing them down the street and sighed. "I had hoped," she said carefully, "that we would have separate rooms."

Will shrugged; his eyes danced with mischief. "Life is full of disappointments," he noted.

"Is there anything wrong in not wanting to sleep with a man on the first date?"

"Of course not," he said reasonably. His eyes sparkled even brighter when he added, "There *is* something wrong with not wanting to sleep with your husband on your honeymoon."

"I always wanted to go someplace exotic on my honeymoon," she complained. "Someplace with palm trees, and tropical drinks with little umbrellas sticking out of them."

"Maybe the Ludens can whip up a daiquiri."

"Will, we're in Ohio."

"I'll bet they've heard of daiquiris in Ohio," he countered. "Think of it this way—the last time you were in Ohio you slept in a sow's pen. Compared to that, the bridal suite ought to be a real thrill."

That the bridal suite might be a thrill was exactly what she was afraid of. "Maybe they'll figure out we're not married, and they'll insist that we take separate rooms," she said hopefully.

"Why would they think we aren't married? We make such a perfect couple."

"I'm not wearing a wedding band."

"You can turn that ring around so only the band shows," he suggested, glancing briefly at the simple opal birthstone ring she wore on her right ring finger.

Instead of scoffing at his suggestion, she switched the ring to her left hand and twisted it around so the stone was concealed against her palm. She studied the back of her hand for a moment, then made a face, irked by how nice it looked.

"I know, I know, it isn't as exquisite as the ring Ken gave Barbie," Will conceded. "If I'd had some warning, I would have done you proper. A two-carat diamond, a matching platinum band, the works."

"What a guy," she grunted, then smiled in spite of herself.

"That must be the place," Will said, slowing the van. A gravel driveway arced in a semicircle in front of a two-story farmhouse of clean white shingle, with dark green shutters and a peaked roof. From the front it appeared to be modest in size, but a long section extended off the back, easily tripling the dimensions of the house. Another gravel road branched off from the driveway to the adjacent barn. Will parked the van there and turned off the engine.

By the time they had gotten out, the front door of the house had been thrown open and a handsome older couple bounded onto the porch, flinging handfuls of light brown seeds at them. The couple had slate gray hair, broad faces, square shoulders and strong, healthy physiques.

"Is it planting season?" Chloe whispered, wondering even as she spoke why these people would be sowing seeds on the wooden steps of their front porch.

Will let out a laugh. "Haven't you heard? People don't throw rice at weddings anymore, because birds eat it and choke. The ecologically approved alternative is birdseed."

"They're throwing birdseed at us?"

"Yes, dear. Because we're newlyweds." He made a big show of kissing her cheek, then climbed out and raced through a hail of seed to assist his reluctant bride out of the van.

Birdseed. An ersatz wedding band. As Will led her around to the back of the van to unload their suitcases, she saw the tangled strands of colored yarn dangling from the rear axle, the dented soup cans and the wrinkled banner proclaiming her and Will "Just Married."

"Welcome!" the woman said, hurling a fistful of sunflower seeds at Chloe while the man relieved Will of the suitcases. "I'm Anna Luden, and this is my husband, Frank. I wish we'd had more warning—we would have gotten a bottle of champagne. But—well, come on in!"

Will slung his left arm around Chloe, and she didn't dare object to this show of spousal affection. "Hi," he said, offering Mrs. Luden his free right hand. "We're Will and Chloe Turner. This is quite a place you've got here."

"Well, it's a place, anyway," Mrs. Luden granted as she beckoned them inside. "We can't compete with the motel chains, but we try to make it up to you in service and price. I'm sure you folks are used to more sophisticated trappings."

"Who, us? Nah," said Will. Chloe was disconcerted to hear him use the word "us" in reference to her and himself. It flowed so naturally. So did his introduction. *Will and Chloe Turner,* she thought, bemused. It should have sounded strange to her, but actually it sounded kind of nice.

Having his arm around her felt just as nice. She relished its easy fit about her shoulders, and the light caress of his fingers along her upper arm. She had to exert herself not to nestle against him, not to sigh and call him hubby.

"We're putting you in our very best room," Mrs. Luden said, guiding them through a spotlessly clean center hall and up a flight of stairs covered with a patterned maroon runner rug and flanked by a polished oak railing. At the top of the stairs Mrs. Luden led them down a corridor to the door at the end. "This is definitely the nicest room we've got. You'll have your own bath and privacy."

"Lots of privacy," emphasized Mr. Luden, who followed them down the hall with the suitcases. "Make all the noise you want, kids. Nobody'll hear you back here."

"And this room has the best view," Mrs. Luden said.

"As if anyone's going to be killing time gazing out the windows," said Mr. Luden with a wink.

Mrs. Luden scowled disapprovingly at her husband, then bent her head toward Chloe. "All the years we've been married, and he still doesn't understand that a woman likes a beautiful view to put her in the mood."

"Who said a woman doesn't like a beautiful view?" Mr. Luden defended himself. "All I'm saying is, the view doesn't have to be out the window. There's much more interesting things to be looking at right there in the room."

Chloe blushed for the umpteenth time since she had left Boston with Will. She had never been much of a blusher before, but now she felt as if her face were running a permanent temperature of a hundred and ten.

"I believe Jay told you we charge thirty-five dollars a night for this room," said Mrs. Luden, changing the subject and sparing Chloe further embarrassment.

"Yes, he did," Will confirmed.

"That includes breakfast, of course." Mrs. Luden opened the door, then stepped aside so Chloe and Will could enter.

Protruding from the wall opposite the door was a raised queen-size four-poster covered with a lacy white spread. Windows on either side of the bed were curtained in the same eyelet lace, and braided oval rugs covered the hard-wood floor. Embroidered runners adorned the solid maple dresser and chest. In one corner stood a cane rocker, in another a maple valet stand with a patchwork quilt folded over the lower crossbar. The matching night tables held twin lamps of brass and milk glass.

Unable to stop herself, Chloe raced to one of the windows to check out the view Mrs. Luden had extolled. A small apple orchard, perhaps forty or fifty trees in all, spread south from the rear of the house, the branches dappled in the pale green and delicate pink of budding leaves and blossoms.

She loved it. Everything about the room was perfect: the view, the linens, the furnishings, the groom....

"...and the bathroom's right through here," Mrs. Luden was saying as she pushed open an inner door. "We haven't got a switchboard or anything like that, so if you need something you'll have to come downstairs and find me or Frank. But we're always around."

"We live here," Mr. Luden reminded them.

"Now, I don't know if anyone told you, but we host a weekly poker game here, every Saturday night," said Mrs. Luden. "Just a few neighbors come around, and the young fellow we've got boarding at the present. But that shouldn't bother you up here, way at the end of the hall. As I said, this room is very private."

"Of course," Mr. Luden said, addressing Will directly, "you're welcome to join the game. Nickel a hand—ten-dollar limit."

"Now, Frank, don't you think he's got something better to do than play cards with you and the others?"

"I'm just saying—"

"He's just saying," she snorted, giving her husband a shove. She eyed Chloe knowingly. "If this man of yours wants to play poker tonight instead of you-know-what, you make sure he knows enough to make an early night of it. Come along, Frank, let's let them get settled in." With that, the Ludens departed, closing the door behind them.

Unable to contain her pleasure, Chloe waltzed around the room, admiring the vista beyond the windows again, running her hand over the polished maple headboard, swinging around one of the vertical posts at the foot of the bed and finding herself face-to-face with Will. The dusk light filtering in through the windows played on the coppery highlights of his hair, and his eyes glowed with all the blue wattage of a state trooper's warning lights. Had Chloe actually thought he wasn't gorgeous when she'd first met him?

"I love poker," he said.

Jolted, she froze. Here she'd been ready to abandon reason, to exult in the illogic of the moment, pretend she was his bride—and *he loved poker*.

"It's a great game," he asserted in answer to her startled expression. "I haven't played since I moved to Boston. You don't mind if I play a few hands tonight, do you?"

"Why should I mind?" she asked archly. If he'd rather play cards than try to seduce her, let him play. She hoped he suffered humiliating losses. "I'd like to take a shower," she said in a glacial tone, "so if you want to use the bathroom first..."

Ten minutes later, Will had cleared out, leaving Chloe to wash in private. She took her time, dawdling under the hot spray until her skin began to pucker. She had no idea what she was going to do once she was done. Watch Will play poker? Curl up in that big, beautiful bed and resent him for not making a pass at her?

Still fuming, she dried herself off and dressed in the black jeans and sweater she had brought into the bathroom with her, on the chance that Will might have changed his mind and returned to the bedroom, ready to test the limits of her trust.

She exited the bathroom to find herself alone.

She hated him, and then she hated herself for hating him. *Lucky in cards, unlucky in love,* she grumbled under her breath.

After donning her earrings, she reached for her opal ring. She started to slide it onto her right hand, then changed course and put it on her left ring finger, twisting it to hide the stone in her palm. Seeing how lovely her finger looked in a wedding band only made her hate Will even more. Not wanting to linger in the same room with that taunting bed, she stormed out.

At the bottom of the stairs she heard men's voices coming from somewhere to her right and women's voices coming from the rear of the house. Chloe followed the men's voices first, tracing them to a spacious dining room, most of which was taken up with a large circular table covered with a green felt tablecloth. Six men sat around the table, each armed with a bottle of beer, one of them puffing on a cigar. Frank Luden appeared to be the oldest of the group, although another man was not much younger. The cigar smoker looked about forty, and the other two men appeared to be about Will's age.

Will was leaning back in his chair, assessing the cards fanned out in his hand, his expression impassive. His lips were set in a straight line, his gaze concentrated. A stack of white chips stood neatly before him.

He and the other players glanced up at her entrance. They smiled, and the older ones made a halfhearted show of rising from their seats. "How was the shower?" Frank Luden asked. "Water hot enough?"

"It was fine, thank you."

"The ladies are in the kitchen, if you'd care to join them," said Frank. "If you just head on down the hall—"

"I'll find it, thanks," she said, deliberately omitting Will from her smile.

She headed down the hall to the kitchen. Like every other farm kitchen she had ever been in, this one was big and bright, but despite the room's spaciousness, the four women in it seemed to fill it.

Anna Luden was bent over the oven, sliding two heat-and-serve pies in to warm; a stocky woman with a dashing orange scarf tied decoratively around her neck was pouring white wine from a gallon jug into glass tumblers at the table, a woman on the shy side of middle age was plugging in a twenty-four-cup electric coffee urn and a woman no older than Chloe sat on one of the chairs, her sweater bunched up under her arms as she nursed an infant. On the floor next to her was a baby chair and a diaper tote. All four women chattered simultaneously. The room's atmosphere was warmed not only by the mild spring night and by the oven's heat but by their friendly nonstop banter.

Chloe hovered in the doorway for a moment, feeling even more like an intruder here than she had in the dining room. But when Anna straightened up from the oven and caught her eye, the smile she gave Chloe instantly vanquished her bashfulness. "Well, come on in, have some wine!" she greeted her.

The other three women fell silent, appraising Chloe as she entered the room. Then they all began yakking again. Amid the verbal confusion, Chloe discerned that the nursing mother was named Gwen, her son was five weeks old, the woman with the coffee urn was either Jodie or Joanie and Chloe simply had to have some wine. Before she could speak a tumbler full of chablis was pressed into her hand. "It ain't the fanciest stuff in the world," said the orange-scarf woman with a grin, "but after a couple of glasses, who cares?"

Smiling shyly, Chloe took a seat across the table from Gwen. The orange-scarf woman crossed to the sink, opened the window above it, and lit a cigarette. Joanie lit one, too. "This isn't bothering the baby, is it?" Joanie asked.

"Not if you blow out. What's your name again?" Gwen asked Chloe.

"Chloe Verona—I mean, Chloe Turner."

"She's a new bride," Anna announced, helping herself to a glass of wine. "It takes time to get used to your married name, doesn't it?"

Sure, Chloe thought—especially if you weren't married and it wasn't your name. "This wine isn't so bad," she said, taking another sip.

Gwen ran her fingertip absently over the baby's tiny hands as he nursed. "Newlywed? When'd ya get married?"

"Oh—uh—yesterday," Chloe fibbed, wondering what Will would say if one of the men asked him.

"Yesterday? Hey, you're an old hand at it, then, aren't you," the woman in the orange scarf joked.

"I don't care how old a hand she is," Anna interjected, taking a seat beside Chloe. "You give that boy 'til ten o'clock and not a minute longer. Then you take him upstairs where he belongs."

"He belongs up there with her now, if they're newlyweds," said Joanie.

"Uh-uh," the orange-scarf woman said. "Give him his inch, sweetheart."

"And he'll give you his eight inches later," Gwen teased. Chloe practically choked on her wine.

"You shouldn't talk like that in front of the baby," Joanie scolded.

"Why not? Someday he'll be taking care of some bride, too. I hope he takes as good care of her as my Jimmy takes care of me."

"Yeah," the orange-scarf woman teased, snubbing out her cigarette and returning to the table. She nodded toward the infant. "Look how good he took care of you."

"Now, Mildred, we wanted this baby very much and you know it. And we'll have more—just as soon as Jimmy Junior learns to sleep through the night so we can get to work on it. And believe you me, I can't wait." She turned to Chloe. "Are you planning to have a family?"

"I—I guess so," Chloe stammered. "I mean...we only just got married." They hadn't even consummated their union—and they never would, as long as Will was the kind of jerk who thought playing cards was more fun than what he could have been doing upstairs with Chloe.

"Children are the greatest blessing in the world," Anna declared.

"They are not," Mildred scoffed. "They're the *result* of the greatest blessing in the world."

"Oh, Mildred, you're awful," Joanie said with a laugh. She extinguished her cigarette, too, and returned to the table. "So tell me, sweetie," she said to Chloe. "How come your husband is playing poker on your honeymoon?"

"Your age is showing, Joanie," Gwen reproached with a grin. "Nowadays, a honeymoon doesn't have the same significance as it used to, if you know what I mean."

"I don't care how far you've gone with the fellow before you exchange vows," said Joanie. "Once those vows are exchanged, the experience is entirely different. Don't you agree?" she asked Anna.

"I wouldn't know," Anna replied, her tone devoid of piety. "I never did it before we exchanged vows."

"Ah, the good old days," Mildred snorted. "Anna, you were the last of the genuine virgins. I'll tell you, the only real difference between girls like Gwen and Chloe and girls like us was that they didn't have to be so sneaky about what they were doing. With us, we had to pretend to be good."

"I didn't have to pretend," Anna pointed out. Then she patted Chloe's wrist and whispered, "Let me tell you, being good isn't all it's cracked up to be. I wish I'd had Mildred's guts. The more you learn before, the more you can start enjoying after."

Chloe bit back a laugh. It was peculiar to discuss premarital sex with these strangers—and yet she didn't feel strange about it at all. She listened, and smiled, and let them ramble on.

"Let me give you some advice, honey," Mildred confided, leaning across the table and patting the hand Anna hadn't claimed. She paused for effect, and the room filled with the sigh and gurgle of coffee percolating in the urn by the sink. "If your husband wants to play poker, let him. Set a limit on how much he can bet and then let him play."

"Mildred knows what she's talking about," Gwen informed Chloe. "She and Duke are going to be celebrating their thirtieth anniversary this June."

"Your thirtieth? Congratulations," said Chloe.

"If I learned one thing about how to make a marriage last," Mildred revealed, "It's this—give the man his ten or twenty dollars and let him play poker."

"Why?" Chloe asked. "Why is that so good for a marriage?"

"A man needs to prove himself," said Anna. "He thinks he's got to prove his manhood by taking risks. The key is to make sure the risks are manageable—and you're the one managing them."

Chloe gazed around the room. Gwen was still grinning, Anna was placidly tapping her fingers against the chrome edge of the table, Joanie was lifting her wineglass, and all four of them were nodding. Since Chloe wasn't married, the discussion was merely academic to her, but she was fascinated just the same. "In other words, if you don't let your husband play poker he's going to wind up taking up skydiving?"

"Skydiving, nothing," Joanie corrected her. "She's talking about running around on you."

"You can keep your man from running around by being good in bed yourself," Gwen argued.

Mildred shook her head. "If he's doing it with his wife, it ain't a risk. But the thing with poker—if he wins, he's a stallion, you know? Full of all that self-satisfied energy, and he's going to share it with you because you were the one who told him to play in the first place."

"And if he loses?" Chloe asked.

"Then the poor boy needs comforting, and you're his sweet mama, and if anyone can give him back his ego it's you, and he's so grateful.... You see? For a stake of ten dollars, the wife wins big, either way."

"Isn't that kind of...I don't know, manipulative?" Chloe asked.

The women erupted in raucous laughter. "Of course it is," Mildred confirmed once she stopped guffawing. "So what? It keeps them happy, it keeps you happy, and thirty years down the road you wind up having a slam-bang anniversary party."

"It does make things lively in bed," Gwen concurred.

"You mean—all you women bring your husbands to this poker game so you can have a lively time in bed afterward?" Chloe asked, astonished.

They nodded in unison.

"But what about—I don't know, candles and lacy underwear? What about dim lights and soft music?"

"That turns *us* on, not them," Joanie explained.

"Except the lacy underwear," said Gwen. "I know my Jimmy really goes crazy for that. You buy any lacy underwear for your honeymoon, Chloe?"

Chloe nodded—in fact, most of her underwear was more lace than fabric. But she hadn't packed with a honeymoon in mind, and the fact that she'd revealed something as private as her taste in lingerie to these women flustered her so much she gulped the rest of her wine in a single swallow.

"Good thinking," Gwen said calmly. "Poker and lace. That's what solid marital relations are really all about."

"'Specially when he comes a'calling on your lace with his poker," Mildred cracked.

Chloe really should have been shocked. But the wine combined with her mood to make her laugh, instead.

WILL SLID THIRTY-EIGHT dollars—twenty-eight of them pure profit—into his wallet. The money he'd won could be used to pay for a second room without diminishing their original cash supply. If he were a true gentleman he would offer to take a separate room for the night.

But then the Ludens would think the newlyweds had had a spat, and after an evening of wink-wink advice from the stud-poker studs of central Ohio he didn't think he could face that. He'd spent the past couple of hours being advised on such subjects as how to soften Chloe up, how to get her to try new positions, how to use back rubs to his best advantage and—most relevant, given Chloe's fraudulent migraine claim—how to cure a make-believe headache. By the time he'd called it a night, his money supply was not the only thing that had more than doubled in size.

Back rubs, he thought, wondering if they were as effective as Frank Luden and Simon had claimed. "If you dig your thumbs right in at the base of her neck, she'll do anything for you," Simon said. "Forget about erogenous zones. The base of the neck—that's all you need to know."

Then again, Simon was currently living in the Ludens' boarding house because he and his wife were separated. "I'll tell you this—she kicked me out, but it wasn't on account of I didn't satisfy her in bed. She had no complaints there, buddy. None." One of the other men had confirmed this, saying Simon's estranged wife worked with his own wife at a downtown store and talked about Simon's prowess from opening time 'til closing time.

So now what? Should Will sidle up behind her and give her that extraspecial back rub? Or should he wait for a sign from her? She knew he desired her; all she had to do was hint that the desire was mutual. One little hint and they would have a wedding night for the record books.

He tried not to stare at her as she stood in front of the framed mirror above the dresser, brushing her extravagantly curly hair. She'd removed her shoes, and as he glimpsed her socks he recalled her toes with their peach-painted nails. He recalled the way she'd stroked his calf with her foot when they'd lain together in the back of the van that morning.

Go ahead, rub her neck, a voice whispered inside him. *Just do it and see what happens.*

He started toward her, but when he was still halfway across the room she put down her brush, turned away from him and bent to lift her suitcase onto the bed. He let his gaze linger on the enticing roundness of her bottom. His jeans felt uncomfortably tight.

"Are you going to shower?" she asked.

Was that the hint he was waiting for? Or was it her way of getting him out of the room? Not trusting his voice, he didn't speak.

"You can have the bathroom first, if you want," she offered.

"Okay," he said in a gravelly tone. He carried his suitcase into the bathroom and closed the door. As he undressed, he imagined her undressing in the other room, sliding her slacks down those long, graceful legs, lifting off her sweater, unfastening the clasp of her bra—

God, it was torture just thinking about it. Forget all the how-to's his card-playing companions had shared with him—the real question was how Will was going to endure a night in bed with her when he knew that, for all her responsiveness to him earlier that day, deep in her heart she didn't want him making a pass at her.

He was an adult; he had a respectable supply of willpower. But his willpower had never been tested by someone like Chloe Verona.

He set the shower to a cool temperature. As streams of water flooded his face and skittered down his body, he tried to map out a survival strategy. He hit a snag right at the start: sleepwear. He hadn't packed any pajamas. He didn't own any.

Would she trust him if he wore underwear?

Not if she made the mistake of looking at him. He was fully capable of controlling his actions, but he couldn't control his *reactions*, and underwear didn't hide much.

What alternative did he have? It was either sleep in his clothes—too constricting—or sleep naked, and she would probably lock him out in the hall if he tried that.

Not that it mattered. She undoubtedly slept in a high-necked, ankle-length, long-sleeved nightgown, virginal pink flowers on white flannel. One look at her and he would wilt.

He put on a clean pair of jeans and emerged from the bathroom, his towel slung around his neck. She was leaning over the bed, turning down the lacy white spread. Her nightgown was also white, but to his distress—and irrepressible delight—it was far from virginal. The lightweight fabric flowed loosely to her ankles, revealing the willowy silhouette of her body underneath, and it was held up by thin white straps of lace. He stared at her arms, as long and graceful as her legs, and at her smooth, creamy shoulders, and at the slender arch of her neck. And at her face, growing rosy as she straightened up from the bed and discovered him ogling her.

"I don't have any pajamas," he informed her.

She swallowed. "What are you planning to do?"

Her voice sounded curiously breathy. The tremor of anticipation in it streaked along his nerve endings, making the muscles in his abdomen contract.

"I was hoping," he said in an admirably level tone, "you wouldn't mind if I slept in my underwear."

She dropped her gaze from his face to his torso. He wondered if her tastes ran to hairy chests. If so, his was sure to disappoint. No manly pelt covered the stretch of skin from his shoulders to his navel; no cloud of curls carpeted his pectorals. What she saw was a smooth, supple body honed by frequent squash games and distance swims. She saw sinewy arms, tawny skin. She saw his dark nipples and his narrow navel. And his jeans, barely hiding what they had to hide.

He noticed a movement in her throat as she swallowed again. "I've got to brush my teeth," she mumbled, hurrying past him to the bathroom door. Gripping the knob, she turned back to him and said, "I really hope we can be adults about this."

"Meaning?"

"You can sleep in your underwear, but please get under the covers before I come out." She darted in and slammed the door with hinge-rattling force.

Will chuckled, partly to release some tension and partly because it did him good to know she was as tense as he was. He shed his jeans and arranged himself chastely under the blankets. After a while she inched the bathroom door open and took a quick peek to make sure he was safely tucked in before she emerged from the bathroom. Avoiding eye contact with him, she glided about the bedroom, placing her toiletries bag on the dresser next to her comb and brush, checking her reflection one last time in the mirror before she came to bed. He admired the swirling flow of her gown, the way the hem danced around her ankles.

He took a deep breath, held it until his body unwound, and them emptied his lungs. As soon as Chloe pulled back the corner of the blanket on her side of the bed he turned off the lamp.

In the dark, he felt the mattress shift beneath her weight. He had left her a full half of the bed, yet she perched herself at the very edge of the mattress, as far from him as possible.

"Chloe..."

"So, how was the poker game?" she asked in an absurdly conversational tone.

He wanted to tell her to get away from the edge before she fell off the bed. "It was fun."

"How much did you lose?"

"I won."

She clung precariously to the edge of the bed.

"Chloe?"

She sighed. "What?"

"Trust me."

A moment elapsed in silence, and then she issued a tiny laugh. "Did you ever play that game?"

"What game?"

"'Trust Me.'" The mattress flexed under him as she rolled onto her back, away from the edge. He inhaled her familiar almond-blossom smell; he felt her warmth filling the space between the bottom and top sheets. He commanded his body not to respond.

"Is it like poker?" he asked.

She laughed, a fuller, more confident chuckle. "No. It was a game teenagers played, girls and boys."

"Boys against girls?"

"Actually, it was just one girl and one boy, and they weren't exactly on opposite sides. You'd play it in a secluded place, lying down and sort of touching each other—"

"I know that game. Only where I come from, it was called foreplay."

"No," she corrected him with another laugh. "The way it worked was, the boy would touch the girl somewhere— say, her stomach—and say, 'Trust me?' And if she said yes, he'd inch his hand higher and say, 'Trust me?' And if she said yes again, he'd inch his hand higher yet, up on her ribs, and say, 'Trust me?' And each time she said yes he'd move his hand closer to her breasts."

Will took a moment to digest this. As games went it wasn't much. As foreplay, though, it sounded great. "What if she didn't say yes?"

"Well, then the game was over. It was kind of a game of chicken, you know? There was always a chance the guy would chicken out before the girl."

"I can't imagine a guy chickening out before a girl."

"It wasn't played by experienced lovers, Will. It was just an excuse to touch, to experiment."

"You played this game a lot, I take it."

She must have heard the mocking humor in his voice. "No, of course not. But it was very popular at the beach, the summer my family lived in Key West, when I was fourteen. They also played it in Michigan when we lived there, and down in New Mexico...."

"Heaven knows why it didn't make it to Rowayton. If it had, I would have gone out for the varsity team."

"Oh, and now I'm supposed to trust you?"

"I'm not fourteen years old, Chloe. You were the one who said we should be adults."

She lapsed into silence. Will lay on his back, acutely aware of Chloe a foot away from him, her pillow abutting his, her vision trained on the same darkness above them. He couldn't guess what she was thinking, but what he was thinking was that if they were adults they would be kissing right now, indulging in the sort of thrills adults who were attracted to each other indulged in when they found themselves in bed together.

Instead, he was going to spend the night on his side with his back to her, trying futilely to ignore the rhythmic whisper of her breathing, the fragrance of her skin, the nearness of her lips. He was going to spend the night burning with frustration just to prove that he was a trustworthy guy.

So there was a game called "Trust Me." So high school kids in Key West and Michigan and New Mexico were having more fun than Will was tonight.

What a honeymoon, he thought grimly as he mumbled a good-night and rolled away.

Chapter Nine

Sometime when the night was still dense around her, she almost woke up. She wasn't sure what was pulling her toward consciousness—the searing warmth of Will's chest along her back, his knees against the backs of her thighs, his arm arched protectively around her waist. His hand flat on her belly, his fingers moving in slow, vague circles, drawing sensations down through her flesh.

His hardness pressing into her softness as his hips cradled her derriere.

She tried to force her eyes open. If only she were awake she could yell at him to leave her alone. But as long as she was still half-asleep she lacked the fortitude to stop him. His hand felt too good where it was, caressing her through the silky fabric of her gown. His firm, sleek chest felt too virile, and his legs lining hers, and the steel-hard shaft of him wedged against her bottom.

She stopped breathing for a moment. Apparently he was sound asleep; he continued to inhale and exhale with lulling regularity, his breath a ruffle of warmth through her hair. His fingers moved aimlessly, meandering down as far as the edge of her panties.

Tell him to stop, she ordered herself. But the core of aching heat just below his fingertips sent out its own message, and without meaning to she rocked her hips against him.

He groaned and slid his hand back up to the relative safety of her stomach. It proved not to be a safe retreat, after all—he splayed his long fingers across her abdomen and urged her tighter against himself. Through her gown and his briefs she felt him seeking, his need complementing hers.

"Will." Her voice emerged in the faintest whisper. Her body defied her common sense, writhing against him, provoking another groan from him.

He moved his hand higher, over her midriff, over her ribs to her breast. She thought about the silly adolescent game she'd described to him when they first climbed into bed. She thought about shouting, "No, I don't trust you!" Thought about rolling out of bed, whacking him in the head with her pillow.

Thought about turning in his arms and submerging herself fully in the erotic fever that burned through her as his hand curved along the underside of her breast.

She felt his lips move against her hair and braced herself for whatever he might have to say. He would probably implore her to let him continue. Maybe he would apologize for his forwardness before pointing out, with complete justification, that she was responding to him as fervently as he was to her. Whatever he said, she would have to insist that he stop. She wasn't ready for this. She wasn't.

He said nothing at all. He only grazed through her curls until he could close his lips tenderly over the edge of her earlobe.

This time she was the one who groaned, as tremors of arousal spread from his kiss down to the breast he was touching and then further, following the course his hand had taken and continuing beyond where he had ventured. She felt overheated, restless, torn.

She twisted her head with the idea of wriggling out of his embrace, and the motion freed his lips to browse along the sensitive skin below her ear. His hips continued to grind against her; his hand continued to cup the underside of her breast.

It would be so easy to give in. So easy to let her mind follow her body into bliss.

"Will. Stop." Her voice emerged in a breathless croak, and she tried again, louder. *"Stop."*

He groaned once more, opened his eyes and then recoiled in shock, his hand flying from her, his head jerking back as he hurled himself onto his half of the bed. He gulped in a great, ragged breath of air.

"I'm sorry," he said.

His sudden withdrawal left her shivering. She curled into a ball and clutched the edge of the blanket to her chin. Underneath the cover, parts of her body still simmered and seethed. Her shivering was not so much from the loss of Will's warmth as from sheer panic.

"Chloe?" He seemed to be calling to her from a great distance.

She was too chagrined to answer.

He cursed. Over her shoulder she glimpsed him sprawled out on his back, one arm flung across his forehead. The blanket had dropped to his waist, and she could see his naked chest rising and falling as he struggled with his breath. Below the blanket, below his waist... It was just as well she couldn't see what was going on down there.

"I thought I was dreaming," he mumbled.

She closed her eyes and commanded herself to stop shaking.

"I swear to God, Chloe, I didn't...I didn't mean to do that. I don't even know exactly what I did. What did I do?"

"Nothing much," she rasped. It wasn't true; he'd done way too much. But whatever he'd done, she'd done half of it.

"Tell me. I was asleep. I honestly don't remember."

A hoarse sound escaped her, laughter tinged with bitterness. "Wow. I must be awfully memorable, if you can't even remember what happened."

"Oh, Chloe, don't..." He sighed and rose onto his side so he could look at her. Her eyes had adjusted to the gloom enough for her to make out his tentative smile. "Don't say that. I'm awake now. If we go at it again, I swear I'll remember everything."

"Go at it again? Not on your life," she snapped. "Certainly not after you've proven how trustworthy you are." That wasn't fair. She ought to accept her share of the responsibility. But she was too anxious, too upset with herself as well as him, too infuriated by the whole thing. Too dangerously frustrated.

Turning away from her, he sat up, kicked off the covers and stood. "I'm going to the bathroom," he muttered, then stalked through the dark to the bathroom and banged the door shut behind him.

She lay in bed, listening to the rush of running water in the sink. She wondered whether he intended to spend the night in there, or get dressed and find another room. She wondered whether she should go after him, tell him all was forgiven.

Sure. She should go on in there, throw herself at him and invite him to join her in bed. She should tell him that she would try not to tempt him anymore, and that if he accidentally did touch her in his sleep she wouldn't rub up against him and drive both of them insane.

She should beg *him* to trust *her*.

The pulsing heat below her abdomen began to wane. The water in the bathroom shut off. After a minute Will came out. She kept her gaze resolutely on his face.

He got into bed, stretched out on his side with his back to her and yanked up the blanket. "Sorry," he said tersely, biting off the word as if he were sick of the whole thing, sick of apologizing, sick of her.

"I'm sorry, too."

He said nothing.

Too little, too late. She had allowed him to bear all the blame, and he hated her for it, and he would never kiss her again.

Now *that* was a scary thought.

HOW MANY SHOWERS? he thought, letting the stinging cold water rush over his upturned face. He'd awakened early and vaulted out of bed, refusing to remain in her vicinity a second longer than necessary. She'd continued to sleep, her tousled hair splayed out on the pillow and her arm draped over the blanket, which had slithered down below her breasts. In the pearly morning light he could almost make out her nipples, two round shadows pressing up against the filmy material of her nightgown.

She'd looked so damned relaxed, her eyes closed, her lashes thick and dark against her cheeks, her lips slightly parted. She'd probably been dreaming about capital gains and tax shelters.

Swearing under his breath, he turned off the faucets and reached around the shower curtain to grab his towel, which was still slightly damp from last night's cold shower. He reviewed his situation as he dressed in the narrow space between the tub and the sink.

Granted, he and Chloe hadn't known each other long. Some women measured a relationship in terms of longevity rather than intensity. Maybe she was just a prude—although, judging by the way she'd slithered against him last night, the way she'd twitched her tight little rear end against him until he thought he'd explode... No, he didn't really believe she was cold.

She had told him she was confused. Will was confused, too. He was baffled by what had happened between them. He'd never tried to seduce a woman in his sleep before.

He had a vague recollection of dreaming about her body cuddled up next to him, about the feminine curve of her belly, the sweet weight of her breast filling his hand, the velvety skin below her ear. He recalled dreaming about taking her, filling her, feeling her hot and pulsing around him. He'd gotten aroused. It was normal. It was healthy.

But to act on it? *In his sleep?*

Swinging open the bathroom door, he gazed at her for a long minute. She hadn't moved since he'd left the bed. Her hair still tumbled in voluptuous dark curls across the pillow; the blanket remained at her waist; her nipples still strained against her nightgown when she inhaled. And he still desired her.

Actually looking at her, he remembered other parts of his dream, parts not limited to her physical attributes. There had been more to it last night than just two bodies in bed. Much more.

In his dream he'd heard her laughter. He'd seen the righteous indignation in her eyes, and the determined set of her chin. He'd heard the unspoken *uh-oh* in her voice when she inadvertently let on that she'd lied about her appreciation of opera. He'd seen the rhapsodic joy in her face as she pranced around the bridal suite, and the almost maternal smile she got whenever she supplied him with a snack from the tote. In his dream he had reveled in her girlish humor as she described that "Trust Me" game to him last night.

Good God, an accountant. Just what he needed in his life: an accountant with a dingbat brother and great legs.

Needed. Will needed her. This had gone way beyond wanting. It had to do with stimulating conversation, with sharing a woman's deepest secrets about Barbie dolls, with someone so strong and independent she wasn't afraid to expose her weakness. It had to do with bridal suites.

He left the bedroom, closing the door quietly so as not to wake her up. He had to get away from her to straighten out his head. The longer she slept, the more time he would have.

Downstairs in the dining room he found Frank Luden and Simon, the Ludens' current boarder. The green felt cloth that had covered the round table for the game had been replaced by a white damask cloth, and a lazy Susan at the center held a creamer, a sugar bowl, salt- and pepper-shakers, a butter dish and a ceramic bowl of jam. A huge electric urn stood on the side table beside a half-dozen coffee cups; Frank was filling a cup with coffee. A blend of aromas, bacon and freshly baked pastry prominent among them, wafted down the hall from the kitchen.

Both men turned to Will as he entered, and he greeted them with as chipper a "good morning" as he could manage.

"The cardsharp needs coffee," Simon said, diagnosing Will's sour mood.

"After last night, I'm not surprised," Frank returned, winking and jabbing his elbow into Simon's ribs. "Wore you out, did she?"

She'd worn him out, all right, but not the way they meant. "I'd love some coffee," he grumbled.

"Is the wife on her way down?" Frank asked, as he placed two cups on the table.

"No, I'm letting her sleep in."

"Watch out," Simon warned. "My wife always slept late, and look where I am now."

"Well, there's no harm in her sleeping a little late today. We're on our honeymoon, after all," Will said, staggering under the weight of his own irony.

"That's true," Frank commented. "If there's ever a time you want her 'specially well rested, it's on your honeymoon."

"Sure," Simon agreed. "Let the lady sleep in. That way she'll have more energy tonight."

"I don't know about our groom, though," Frank joked. "He looks tuckered out. We better get some food into him." He left the dining room.

"Have some coffee, Will," Simon said, bringing him a full cup. "Get your strength up. You ever try Vitamin E pills? They can really rejuvenate a tired man."

Will smiled so he wouldn't seem rude, then took a long sip of the black coffee.

"So, where does your honeymoon take you next?" Simon asked.

"Up to Minnesota." He really wasn't in the mood to talk, but Simon was trying so valiantly to get a dialogue going, Will didn't have the heart to disappoint him.

"Me and Diane went to Niagara Falls on our honeymoon," Simon told him. "It's unbelievable. You ever been?"

"No."

"You ought to go sometime with the wife. All that spuming foam does something to women. It's kind of like the tides with them, you know? All that moon tide and water stuff."

Will struggled to shape another smile. He was rescued from having to speak by Frank, who returned from the kitchen carrying a platter of fresh baked corn muffins. "Get 'em while they're hot," he boomed, then looked toward the door. "Ah, here comes the missus."

Will looked toward the hall, expecting to see Anna Luden bringing in the rest of their breakfast. The "missus" Frank was referring to, however, was Chloe.

She was dressed in a short-sleeved pink sweater and the black jeans she'd had on last night. Her hair was brushed back from her face, and she offered a brave smile to Frank and Simon before glancing at Will—and then right past him, very quickly.

"Good morning," she murmured.

Frank already had a cup of coffee filled for her. He placed it in front of the chair next to Will's, refusing her the option of sitting further away from her alleged spouse. Somehow she managed to take her seat without allowing her gaze to intersect with Will's or her arm to brush his. She occupied herself by mixing spoonful after spoonful of sugar into the coffee.

"Did you sleep well last night?" Simon asked in a great show of neighborliness.

"Yes," she said curtly. She added some cream to her coffee and stirred for all it was worth. "I slept very well. We both did."

"Enjoy it while you can," he said.

Her eyes flashed at Simon. "Enjoy what?"

"Holy matrimony."

She stirred her coffee even harder. Will began to worry that she would break the cup.

"Incidentally," Frank piped up, "we've got a real nice church in town, if you folks are interested in attending services this morning."

"Sin on Saturday, save yourself on Sunday," Simon remarked.

"They're married, Simon," Frank reminded him. "They're allowed." He turned back to Chloe and Will. "Very nice young minister we've got here. We could have him say a special prayer for you, as you start your new life together."

"I don't think—" Will said.

"No, we can't—" Chloe said simultaneously. They glanced at each other, on the verge of sharing a smile at how well their sentiments meshed. But the moment Chloe's dark eyes met Will's her smile vanished, and she swiftly turned back to her coffee.

"We've got a lot of miles to cover today," he explained.

"A long trip," she emphasized before sipping her coffee.

"We need to get an early start."

"A very early start."

Silence descended upon the room. It lasted until Anna Luden arrived with a steaming platter of scrambled eggs in one hand and a small bowl heaped with bacon strips in the other. Chloe's expression brightened when Anna entered; she invited her to sit down and join them for breakfast. When Anna said she had business to take care of in the kitchen, Chloe's face resumed its pinched, distant look.

More silence. Reaching for the butter, Will accidentally bumped Chloe's arm with his hand. They jumped apart, as if they had given each other electrical shocks. He hazarded a quick glance at her, wondering whether she expected him to apologize for the inadvertent contact. She kept eating, though, her eyes on her plate.

He slathered butter on his muffin with such belligerence it crumbled in his hand.

"Wedded bliss," Simon pondered, taking in Chloe and Will with a fond gaze. "Kind of leaves you speechless, doesn't it?"

"Kind of," Will muttered.

"I remember when things were good between Diane and me. There were some nights when everything that had to be said got said without words. I know the feeling. Just one glance and you're sharing a world of memories."

Chloe stirred her coffee again.

"That look, Will—the glow of a woman well satisfied... There's nothing quite like it."

"Sure," Will mumbled.

"Go ahead, Will—give her a kiss. I won't look."

"That's quite all right," Chloe said quickly, dropping her spoon onto her plate with a loud clatter. "If we're going to get an early start, Will, you'd better go upstairs and pack. I've already packed my things."

"Oh. Sure." She'd reduced him to monosyllabic grunts, but he didn't care. He stood, sent a final wan smile Simon's way, and left the dining room.

It didn't take him long to throw his things into his suitcase. He checked the dresser top to make sure nothing had been left behind, and the floor, and the bathroom. Returning to the bedroom for one final inspection, he confronted the bed.

Staring at the misshapen pillows and the rumpled sheets, he felt his anger subside. She hadn't exactly rejected *him,* he reminded himself. She'd rejected his seduction attempt, but not *him*. And before she'd done any rejecting, she'd responded. Oh, God, how she'd responded.

There was hope yet. He had already slept with her twice. What was the old saw about the third time being a charm?

He carried their bags from the room, through the long hall and downstairs. Chloe was standing in the wide entrance hall with the Ludens, smiling and talking as if everything were just fine and dandy. The minute Will's foot hit the bottom step, though, she flinched and fell silent for a minute.

"Well," she said to the Ludens, turning her back to Will, "thanks again for everything."

Will set the bags down with a thud. "Don't we have to settle accounts?"

"I already paid."

"I see how it works," Frank teased. "You win the money, she spends it."

"Now, you folks drive safely, and make sure you come see us next time you're in town," said Anna.

"You can count on it," Chloe promised.

"Unless it's a Saturday night," Frank joked again, shaking Will's hand. "I don't know if I can afford playing poker with you again, Will." He turned to Chloe. "Your husband's quite a bluffer, Mrs. Turner. He's got a killer instinct you just can't trust."

"Tell me about it," she muttered in agreement.

Will held the door open for her, then lifted the bags, insisting that the Ludens didn't have to see them out. He suddenly felt anxious to depart from the house and its strange undertow. He wanted to get away, to get back in gear, to cruise the highway until he and Chloe figured out how to feel comfortable with each other again.

Chloe climbed into the passenger seat while he stowed their bags in the back of the van. When he took his place behind the wheel, he noticed that she'd donned her sunglasses, blocking a major portion of her face from him. Leafing through the road atlas, she didn't even acknowledge him when he strapped himself into the seat next to her.

He acknowledged her, though. Her almond-blossom scent filled the atmosphere. Her curly hair spilled enticingly over her shoulders. Her sweater hinted at the contours of her bosom and her formfitting jeans advertised her long legs. Her presence permeated the van like an intoxicating mist, seeping through his pores and filtering through him.

Keeping his face expressionless, he steered around the gravel driveway to the road, retracing the route they'd taken the previous evening. He focused on the view through the windshield, his lids lowered against the morning glare, his fingers hooked casually around the steering wheel, his foot light and steady on the gas pedal. And inside his chest his heart drummed: *I want her. I want her. I want her.*

Peggy hadn't had this effect on him. Peggy had had her pluses and minuses—too many of the latter, as it turned out—but one thing Will had to say for her: she had never been hesitant about sex.

But then, he'd never made love to her when his brain was in Z-land and his body was operating on its own. He had never ravished her without even being aware that he was ravishing her. He had never reached for her as he'd reached for Chloe, and pulled her against him and believed, in some deep, inscrutable part of his soul that if only he held her close enough he could absorb her into his dreams.

Peggy had made him crazy in plenty of ways, but never like the way Chloe had made him crazy last night.

"We need to stop for gas," he remarked.

Chloe nodded. "I've got to make a phone call, too."

"Your brother hasn't got a phone."

"I'm not calling him."

"Who are you calling?"

"I do volunteer work at a hospice in Boston on Sunday afternoons," she said. "Obviously I'm going to miss my shift today."

Volunteer work. Well, wasn't she a goody-goody. She could break his heart, break his spirit—but, oh, what an altruist Chloe Verona was. Wasn't charity supposed to begin at home? At the moment, home happened to be Will's van.

Not that he would accept anything she gave in charity. She didn't have to do any of her good works on him. He wasn't that hopeless.

They found the highway without any problems, and took the westbound entrance. The sun was behind them; Chloe could have removed her sunglasses if she'd wanted to. But she kept them on. She stuck her chin forward at a pugnacious angle. Her lips were thin and rigid, neither smiling nor scowling. Her hands resided in her lap, folded prissily, her fingers interwoven. Her knees were pressed together.

"How long do your moods usually last?" he asked.

"What's that supposed to mean?"

"What it's supposed to mean," he said, hearing the first strains of impatience sifting through his voice, "is that what happened last night wasn't such a big deal. I mean, all right, it happened, I said I was sorry—and you haven't, by the way—"

"What am I supposed to apologize for?" she asked sanctimoniously. "Refusing to let you manhandle me?"

"*Manhandle* you?" He snorted. "Excuse me, but were you and I in the same bed last night?"

"Yes. That was the problem, as I recall."

"The problem, lady, was that you were as turned on as I was. I wasn't the only one moaning and groaning. You were there, all the way, and I'm willing to admit it and you aren't."

"Wrong," she said, her tone as chilly as his was heated. "The problem was, you told me I could trust you, and the next thing I knew you were—you were—"

"Say it, Chloe. I was touching your breast. I was kissing your ear. Say it."

"Why should I say it? What is this, Will? Why should I say any of this?"

"Because you're repressed, that's why."

"Oh." She pursed her lips and made a huffing sound. "I'm *repressed*. Is that a fact?"

"Yes, Chloe, that's a fact. Not only that, but you're judgmental. You've already crossed me off your list because I do the art for my books, right? I work at a drafting table, so I'm not good enough for you. How about ol' Boris? Your brother's best friend—he's an artist, too, so he's no good, either. Right? Man, we could compile a really juicy case history on you, starting with your artist father—"

"How dare you!"

"'How dare you!'" he mimicked in an affected tone. "What are you, a refugee from the Victorian era?"

"No. I'm a woman under assault. Good God, Will—I suppose I'm lucky you're driving. If you weren't, you'd probably be beating me with your fists."

"Who me? No. I'd be trying to get you to commit carnal acts on sensitive parts of my body."

"I believe it."

"Have you always hated men?"

"Have you always practiced psychoanalysis without a license?"

"No. I only do that when I unintentionally respond to a woman in bed, and she acts as if I'm highly contagious."

"I didn't say you were contagious. All I said was, you told me I could trust you, and I did, and you broke that trust. I wasn't ready for what you wanted last night—"

"For what *we* wanted, Chloe."

"For what *you* wanted," she stressed. "I wanted to sleep last night. You wanted sex. After this morning, I will *never* want to have sex with you. If your fragile ego can't take it—"

"Keep my ego out of it."

"Your ego was poking into the small of my back all last night. *You* keep your ego out of it, and we'll both be fine."

He tossed back his head and led out a loud, scornful laugh. Why did he feel as if he were fighting not just Chloe, not just last night, but some huge, dreaded enemy, some looming, lurking monster from her past? This was not the Chloe who had been so soft and compliant in her sleep. This wasn't the Chloe he wanted to hold to himself with joy and laughter and tenderness, someone he wanted to explore forest glades with, and waterfalls, and the mysteries of his books' characters and—why not?—the mysteries of the IRS tax code.

This was someone else, someone mean and temperamental and anti-men.

"It's your father, isn't it?" he asked, no longer caring about whether he was overstepping the bounds of civility. "He fooled around with other women, so now you're taking revenge on the male species?"

This time it was her turn to give a disdainful laugh. "All I did was turn you down last night, Will. Why must you assume that, just because I don't want to have sex with you, I've got it in for the entire male species? Hasn't anyone ever said no to you before?"

He lacked a quick answer to that. Of course women had said no to him before. But it had never bothered him the way Chloe's rejection bothered him. She was different. He couldn't imagine wanting to drive any other woman across the country, any more than he could imagine making love to another woman in his sleep. He couldn't imagine becoming so compulsive about breaking through to a woman, or going slightly berserk just because a woman had said no to him.

What was it that Scott had said just before Will had walked blindly into her life? Something about using his imagination on her. Will's imagination was so full of Chloe right now, that he couldn't think straight.

"There's a sign," she said tersely. "'Rest stop, one mile.'"

"Great," he said, with the same degree of enthusiasm.

The next minute passed in tense silence. Then he spotted the exit ramp to the rest stop and flipped the directional switch.

"Do you need to use the facilities?" she asked quietly. She seemed exhausted. The weary quality of her voice almost made him feel sorry for her.

"No. I'll fill up the tank while you go inside and make your call. Once I've got the van gassed up, I'll swing around and get you."

"Okay."

He pulled to the curb and she climbed out, slinging the strap of her purse over her shoulder. Without a word or a wave, she marched briskly up the paved walkway to the glass doors of the rest-stop building and disappeared inside.

Sighing, he drove over to the fuel plaza. His rage was fading away, leaving in its place a sorrowful emptiness. He hadn't meant to draw her into a fight. He certainly hadn't meant to pick apart her past. It had only been his frustration talking, his irritation at her refusal to acknowledge what was happening between them. They liked each other; they desired each other. It all seemed so simple to him.

The van guzzled fourteen gallons. Will let the attendant check his oil and water and clean the squashed bugs off the windshield. Crossing his arms over the steering wheel, he rested his head against his wrists and prayed for patience.

Eight minutes elapsed from when she'd left the van until he'd U-turned, cruised back to the building and parked. She must be done with her phone call by now, but he didn't see her anywhere.

He left the van and sauntered through the mild morning air to the building, a boxy cinder-block structure nearly identical to every other boxy cinder-block rest stop they'd visited since they started this trip. He entered to find himself in a bustling lobby area, swarming with travelers. He located the telephones, but not Chloe.

Will jammed his hands into his pockets and walked to the women's rest room. The door flapped open and shut, open and shut. A heavy older woman trudged in, her body heaving from side to side with each step. A slim younger woman came out dragging a whining toddler by the wrist.

Two giggly teenagers with oceans of hair scampered toward the door, with their heads bowed together and their shoulders bumping as they exchanged breathless secrets.

The heavy older woman trudged out. Two nuns in street clothes, identifiable only by their modest wimples, went in.

Will glanced at his watch.

Maybe Chloe wasn't in there. Maybe she'd gone into the food area to buy a snack. He darted toward the restaurant and gave the room a fleeting survey. The din of people's voices was nearly deafening, and it was overlaid with syrupy music. Coins rattled, a computerized cash register beeped, babies bawled and adolescent boys cheerfully snarled profanities at one another.

No Chloe.

He hurried back to the area near the women's room. The two nuns came out.

"Excuse me," he said, approaching them and smiling deferentially. "Did you happen to notice whether there was a woman with curly black hair and black pants in there?"

The two nuns looked at each other and shrugged. "I'd say there were at least a few women who'd fit that description," one of them said.

"Curly hair is very 'in' these days," said the other.

Thank you for that update from the fashion front, he thought. "She had on a—a light purple sweater, I think. Or maybe it was pink. I . . . I don't exactly remember."

The nuns looked at each other and shrugged again. "She might have been in there," the first nun said. "I can't be sure."

"Thanks, anyway." He stepped aside, dismissing them with a polite nod. His vision snagged on a middle-aged woman about to enter the women's room and he raced after her. "Excuse me," he said, grabbing the sleeve of her colorful warm-up suit before she could swing the door open.

She spun around, evidently terrified by his aggression. He immediately dropped his hand from her.

"I'm sorry—I'm just—" He took a deep breath and tried to present himself as saner than he actually felt at the moment. "I'm worried about my—my wife. She went into the ladies' room a while ago, and I've been waiting here, and…I was wondering if you could check on her for me."

The woman glowered at him. "What, am I supposed to peek under the doors?"

He flashed a nervous smile that was really more a grimace. "No—no, of course not. Just see if she's putting on her makeup or something. She's wearing black jeans and a pinkish top, and she's got dark, curly hair and sunglasses. Her name is Chloe."

The woman sized him up with a long, skeptical gaze. Apparently she concluded that he wasn't a psychopath, because as she shoved open the door she said, "I'll check." The door swung shut behind her.

He waited. He paced. He entertained the appalling notion that Chloe had run away, that she'd climbed through a back window and was right this very moment begging for a ride from a stolid midwestern family with two apple-cheeked children and a U-Haul trailer chained to the back of their station wagon.

She would do anything to get away from Will, wouldn't she. After all, he'd had the audacity to kiss her throat and stroke her breast. He was obviously an animal, posing a grave threat to a virtuous damsel like her.

She was gone. She'd gotten away. He had lost her in a rest stop in Ohio, and he felt like kicking a wall and screaming.

The woman in the colorful warm-up suit pushed open the door and stepped out. "She's in there," she said.

Only then did Will realize he'd been holding his breath. He released it in a long sigh, then gave the woman his most grateful smile. "Did you tell her I was waiting here for her?"

"Was I supposed to tell her that?"

He exhaled again. "No... that's all right. I'll just keep waiting."

He took heart in the news that Chloe hadn't fled from him. What little encouragement that brought was dashed by the understanding that she *was* hiding from him. He tapped the arm of an athletic-looking young woman in a University of Indiana windbreaker who was jogging toward the women's room. "Excuse me," he said. "Could you do me a favor?"

Like the last woman he'd enlisted, she appeared less than eager to help. She looked strong, though, her blond hair pulled back into a bouncy ponytail and her feet shod in serious leather running shoes. She had the demeanor of a jock. If worse came to worst, maybe she could wrestle Chloe out of the bathroom.

"There's a woman in there. Her name is Chloe Verona. I know she's in there." He described her clothing, then presented what he hoped was a properly humble, beseeching smile. "Would you please tell her that Will wants her to come out? Tell her I'm waiting."

"You're waiting," the girl repeated.

"If that doesn't work... tell her I'm desperate." What the hell. Right now he needed to get her out of there. Exaggerating wasn't a crime. If it *was* an exaggeration, which he wasn't sure it was.

"You're waiting and you're desperate." The girl nodded dubiously and shouldered open the door. "Hey, is there someone here named Chloe Verona?'' he heard her bellow just before the door whipped shut, muffling the noises inside.

He waited. He brooded. He conjured up every example of foolishness on Chloe's part. He should have guessed she would be more trouble than she was worth. Here was a woman who would turn the universe upside-down over a box of glorified gravel, who would fake a migraine to get out of a date, who would condemn an entire profession—an entire gender—just because her father and brother weren't perfect and some clown of a boyfriend rained on her New Year's Eve celebration.

She could cut through the garbage, all right—and she could generate more garbage than anyone he'd ever met. The woman was intolerable. He ought to get out of here, hop back into the van and drive off. He ought to desert her, just take off and leave her stewing in her own juices. It would damned well serve her right.

A minute passed. The athletic blond girl strode out. "She's in there," the girl reported.

"I know she's in there."

"She doesn't want to come out."

"Why?" he fumed. "What the hell is she doing in there?"

"What do you mean, what's she doing? She's in there, that's all."

"She's sick. Oh, no, is that it?"

"She looked healthy to me."

"Did you tell her I was waiting for her?"

"Yeah. I—uh—I didn't tell her the desperate part, though. I was going to, but before I could, she said, 'Let him wait.'"

A fresh burst of fury seized him, followed by panic. Followed by genuine, no-holds-barred, sky's-the-limit desperation. He wanted her out of there, in the van, by his side where they could talk this thing through.

He turned toward the women's room door, marched up to it and hollered, *"Chloe!"*

Pressing his ear to the door, he heard a chorus of nattering high-pitched voices. Then silence.

"Come on, Chloe, come out!"

He waited.

The blond girl sidled over. "What you've got to do," she said helpfully, "is change her mind."

"Change her mind?" he asked crossly.

"Sure. If she doesn't want to come out, you've got to give her a reason to come out."

Of course. It was obvious. She didn't want to face him, so he had to give her a reason to face him. She didn't trust him, so he had to give her a reason to trust him.

He edged the door open a crack so he could be heard without screaming. "Chloe?" he entreated in a soft, cajoling tone. "Chloe…come on out. Please. I need you out here." He caught his breath and gave her a minute to respond.

She didn't scream at him to go away. She didn't say anything at all.

He sent her a silent plea: *Give a little, woman. Meet me halfway.* "Come on out, Chloe," he implored, closing his eyes and resting his forehead against the door. "I love you, okay?"

Chapter Ten

"Wow," sighed the skinnier of the two adolescents who had been sharing a cigarette in the rest room. She gazed worshipfully at Chloe. "Did you hear that? He said he loves you!"

Her companion twisted the faucet of the sink where she'd been scrubbing the cigarette smell from her face. "In public, too. You are so-o-o-o lucky to have a guy, like, do that."

"It's so neat that he's, like, willing to make an ass of himself in public, just for you."

Well, Chloe thought, that was true love in a nutshell: the willingness to make an ass of oneself in public.

She smiled at the earnest teenagers with their damp faces. She couldn't take them too seriously—she couldn't take seriously anyone who would voluntarily subject her hair to a beauty treatment that would render it as unmanageable as Chloe's. But the frizz twins were kind of cute in a delirious-teenybopper way.

It wasn't as easy to dismiss the others in the rest room: the elderly woman with the blue-rinsed hair, who wagged an arthritic finger at Chloe and said, "If you don't go out and make up with him, young lady, you'll never forgive yourself. You've got to grab the gold ring when you have the chance, because it may not be there the next time the merry-go-round goes 'round.''

And the middle-aged woman in stretch pants who said, "If my husband verbalized his feelings like that, I'd never have to write to Ann Landers again.''

And the woman in her mid-thirties who said, "Grab him, honey—the older you get, the tougher it gets.''

Dear God, Chloe thought, *can't a person have a private crisis?*

She glimpsed her reflection in the mirror above the row of sinks. She looked drawn, her lips bitten raw and framed with lines of tension. She wanted to look beautiful when she faced Will—*if* she faced Will. Given her wretched appearance, she wasn't sure whether she should leave the rest room or flush herself down a toilet.

She felt despicable, undeserving of forgiveness. She was torturing the poor man not because of anything he'd said or done but because she couldn't figure out whether or not she wanted him.

Not true. She knew damned well she wanted him—and she knew she shouldn't. She didn't love him. She *couldn't* love him. He was an artist, for heaven's sake. He picked up and moved every few years. He was the descendant of a witch. He loved poker.

Anyway, this was their first date. It didn't matter that it was lasting for days. She couldn't make love with him on their first date. It just wasn't right. She shouldn't want him that way.

But she did. And he knew it.

She tore her gaze from the mirror and eyed her cheering squad. Shoring up what little courage she had, she gave them a brave smile. "Okay," she said. "I'm going.''

"Go for it," one of the teenagers said with a giggle. "This is, like, so-o-o-o romantic.''

Chloe marched to the door, refusing to slow her stride, refusing to look back. She shoved it open and discovered Will standing just a few feet away, surrounded by his own small band of cheerleaders—a couple of truck-driver types, a salesman armed with a bulky samples case, several teenagers in biker jackets, two nuns carrying take-out bags from the restaurant, and the bouncy blond athlete who had delivered Will's message. As soon as Will saw her his expression brightened, his mouth curving into a tentative smile. The circle of onlookers burst into applause.

Chloe had never felt so embarrassed in her life.

Before she could duck back inside the rest room, Will grabbed her hand and hauled her across the lobby to the door. She was more than willing to be hustled out of the building, especially when a few of the men shouted what they no doubt intended as congratulatory remarks: "You pushed her button, man! She's all yours! You know how it is with chicks—it don't matter what you do, as long as you tell 'em you love 'em!"

The instant she saw the van she broke into a run.

They both hurried inside the vehicle, slammed the doors behind themselves and settled in their seats. Chloe kept her hands in her lap; Will drummed his fingers against the steering wheel. She stared at her cuticles; he stared at the fuel plaza occupying the far end of the lot.

For no good reason, tears welled up in her eyes. Her sunglasses hid them from Will's view, and she batted her eyelids furiously to blink them away before he could see them.

Why did this hurt so much? Why did she suddenly feel a deep, bruising pain inside her?

You pushed her button, man. That was what the theatrics inside the building had been about. Will's declara-

tion had nothing to do with love. It was simply a ploy to
lure her out of the bathroom. He didn't mean any of it.

Fine. Of course he didn't mean it. So why should she be
hurting? Why should she even care?

He let out a long breath, turned toward her and reached
for her hand. When he'd grabbed her hand in the rest-stop
lobby, she hadn't felt in his clasp anything more compli-
cated than a desire to keep her from escaping again. Now,
however, he was holding her to connect with her, to com-
municate something. His touch set off sparks beneath her
skin, sending a tremulous heat up her arm.

She cautioned herself not to overreact—not to react at
all.

"It occurred to me," he said slowly, apparently select-
ing each word with care, "that I was under no obligation
to wait for you. You could have stayed in the women's
room and I could have left, and when I got to the next exit
on the interstate I could have turned around and driven
back to Boston. I mean, really, what do we owe each
other?"

Nothing, she answered silently. They owed each other
nothing and—damn her tears. Will Turner was not worth
crying over.

"But I couldn't do it. I couldn't leave you. Plain human decency, I guess. I just couldn't abandon you in the
bathroom like that."

"Sure. Great."

"I know that scene in the lobby was kind of humiliating—"

Kind of! Half the rest stop had witnessed their idiotic
behavior. Someone had probably caught them with a cam-
corder, and they were going to see themselves on some
"Goofy Home Videos" show, between the dancing cat

and the toddler whose pants fell down at the nursery-school picnic.

"I can handle a little humiliation," he said. "I couldn't handle deserting you."

"Okay. You've made your point."

"I would have said anything to get you out of there, Chloe. I would have tried anything. If talking to you through the door hadn't worked, I probably would have barged in and carried you out over my shoulder."

"How very Neanderthal."

He tendered a faint smile. "Fortunately, talking to you worked. We were able to remain civilized."

Oh, yes, so civilized. He'd done what was necessary. He'd spouted empty words, meaningless sentiments, sweet nothings. He'd pushed her button, as that eloquent gentleman near the gift shop had so cleverly put it. And it had worked, hadn't it. He'd said the word love, and Chloe had come running.

"So..." He stroked his thumb gently across her wrist, sending a fresh current of sparks up her arm and through her flesh, a sensation uncomfortably similar to what she'd felt last night when he'd kissed her and run his hand over her nightgown, over her body. "If we're ever going to get to Minnesota, we'd better hit the road."

"I guess we'd better."

He released her hand and turned on the engine. Neither of them spoke as he backed out of the space and maneuvered through the lot to the highway ramp. Not until he had accelerated into the flow of thruway traffic did he glance her way. "You're upset, aren't you?"

"Why should I be upset?"

"You're mad at me for saying what I said outside the bathroom."

For lying like a dog, she thought bitterly. For operating on the assumption that all he'd had to do was mention an insipid four-letter word and she'd be squealing and gushing like those thirteen-year-olds, thinking it was so-o-o-o romantic. No, she wasn't mad at him. She hated him. He didn't deserve it, but she hated him for doing this to her. She hated Orin for starting this mess, and she hated Will for becoming a part of it.

She ought to be home right now, doing the Sunday *Globe* crossword puzzle and sipping her third cup of gourmet ground coffee. She ought to be fondling one of her smooth round abalone beads and enjoying a stress-free Sunday.

Instead, she was on I-80, swallowing down a lump of tears the size of Mount Rushmore and hating a man for throwing around the word love as if it didn't mean a thing.

"No, I'm not mad at you," she said, figuring that if he could lie, so could she. "Are you mad at me?"

He was accelerating to pass a three-rig convoy, and he didn't speak until he'd merged back into the right lane. Then he glanced briefly her way and shrugged. "Why should I be?"

"Because of last night."

"You mean, the way you tempted me?"

"The way I made you stop."

He chuckled. "Oh, I think my ego and I will survive. How about it, ego?" he addressed his groin. "Are you going to survive?"

"Sure. I'm tough," he answered for his ego in a raspy little voice.

"Don't make jokes, Will. I feel lousy about what happened—not just what you did, but the way I dealt with it. I didn't handle the situation well."

"I can't argue that." He grinned mischievously. "Perhaps we can come up with a way for you to make it up to me. I've got a few ideas—"

"Will," she said sternly.

"No," he finally answered, all traces of humor gone. "I'm not mad at you."

She fell silent. That was it, then. Every score settled, pardons all around. She had no right to expect more.

But she wanted more, much more.

"It has nothing to do with my father, you know," she said.

He shot her a puzzled look that lasted long enough to cause him to swerve across the broken line. He turned back to the road and corrected his steering. "Take off those sunglasses, would you?"

"What?"

"The sun's behind us. Take the damned glasses off, so I can see your face."

She knew her eyes were watery and red-rimmed, her lashes all spiky from her tears. But she'd done enough hiding for one day—for one lifetime, probably. Sighing, she removed her sunglasses and stowed them in her purse.

He peered at her again, this time without losing control of the van. "Okay," he said with satisfaction. "What has nothing to do with your father?"

"All that stuff you said, your cheapo Freudian analysis of my relationships with men."

"I shouldn't have said those things, Chloe—I was way out of line."

In spite of herself, Chloe smiled. "Actually, it was a reasonable thing to say. It just happens to be wrong. I loved my father."

"Even though he was selfish, arrogant and unfaithful, and he never gave you a real home and he never changed your diapers, and he painted ugly green squares?"

"We all have our faults." She relaxed slightly, crossing one leg over the other knee and leaning back into the velour upholstery. "I envied him. I always wished I could be more like him. He always knew where he wanted to go, and then he went. With me..." She sighed. "Sometimes it seems like I'm not going anywhere. I'm just the reverse. I'm always backing off from things."

"Like the way you backed off from me last night?"

"Last night was sex. I'm speaking spiritually now."

"Sex can be a spiritual thing."

"I don't want to talk about last night. I want to talk about the direction a person takes in her life, the choices she makes, the goals she aims for. My father had dreams. What do I dream of? Finding the best possible tax shelter for a client? Wringing the biggest possible refund out of the government?"

"Those dreams are more relevant to most people than anything your father ever painted," Will remarked.

It took her a minute to decide he wasn't joking. She was relieved. If he dared to kid her about her insecurities, she would kick him in his ego.

She stared ahead at the highway, a monotonous strip of gray stretching out before them. "My father had such power, such magnetism. He could make people rearrange their lives for him. I can't get people to do that for me."

"Wait a minute, wait a minute." Will held up his hand for emphasis. "Correct me if I'm wrong, Chloe, but aren't we a thousand miles from Boston right now because you wanted to repossess some rocks? Didn't *I* rearrange my life?"

"This trip doesn't count," she argued. "You offered to come along because you didn't have anything better to do."

"Oh, of course, you're absolutely right. If you hadn't offered me an excuse to drive to Minnesota, I would have gone by myself, anyway, just to get away from my work. Hell, I probably would have driven all the way to Seattle."

She opened her mouth to object to his sarcasm, then pressed her lips together without saying anything. It didn't seem possible that Will could have participated in this journey simply because she'd asked him to. In fact, she *hadn't* asked. She had only said she had to go to Minnesota, and...

And he'd rearranged his life. For her.

But he didn't love her. Heaven knew whether he felt anything for her, other than frustration. He'd taken her to the opera because he'd thought he would get her into bed, and he'd agreed to take her to Orin because he'd thought he would get her into bed, and, lo and behold, last night he'd gotten her into bed.

And she'd turned him down. So now what? Was he going to keep trying?

Was she going to keep turning him down?

Would someone please give her a pebble to squeeze, so she could think straight?

HE STILL WASN'T sure why he had said *I love you* at the rest stop. It had been the first thing to pop into his head ... but *why?*

He wanted her, even needed her. No question about it. But *love?* He shouldn't have used that word. It had done the trick, but he shouldn't have used it, because using it seemed to have hurt Chloe in a way he couldn't begin to fathom.

She reached for the radio dial and gave it a twist. After running through a few bands of static, she hit an album-rock station out of Toledo. "Minute by Minute" by the Doobie Brothers was playing.

"What is this song about?" Will asked as Chloe leaned back.

"Beats me."

"The singer mumbles all the words. Ever since this record came out I've been trying to figure out what he's saying, but I can't. He sounds like he's got pebbles in his mouth."

She gave him a canny look. "I wonder if Orin stole my pebbles to improve his singing."

"Tell me the truth, Chloe—why do you think he stole your pebbles?"

"I wish I knew," she said with a sigh. "Orin generally operates on one of three basic principles—he needs money, he wants glory, or he's looking for fun."

"Could the pebbles be worth any money?"

She shook her head. "They're rock chips. The humidor might be worth something. It's mahogany and it's got a beautiful carving on the lid. But even that couldn't be worth more than a hundred dollars."

"Glory?"

She snorted.

"Fun, then?"

"I suppose it says something about Orin, that his idea of fun is to hop on a plane to Boston, let himself into his sister's apartment, steal her favorite possession and fly back to Minneapolis."

"I don't get it."

"There's nothing to get. It's just the way he is." She sighed. "Do you have any crackpot siblings?"

"I've got two brothers, but they aren't crackpots. James is an attorney. Michael is working on a Ph.D. in botany. He's into fungus."

"Fungus. How nice." Her eyes, he noticed, were no longer glistening with unshed tears, and the tendons in her neck no longer protruded. Her tension seemed to have melted away.

"Maybe they *are* worth money."

"What's worth money? Fungus?"

"The pebbles."

"Not a chance."

"Not in and of themselves, maybe, but... what about as a possession of the famous painter, Aldo Verona?"

Chloe considered the possibility, then shook her head. "They weren't his. They were my mother's."

"The widow of the famous painter, Aldo Verona."

She considered some more. "It's not like any of his other possessions got auctioned off for millions of dollars. Nobody even cared about his old paintbrushes. My mother donated his palettes to the Guggenheim, but the museum took them only because she was also donating one of his 'Sky' paintings."

"His 'Sky' paintings?"

"Big squares of blue."

"I should have guessed." Will meditated. "So, you think your brother took the pebbles for fun?"

"I don't know. I hope so. He's always sponged off me, but he's never actually stolen anything. I'm his sister. We love each other. I can't figure out why he would have taken the one thing that meant so much to me. He had to know I'd come after him to get it back. And so help me, if he *did* find someone who wanted to buy the pebbles—

for whatever reason—he's just going to have to buy them
back. They weren't his to sell. I swear, if it comes to that,
I'll have the buyer arrested for trading in stolen property."

Will enjoyed having her target her anger at her brother
rather than at him for a change. "Do you want to stop for
lunch?" he asked.

"No."

"I'm not exactly starving, either. A few chocolate-chip
cookies would probably hold me for a while."

She bent over and pulled the cookie package out of the
tote. Her hair tumbled forward, a rippling curtain of
darkness across her face. Then she straightened up and he
was able to see her again, his quick glimpses taking in her
smooth honey gold complexion, her sharp nose and the
hollow of her cheek. Her left side—the side he could see—
had been pressed into the pillow last night; her right side
was the one he'd kissed. He wished he could have nibbled
as far as her cheekbone, as far as the delicate indentation
below her mouth—as far as her mouth.

He wished he could kiss her the way he'd kissed her at
the waterfall, a deep, hungry kiss, one of those devour-
ing kisses that soften a man's bones and harden his flesh.
He wished he could kiss her mouth and then her shoulders, her finely sculpted collarbones and her breasts. He
wished he could keep kissing all the way down her body,
until she was writhing and gasping the way she had last
night, until he reached her cute little polished toenails and
reversed course, retracing his path upward until . . .

Not a safe subject to contemplate while he was driving.

He thanked Chloe for the cookie she passed him. The
day was young, and another night loomed ahead before
they reached her brother. Another night filled with pos-

sibilities. Chloe claimed she wasn't going anywhere, but that wasn't true. Right now she was definitely headed somewhere—and Will wasn't thinking of Minnesota. He had other destinations in mind.

He munched on his cookie and weighed the chances that a sweeter treat would be waiting for him not too far down the road. Despite her unpredictable state of mind, he liked the odds. He liked them a lot. If this trip were a card game, he'd wager every chip and call her bluff—and he'd probably win. Big.

"THERE'S A MOTEL," she said.

The sun was low on the western horizon. Chloe had donned her sunglasses once again, and Will didn't complain. In fact, he wished he had a pair himself. He'd been driving into the glare for over an hour now.

A motel. Not a quaint rooming house, oozing charm and populated with crackerjack folks spouting X-rated suggestions to a couple of antagonists masquerading as honeymooners. The motel Chloe was pointing to overlooked the highway from behind a chain-link fence. It looked like a poor man's Ramada Inn, bland and impersonal, with a glaring neon sign illuminating its nondescript logo.

"Let's stop," he said. "I'm beat."

"We're getting separate rooms," she reminded him.

So much for the odds. He ought to have been grateful that he hadn't actually bet real money on the likelihood that he'd make love with her tonight, but he wasn't grateful, not at all. "Separate rooms," he grumbled.

"Please don't take it personally, Will. You know as well as I do that we'd be better off in two rooms."

"We'd be better off in one bed," he argued, coasting down the ramp to the motel.

"I'll pay for your room."

"Gee. You're so afraid of me, you'll actually pay me to stay away from you. That's all right, Chloe. I'll pay for my own room."

She pressed her lips together in that huffy Victorian way of hers and stared resolutely at the glass door of the motel office as Will parked in a nearby space.

The motel's interior matched the exterior: cheap carpeting, vinyl furniture, and a few plastic plants.

"Two rooms?" the clerk behind the desk repeated in response to Chloe's request. "You're in luck—we have only two vacancies. One is a double room, and the other is the penthouse."

"The penthouse," Will drawled.

"The double room costs forty-two fifty a night. The penthouse goes for a hundred and twenty."

"Dollars?" Chloe asked.

"Oh, it's worth it," the clerk assured her cheerfully. "It's got a Jacuzzi, a circular bed and free champagne."

"For a hundred and twenty dollars, it must be Dom Perignon," said Chloe.

"I just changed my mind," Will resolved, trying to suppress his grin. "You can pay for my room, after all."

"I'm not going to pay all that money so you can sleep in a circular bed," she snapped.

"Fine. I'll take the double. You can have the circular bed. Thanks for footing the bill. I really appreciate it."

He could tell she was miffed. Troubled. Supremely concerned. She turned back to the clerk. "Are you sure you haven't got any other rooms available?"

"Just that one double and the penthouse. Ordinarily the penthouse is taken. It tends to get booked in advance."

"By whom?" Will asked, glimpsing the highway through the glass door. "Extravagant teamsters?"

"Romantic couples," the woman said. "We've got lots of romantic couples around here."

Not at the moment, Will thought morosely. In front of the clerk right now was only a fifty-percent-romantic couple.

"The double—it has two beds, right?" Chloe asked. When the clerk nodded, Chloe sighed and handed over her credit card. "We'll take it," she said, shooting Will a look of explicit warning.

He read her quite clearly. She was tacitly reminding him that, as far as she was concerned, the space between those two beds literally constituted a no-man's land. She didn't trust him, but her distrust wasn't worth a hundred and twenty dollars.

Frankly, if they weren't going to share a bed, he would have preferred to have his own room. He had gotten through two nights with her, but it hadn't been easy. Tonight would be even harder, because tonight he would have some idea of what they were missing.

But then again, they *were* going to be in the same room, and if the atmosphere was right, and luck was with him...

Forget it. What he'd thought were good odds a few hours ago looked mighty grim now. If Chloe happened to come to her senses later tonight, Will would be thrilled—but Chloe and sense were an iffy combination.

So he would spend the entire night in her room, but not in her bed, not in her arms, not where he belonged. If that was the way she wanted it, that was the way she'd have it.

He wouldn't touch her. He wouldn't even ask. He'd prove to her that she could trust him, damn it.

Chapter Eleven

"Well, we certainly have come full circle today, haven't we?" she asked her reflection in the foggy mirror after her steamy shower. Staring at her bedraggled curls, her pale skin and her bloodshot eyes, she sighed. When that proved insufficient, she cut loose with a few loud curses. Will couldn't hear her. He was out.

She had invited him to join her for dinner in the motel's restaurant. He'd declined, claiming he wasn't hungry. But she knew better. He just hadn't wanted to eat with her. To confirm his dishonesty, the minute she'd returned to the room after dinner, he'd stood turned off the TV and said, "I'm going out."

Out to eat the dinner he'd refused to eat with her—or, heaven forbid, out to pick up a woman.

Wouldn't it be funny if they wound up in separate rooms tonight, after all? Her alone in this double room, and Will off with some accommodating playmate he met in the cocktail lounge off the motel's lobby.

She'd felt ridiculous eating dinner alone. Within minutes of her being seated in the motel's restaurant, no fewer than four men noticed that she was sitting by herself and hastened over to offer their charming company. Now, as she finished blow-drying her hair and adjusted the shoulder straps of her nightgown, she couldn't shake her mental picture of Will seated by himself at the same table she'd sat at, being accosted by a dynamic young businesswoman—the sort who wore a power suit over a skimpy lace bra and garter belt. Or a deceptively tough-looking female trucker, all soft malleability and dimples beneath her denim coveralls. Or a couple of nubile young college girls on the prowl, smiling and winking and inviting him to their room for fun and games.

Let him go, she thought, tossing down her brush and yanking the plug of her hair dryer out of the socket. She'd meant, let him go to some woman's room. But somewhere in her soul, she sensed a deeper message. All he'd ever offered her was a ride. No relationship, no commitment—even his mention of love had been nothing but a ruse. She had to stop wanting him. She had to let him go.

She trudged into the bedroom and turned on the television, hoping the sound of it would make her feel less lonesome. Uninterested in the show, she flipped through the atlas. If she and Will left immediately after breakfast tomorrow morning, they would probably arrive at Orin's place early in the afternoon.

Once she had her pebbles, the world would be a better place.

When Will hadn't returned to the room by ten o'clock, Chloe began to think he really had picked up a willing woman. The possibility hurt so much she was frightened.

Why couldn't he have fallen in love with her, just a little bit? She could have fallen in love with him so easily—too easily, really. Just the dazzling light in his eyes, the infectious charm of his smile, the low, sensual sound of his laughter... she could have fallen head over heels, if only she had sensed the tiniest hint that her feelings would be returned.

At ten-twenty she gave up waiting for him to come back, switched off the light and got into bed. But much as she tried to sleep, every sound outside in the hallway resonated inside her head. She ended up staring at the glowing red digits on the clock radio's face until her eyes stung.

Another noise. She tensed. The noise was close—definitely at her door. A loud click and the door swung open, allowing a narrow tunnel of light into the room. She glanced at the clock: ten forty-six.

Will stepped inside and quietly closed the door, plunging the room back into darkness. Breathing evenly and holding her body rigid under the blanket, Chloe pretended to be asleep. She heard the snap of the safety bolt easing into place, and then the muffled clank of a room key being placed on the dresser's laminated surface. Two muted thuds as Will removed his shoes and dropped them onto the carpeted floor, then the nearly silent tread of his steps as he strode past her bed and into the bathroom. A flicker of light against her eyelids as he hit the bathroom light switch, and then he shut the door behind himself.

Shifting onto her side, Chloe gazed at the stripe of light underlining the bathroom door. She heard the rush of the shower.

She almost wished he hadn't come back. If he hadn't, if he'd instead spent the night with someone else, she would have felt free to hate him.

After a while, the shower shut off. She strained to listen to his movements in the bathroom, tried to picture him drying off, tying a towel around his naked hips, brushing his teeth, shaving. Hanging up the towel . . .

A faint groan escaped her. She told herself once more that they didn't love each other, and that lovemaking without love wasn't worth the effort. She told herself he was as eager to avoid her as she was to keep her distance from him. She told herself a bunch of things, most of which didn't ring true to her.

A shaft of light again wedged into the room as he inched open the bathroom door. Almost immediately, he turned off the bathroom light. He took a step into the bedroom, another step, and then he bumped into the foot of her bed and let out a howl. A heavy mass of cloth struck Chloe in the stomach and she yelped, more in surprise than in pain.

"Sorry," he mumbled. She heard a chafing sound; as her eyes adjusted to the darkness she was able to make out his shadow as he bent over and rubbed his shin.

She lifted the cloth off her stomach. Her fingers identified the fabric as denim. "Here are your jeans," she said.

"Thanks," he grunted none too graciously, managing to grab them without touching her. He tossed them on the dresser, then limped to his own bed.

If he'd been carrying his jeans, he wasn't wearing them. Like last night, he was wearing snug cotton briefs and nothing else.

She closed her eyes. She really wanted to hate him, but her mind was too focused on his broad shoulders and his trim hips, his long, sinewy legs and his auburn hair. She thought about how clean his skin would smell after his shower, how smooth his jaw would feel. She thought about how he hadn't gone to another woman's room for the night, after all. He'd come back to her and was now lying in bed, all big and male and sexy—and beyond her reach.

She began to suspect that her life would never be simple again.

PERHAPS HE HAD ENDURED drearier nights in his life. But if he had he couldn't recall them.

He should have gotten drunk, he thought as he rubbed his bruised shin. If he was going to be walking into furniture anyway, he might as well be blitzed.

He decided that smashing his leg on her no-trespassing bed was his punishment for behaving like a baby: throwing a tantrum, storming out of the room and denying her his wonderful company.

As if she even cared.

Why the hell couldn't she trust him?

He punched his pillow and settled his head into it. Then he closed his eyes and tried to forget about her.

But he couldn't. Not when she was lying only a few feet away from him, when he knew that if he were as untrustworthy as she seemed to think he was, he would have breached the space between their beds by now and covered that prim little mouth until she was kissing him back. If he were all that despicable, he would be in her bed right now, easing the lacy straps of her gown off her shoulders until he could touch her breasts, kiss them, suck them deep into his mouth and feel her blazing with desire. . . .

She's not worth it, he swore to himself, rolling onto his stomach and burying his head under the pillow. *She's not worth torturing myself over.*

But the torture continued. And he knew it would, because she fascinated him, because he had become obsessed with her. Because she had the darkest, most expressive eyes he had ever seen. Because she was the daughter of an artist and the mistress of her own life, because she was sane enough to be an accountant and eccentric enough to be attached to a box of pebbles. Because she loved her crackpot brother, even though he exasperated her. Because the whole damned room smelled of almond blossoms.

She's not worth it.... She's not worth it.... He lay awake long into the night, reciting the words like a litany, still trying to convince himself.

THE CURTAINS WERE too porous. By a quarter to seven, the room was milky with dawn light.

Groaning, Chloe sat up and rubbed the drowsiness from her eyes. She glanced toward Will's bed and found him lying on his back, inspecting the ceiling. His blanket was bunched around his waist, offering her an unsolicited view of his rugged shoulders and leanly muscled chest. But even though she was obviously awake, he made no move to cover himself.

Go ahead, flaunt it, she thought bitterly. *You won't get to me.*

Sighing, she got out of bed. Will said nothing.

She grabbed her suitcase and stalked to the bathroom, determined to take as long as possible. When she finally emerged, Will was already dressed. His hair glittered with coppery highlights in the glow from the night-table lamp as he sat on the edge of his bed putting on socks. At her entry he promptly abandoned them and walked directly to the bathroom, slamming the door behind him.

She sighed again. *Just a few more hours and I'll be with Orin.* Who knew, maybe he would be able to defuse things. Maybe he would persuade Will to treat Chloe with more respect.

Fat chance. But at least I'll have my pebbles back.

About ten minutes later, no sound emerged from the bathroom. She had packed, rechecked the map, and phoned her office.

And still no sound from the bathroom. Maybe she ought to go have breakfast by herself. Apparently Will didn't want to eat breakfast with her any more than he'd wanted to eat dinner with her last night. She marched to the door, tired of waiting.

"Wait," he said, pushing the bathroom door open.

She spun around. He moved slowly through the furniture-cluttered room, pausing to place his toiletries bag on the dresser, pausing again to flick his hair back from his brow. Pausing to stare at her with his laser-beam blue eyes.

His gaze unnerved her. It was too powerful, too discerning. "Why should I wait?" she challenged him.

"I haven't got any socks on," he said, although he didn't go get them.

"So?"

"So they won't serve me in the dining room if I'm barefoot."

"Oh, did you want to have breakfast with me?" she asked with abundant disdain. "My, my. To what do we owe this burst of sociability?"

He opened his mouth and then shut it. She saw the tension in his jaw. "Okay. Go ahead, go have breakfast. I'll catch you later."

"Oh, no, that's all right. I'll wait," she said magnanimously.

"Don't do me any favors."

"I didn't say I'd do you any favors. I said I'd wait for you to put on your socks."

"That's not a favor?"

"No."

Less than a second ago, it seemed, he'd been halfway across the room. Now he was in front of her, inches from her, close enough that he was able to reach around her and flatten his hand against the safety bolt on the door. "What's your idea of a favor?" he asked.

She tried frantically to interpret the glittering emotion in his eyes and the dark innuendo in his words, but she couldn't. All she knew was that things had gotten very hazardous all of a sudden, and if she wasn't careful, she would wind up in a lot of trouble. "I don't want to have this discussion with you," she said in a pathetically tiny voice.

"What discussion do you want to have?"

"Breakfast."

"Really?" He edged closer yet, so close they were sharing the same breath.

"Will, don't do this."

"Do what?"

So close. So close, she could feel the heat from his chest. So close, the curling ends of her hair brushed his forearm.

If he had planned to seduce her, he would have done it last night. He would have done it when they were in bed. He was too close, that was all.

Too close for her to resist.

She rose on tiptoe as he bowed his head. Their lips met, and she wrapped her arms around him, clinging to him as he pressed her back to the door, as his tongue surged deep into her mouth and his hips trapped hers. He felt powerfully masculine, thrusting his tongue against hers in a devastating rhythm as his body rocked against hers.

This wasn't right, she thought as her tongue parried his. He didn't love her and she intended to hate him. The last thing she wanted was this.... As her hands curled into fists at the back of his head, her hips welcomed the pressure of his.

After an endless minute, he pulled back and gulped in a breath of air. "Oh, Chloe," he groaned, coiling his fingers through her hair. "Do me a favor."

"What?" she asked, her voice as ragged as his.

"Don't stop us this time."

"I don't know, Will—I—"

He arched his hips to hers again, compelling her to acknowledge his arousal and her own. "I could hardly sleep last night, I wanted you so much. I want you even more now. Don't make me stop."

She tried to remember all the reasons she *should* stop him, but came up blank. What she remembered, instead, were his kiss beneath the waterfall and his kiss at the rest stop, and his arms around her in the bridal-suite bed at the Ludens', his fingers kneading the softness of her belly and his lips exploring her throat. What she remembered was his virile chest and his rumbling laughter.

His blue, blue eyes looked into her soul and saw that she wanted this as much as he did. "Trust me," he whispered, and then his mouth came down on hers again, hard and hungry.

She was scarcely conscious of making the short journey to his bed. She was hardly aware of tearing at the buttons of his shirt, groping at his belt, wriggling her arms free of her sweater and kicking off her jeans once he'd pushed them down past her hips. She didn't recall tumbling backward onto the covers. Her brain didn't take full hold of what was going on until he was lying naked beside her, one of his legs wedged between her thighs, his hands wandering over her skin and his teeth teasing her lower lip.

I don't trust you, she thought, *I really don't.* But her fingers followed the smooth, warm arch of his back, roaming over the bony contours of his shoulders, along his arms and across his chest, over the taut brown nubs of his nipples and down to his abdomen.

He drew in a breath and inched back. "Slow down," he pleaded, half to her and half to himself. "God, Chloe—your legs are incredible." He let his fingers drift down to her thighs, to her knees.

"My legs?" she asked shakily.

"And your feet." He tucked his hand behind her knee and bent her leg upward until he could cradle her foot in his palm. He studied her toes, then placed a delicate kiss on her instep. "Most people have ugly feet. Yours are spectacular."

"My feet?" She'd never thought one way or the other about them.

"That's not to say the rest of you isn't equally spectacular." He twisted around and caught one of her nipples between his lips. "You ought to spend more of your life undressed."

"That would be impractical."

"All the more reason to do it." He flicked the flushed red tip with his tongue, then shifted to suckle the other breast. His hands stroked her belly as they had the previous night—only this time skin to skin, his fingers tracing their magic across her flesh, skirting the edge of her hair, creeping maddeningly lower with each meandering circuit.

If he didn't reach his goal soon, she'd die. If he kept doing whatever it was he was doing to her breasts, if he kept flexing his thigh against her, if he didn't stop . . . she would die.

If he *did* stop, she'd kill him.

He lifted his head and rose higher onto her, until his eyes were gazing down into hers. "Say it," he whispered.

"Say what?"

His hand moved lower, deeper into the damp thatch of hair between her legs. "Say you're glad you didn't take that penthouse room for the night."

"A hundred twenty dollars is a lot of money," she conceded, not quite prepared to admit that she'd been wrong about any of this. "On the other hand, I don't like having to share a bathroom."

"I'm very easy to share a bathroom with," he argued, skimming his fingers lower yet, finding her, making her burn deep inside. "Admit it."

"Will . . ." Her hips arched and her voice emerged on a broken sigh.

"I happen to be the tidiest person in the world when it comes to bathrooms."

"Your ego knows no bounds," she managed before her voice dissolved into a moan.

"Actually, my ego could use some stroking right now," he said, as his fingers continued to stimulate her with wicked effectiveness.

She filled her hands with him, curled her fingers around him, slid up and down the length of him. He closed his eyes and groaned, flexing in time with her caresses.

"Will." Her voice was a faint wisp of sound. "Will, I'm not—I'm not protected."

"Oh." But he did not stop driving against her palms, did not stop sliding his fingers over her sensitive flesh.

"Will. Please—this is important—"

"Not to worry," he whispered, reluctantly withdrawing from her. He leaned over the edge of the bed and pulled his wallet from the pocket of his jeans.

Her eyes grew round and a startled laugh escaped her. "Don't tell me you've been carrying that thing around since high school."

"No," he said, tearing at the wrapper. "Just since Friday night."

"Friday night?" Her smile faded; her spine stiffened. "You mean—when we went to the opera? You brought that with you?"

Her abrupt chilliness seemed to take him aback. "Yeah, I did. Do you have a problem with that?"

"I most certainly do. It was our first date, Will. Did you honestly think you were going to have sex with me on the first date?"

He chuckled. "I thought maybe I'd get lucky. Scott told me you were a knockout and..." He tactfully drifted off.

"And what?"

He shrugged. "Nothing much."

"What?" she demanded.

"Oh, just that—uh—that you'd be wowed by the opera—"

"Scott obviously doesn't know what he's talking about," she snapped, greatly annoyed. "What else did he tell you?"

"You just said it." Will attempted to mollify her. "He didn't know what he was talking about."

She poked him in the stomach. He laughed and shook his head. "What? What did he tell you?" She continued poking him until he swatted her hand away.

"That you hadn't dated anyone in a while and you'd fall at my feet, and you were an easy score."

"He said that?" Since Scott wasn't around to hit, she pummeled Will instead, jabbing at his abdomen with a blizzard of punches that did absolutely no damage.

He grabbed her wrists and pinned them to the mattress, propping himself up above her and scattering light, playful kisses over her face. "You're right," he murmured, feeling the fight drain from her. "Scott didn't know what he was talking about."

"Will..." She ought to be angry. She ought to be furious that he'd given even a moment's credence to Scott's disgusting insinuations. But as Will moved over her, shifting his hips, nipping at her chin and her throat, as his chest rubbed against the swollen tips of her breasts, her passionate anger gave way to passionate desire.

"That's better," he murmured, running his hand between her legs. "The only smart thing he said was that I was going to have a great time. And I am. We both are."

His mouth took hers as his body did, swallowing her moan, forcing her responses down into the place he inhabited, the hollow he filled. His heat engulfed her, roared through her, melted her flesh into a seething, quivering mass of sensation.

She couldn't breathe. Couldn't think. Couldn't do anything but move with him, rise to meet him, lure him deeper and deeper. Her body burned, hurt, needed him, and he was there, again and again, pushing her beyond her own endurance.

She clutched him, her fingernails moving in a frenzy on his back, her tongue wrestling with his as his hips pumped in a relentless tempo. Her abdomen trembled, her thighs grew unbearably tense—and then ecstasy overtook her, a lush contraction descending through her, and another, and another, until she sank deep into the bed linens with a tremulous cry.

Will drove harder into her, wilder, racing to his own peak. She clamped her hands over his buttocks and held him inside her as he groaned, his body shuddering and his head rearing back, his eyes closed, blinding him to everything but the joy of his release. An endless minute passed before he relaxed in her arms. He groaned again, opened his eyes, and grinned down at her.

"You aren't laughing," she noted, her voice so hoarse she could scarcely recognize it.

"No."

"But you're smiling." She traced the curve of his lip with her index finger. His mouth was as responsive to her touch as his manhood had been; the light caress made his smile grow larger, stronger.

"I'm happy. So are you," he observed, planting a tender kiss on one upturned corner of her mouth and then the other.

"If I'm smiling, I can assure you it's only because I'm in a state of panic."

That made him laugh. "You spend most of your life in a state of panic. Why should this be any different?"

It should be different, she thought, perplexed. Everything should be different. And it *was,* only she couldn't figure out specifically how. This wasn't like a financial form that she could analyze and tally. Everything was different, and she didn't know what to do about it—and that panicked her even more.

"Come on," Will said, climbing off the bed and pulling her to her feet. Clasping her hand, he ushered her into the bathroom. In spite of herself, she liked crowding into the narrow room with him, bumping into him, being unable to escape him as he planted a kiss on her cheek and turned the faucets inside the shower.

"Are we going to take a shower together?" she asked warily. She had never showered with anyone else in her life.

"Unless you know of a waterfall nearby."

"Will."

"Don't be a prig," he said, lifting her over the edge of the tub and nudging her under the spray.

This was not like the waterfall. Not only was it warmer, but it included a bar of soap, which Chloe had never before thought of as sexual paraphernalia. In Will's hands, it was. He ran the slick, sudsy block between her shoulder blades, down her spine, over her breasts until they were slick and tingling, and then down between her thighs. He lathered her, teased her, kissed her until she was gasping, until she had to hang on to him to keep from falling. When at last her body gave in, he gathered her in a powerful, protective embrace, let her rest her head on his damp shoulder and sigh her satisfaction into the curve of his neck.

She reciprocated, washing him as thoroughly as he'd washed her. She skimmed the soap over his back, fretting when she saw the scratches her nails had left on his skin, until he silenced her by turning around and kissing her hard. She soaped his shoulders and arms, his chest and stomach and lower, determined to give him the pleasure he'd given her.

It was more than just giving him pleasure, she admitted to herself. She wanted to make him as defenseless as she felt, as vulnerable, as dependent, as grateful. If she was going to go crazy, she'd damned well make sure he did, too.

And he did, pressing his hands against the tile walls on either side of her head, surging and straining until he succumbed with a deep groan that resounded through the steamy room. Spent, he rested his forehead against hers, his hair slicked back and his breath as hard and hot as the shower spouting down upon them. A low, weary laugh escaped him.

Chloe gazed into his eyes. They were stunningly, painfully blue and full of emotion.

Love. Whatever that emotion was, she was going to call it love.

Serves you right, Will Turner, she thought, astonished to hear herself giggle along with him. *You* do *love me, and it serves you right.*

They were wet, breathless and in love. Will had fallen as deeply as she had, and the understanding made her laugh out loud.

Chapter Twelve

Downtown Hackett, Minnesota consisted of the intersection of two numbered county roads. On one corner stood a church, on another a two-pump gas station, on a third the Hackett general store and post office and on the fourth a signpost displaying arrows that indicated the direction and distance of other, no doubt livelier, municipalities.

"Are you sure they've got electricity here?" Will asked, as he slowed the van to a halt at the intersection. Not that he had to. Around here, he figured, the odds were greater he'd have to brake for a cow than for another car.

Chloe had been fairly quiet for most of the drive, once she'd stopped complaining about what a late start they'd gotten. Not that she had any right to complain. The late start was at least as much her fault as his. When she'd been toweling off his back she'd wound up kissing it, instead.... Granted, he'd taken over from there, but she'd started it.

Owing to that prolonged, glorious interlude in the motel room, they arrived in Hackett much later than planned. In a way, Will regretted arriving at all. He wanted to keep going, to drive right off the edge of the earth with her. Better yet, he wanted to stop driving and make love with her again, just pull off the road and get into the back of the van and make love until they were too tired to do anything but lie in each other's arms, gasping for breath.

Even better: he wanted to find another waterfall. Or a shower. What was it that Simon said back at the Ludens' place in Ohio? Something about women and water and tides. Will wanted to turn around and drive with Chloe to Niagara Falls. This was supposed to be their honeymoon, wasn't it?

Chloe pointed to the general store. Interior lights shone through the plate glass. "They obviously have electricity in Hackett," she said.

Back to reality. Back to the present. Back to the fact that he and this incredible woman were about to face off with her flaky brother.

"So they've got electricity," he said, pulling into the small gravel lot in front of the store. "The question is, how do they generate it? Ten'll get you twenty, they've got a mule harnessed to a wheel out back, walking in circles."

Chloe made a face.

The sign on the glass front of the building said the store closed at five. If they'd arrived in Hackett ten minutes later, they might have had to resort to knocking on people's front doors in their search for Orin's artists' colony—and other than the church and the two retail enterprises occupying the intersection, there were apparently only five front doors in town. At least that was all Will and Chloe had driven past, five farmhouses strewn across the six miles that separated Hackett from the next town to the east.

Stepping out of the van, he stretched his arms above his head and absorbed the rural atmosphere. The sky stretched in a vast dome from horizon to horizon; the few high clouds scattered across it were turning mauve and orange in the fading light. The air vibrated with the loud chirping of crickets and katydids. The wind smelled of dirt and spring, seedlings and manure.

Chloe was clearly not enamored of the scenery. As he helped her out of the van, he felt waves of tension emanating from her. Maybe she was still unsettled by the morning's rapturous activity, but Will chose to interpret her pursed lips and her icy fingers as symptoms of apprehension about confronting her brother.

He wanted to tell her not to worry. He would be right beside her, championing her every step of the way. He'd be her hero, he'd slay her dragons, he'd do whatever she'd let him do. God, he hoped she'd let him do it all. She was so headstrong, so determined to be her own person.... But being her own person didn't mean she couldn't accept help from a man.

They entered the store. Despite its small size, it appeared to carry most of the essentials.

A round-faced man with a brushy mustache greeted them. "Hello, there. What can I do for you?"

Chloe gave him a nervous smile. "We were wondering if you could give us directions to Orin Verona's place."

"Orin's place?" The clerk's pale eyebrows dipped in a slight frown. "You folks artists?"

Chloe's smile grew stiff. "No. I'm Orin's sister."

"His sister?" The clerk broke into a broad grin and extended his hand over the counter. "Well, how do you do! Orin's sister!" He shook Will's hand. "And you're Orin's brother?"

"I'm—a friend," Will said vaguely. He would have introduced himself as Chloe's lover, but he thought that might spook her.

"Orin's sister," the clerk declared, beaming at her. "Welcome to Hackett. What can I do for you?"

"You could tell us how to get to his house."

"It's straight down that road about a mile," he said, pointing through the front window. "Right-hand side. The mailbox says 'Verona Acres' on it."

Chloe curled her lip at the pretentiousness of the name. Will gave her shoulder a gentle squeeze.

"Say, listen," said the clerk, "if you're going down to Orin's, maybe you could do me a favor and drop off this spray gun. He ordered it six weeks ago, and it finally came in." He foraged behind the counter, then set a carton on the countertop.

"A spray gun," Chloe repeated dubiously.

"Yeah, you know—for spraying paint."

"Oh." She eyed the carton distastefully as the clerk peeled off an order form and scribbled something on it. "Now then, if you'll just sign here…" He shoved the pen at her, and she signed her name. "Great," he said, taking the form back. "That'll be forty-nine ninety-five."

"I beg your pardon?"

"Forty-nine dollars and ninety-five cents. He ordered it C.O.D."

"Oh, for heaven's sake! Why can't he pay for it?"

"Well, that would mean we'd have to make up a whole new order form, seeing as you've already signed this one," the clerk explained with a smile. "And then, of course, it's just going to sit here till the next time he drives into town—and knowing him, he won't have enough money to pay for the darned thing. Which means that whatever project he ordered it for is going to stay unfinished, and he won't be able to get a plug nickel for it, and I'll never see my forty-nine ninety-five." His hopeful gaze shuttled between Chloe and Will.

"You don't have to pay for it," Will whispered to her. "It's Orin's problem, not yours."

"Orin *is* my problem," she muttered. On a sigh, she asked the clerk, "Do you accept credit cards?"

Will was sorely tempted to start being her hero right now, but he kept his mouth shut. Sibling relationships were a strange thing.

Besides, he admitted, there was something awfully appealing about Chloe's generosity, even if it did seem rather foolish. For all her external toughness, she was a softy inside, and he adored her for it.

"You didn't have to pay for this," he said a few minutes later, as he hoisted the carton into the back of the van.

"No kidding," she grumbled.

"You know what they say about how no one can take advantage of you unless you let them."

"I'll remember that the next time you make a pass at me."

"I didn't take advantage of you," he protested, trying to convince himself that her grouchiness was meant for her brother, not him. "I seem to recall you enjoyed yourself just fine this morning."

"Oh, yes, it was enjoyable," she conceded dryly. "Much more fun than buying this stupid paint thing. The next time I decide to be taken advantage of, I'll make sure it's for sex and not art equipment. Let's go." Ignoring his hand, she hoisted herself up into her seat and shut the door.

He remained outside the van for a minute, sorting his thoughts. Was he in trouble here? Was her memory of that morning so different from his?

Was something real going on between them, something more significant than a blind date and a morning of sex? Something that might last? Or was she going to turn on him the moment she had her damned pebbles, and declare that she didn't need him anymore?

Stay calm, he ordered himself. She was just overreacting to the impending family reunion. Her peevishness had nothing to do with him . . . he hoped.

He plastered a forgiving smile on his face before he got into the van. If Chloe wanted to take out her anxiety on him, let her. Wasn't that what friends were for?

He glanced at her. She sat facing forward, her arms folded grimly across her chest. Leaning across the gear stick, he kissed her cheek.

"Don't try to soften me up," she snapped.

"All right, I won't," he said, "Stay as hard as you like."

Without looking at her again, he headed the van down the rutted road. When he'd first departed from Boston with Chloe he'd thought of this mission as overtime on the blind-date game clock, affording him another chance to score. Nothing more than that, really. He'd been the first guy off the bench, because he figured that somewhere down the road—literally—he'd get Chloe into bed. She was a challenge.

But now, as the final minutes ticked down, the whole situation had undergone a transformation. He wanted more from her, more than just a check mark in the win column. He had become as attached to her as she was to her pebbles—and if she was going to get what she was after, he wanted to get what he was after, too.

Chloe. In every way, shape and form. In his life. In his future.

She had withdrawn into herself, though, shutting him out. Her entire focus had been diverted from Will to her undeserving cheapskate of a brother, the lord of Verona Acres. Will had been demoted to the role of chauffeur.

She's not worth it, he told himself, just as he'd told himself countless times before—only he couldn't make himself believe it. He didn't think he could bear it, if he wound up with nothing after this journey came to an end.

About a hundred yards ahead on the right-hand side of the road stood a mailbox on a wooden post. Fifty yards back from the road loomed a rambling farmhouse, its outline cast into silhouette by the fading dusk light but several of its windows bright with an amber glow. "That must be the place," said Will.

"I'm sorry," she murmured.

"Sorry about what?" he asked.

"This mood. I'm really nervous."

"That's okay."

"I mean, I'm a wreck."

"I noticed."

"Thanks for the vote of confidence."

"I was agreeing with you, Chloe. Just trying to make you feel better."

"Well, you blew it. I don't feel better."

"Okay. What can I do to make you feel better?"

"Nothing. I don't want to feel better. And I don't want to be softened up. I want to go in there bitter and angry and armed for battle. You can understand that, can't you?"

"Sure."

A shaky laugh escaped her. "You'd never guess how calm and efficient I am at work. You'd never recognize me if you saw me at an IRS audit. I have nerves of steel when it's someone else's business. But when it comes to my brother—"

"Hey, it's all right," he said. "I understand."

"And then Stephen's going to be here. It's not going to be a pretty scene."

"Don't worry," Will said, although worry ricocheted through his nervous system. Stephen. The ex-boyfriend. The one Chloe hadn't seen since New Year's. The one who broke her heart so thoroughly—even if she dumped him and not vice versa—that she hadn't gone on a date with anyone since then. Until now. Chloe was going to see him—on *his* turf—and she hadn't really resolved her feelings about him yet.

This was going to be one hell of an awkward situation. Maybe Will could wait in the car....

And what kind of hero would that make him? Chloe needed him, now more than ever. This was his big chance to prove something to her. The time had come to raise the bid, ask for four cards and hope he got dealt all aces.

"They're little rocks, that's all," she mumbled, no longer attempting to laugh. In the thickening gloom he could see her eyes shimmer as they filled with tears. "I've been trying and trying to figure out why he stole them, and—"

"It doesn't matter, Chloe. You'll get them back. We'll get them back together, and then you can tell him to go to hell."

"I could never tell him that. He's my brother."

"Then *I'll* tell him," Will promised with a bracing surge of courage. "Trust me. I'll take care of everything."

"I don't want it to turn into a big blowup," she insisted.

"Fine. We'll keep it small."

"I just want to go in there, get my humidor and leave."

"And collect the fifty bucks your brother owes you."

"Right."

"Then let's do it," he said in his best General Patton voice.

She inhaled deeply, then let out her breath and shivered. "Okay."

He turned the wheel to head into the driveway, but Chloe touched his hand. He smiled encouragingly at her.

"Whatever happens in there, Will..."

"Yes?"

"It won't change how I feel about this morning."

Her words shot through him. This morning. This morning at the door. This morning in bed. This morning in the shower. This morning with him on top, with her on top, with both of them standing up and water splashing down around them. This morning...and nothing that happened now could change how she felt.

Whatever the hell that means. "How do you feel about what happened this morning?" he asked, wondering whether she could hear his anxiety in his voice.

"I don't know exactly...."

He inhaled for strength. "Do you want to know how I feel about it?"

"No."

"How I feel about it," he forged ahead, "is that this morning meant a lot to me. It meant more than I—" He stopped, afraid of loading her down with a whole lot of psychic baggage she was in no condition to carry. "Whatever happens next won't change how I feel, either."

"Maybe it won't. Maybe it will," she said ominously, releasing his hand and turning her attention to the farmhouse.

He stared at her a moment longer, waiting for her to elaborate. She merely raised her chin to its ready-for-battle angle once more.

Will sighed. What did she think was going to happen in there? How bad could it possibly be?

An uncomfortable chill settled over him. It was like turning over the first card and finding the two of clubs. He turned onto the unpaved driveway and coasted to its end. Next to him Chloe wrung her hands and gnawed on her lower lip. Before he could shut off the engine, she had bolted from the van.

He hurried after her, not catching up to her until they reached the porch. She pounded on the door.

"Take a deep breath," he advised, cupping his hands over her shoulders and kissing the crown of her head. "Pretend this is the IRS."

She gave him a feeble smile and pounded on the door again.

The door swung inward and a man with curly black hair, an angular jaw, dark, thickly lashed eyes and long legs filled the doorway. Will didn't require an introduction.

He didn't get one. "Chloe?" the man exclaimed. "Chloe? Is it you?"

"Who the hell do you think it is?" she volleyed back. "Someone in a Chloe mask?"

"Oh, wow! You're here!" the man shouted, wrapping her in a crushing hug.

We're here, Will thought uneasily, inching back so he wouldn't accidentally get kicked by Chloe as her brother spun her around in the doorway. If the guy felt the merest twinge of guilt about having stolen her property, he revealed nothing.

"Get your hands off me, you turkey," Chloe demanded. A laugh escaped her, though, and she returned his hug.

Well, all right, so she wasn't coming across as a woman warrior—or even a CPA prepared to take on the tax man. The guy *was* her brother, after all.

"I can't believe you actually got in a plane and came here," the man hooted, giving her a final, flamboyant twirl before he loosened his hold on her.

"I didn't," she said, struggling to regain her balance. "I drove. That is, Will drove," she amended. "Will, this is my brother Orin. Orin, Will Turner."

"Will," Orin said with a sincere smile, "thank you for bringing my sister here."

Will could have thanked Orin for having provided Will and Chloe with an excuse to spend the past several days together. But he couldn't shake the sense of foreboding that loomed over him. The past several days had been incredible, but now they were over. Standing on Orin's porch meant something had come to an end.

Will had serious misgivings.

None of them spoke for a minute. Their silence seemed magnified by the tranquil isolation of the farm. Will's ears filled with a symphony of twittering insects and Great Plains wind.

"Well, come on in," Orin finally said, beckoning them inside. Like the Ludens' place, this was a classic farmhouse; unlike the Ludens' place, this was messy and cluttered.

Chloe scanned the entry with a quick glance and then turned back to Orin. "You know why I'm here, don't you?"

"I can guess," he said with a lackadaisical shrug. "But I'd better warn you, Stephen's going to freak out when he sees you."

"He's a big boy. He can handle it."

"I didn't say he was going to freak out *bad*. Well, come on in. I'll bet you could use some drinks. Drove all the way, huh? I tell you, Will, my sister is the stablest, sharpest, most together human being I know, except when it comes to airplanes."

For which Will was thankful. If she had been a seasoned air traveler, this trip never would have happened.

"Did you know," Orin confided to Will, "that Chloe won a tax case before the Supreme Court?"

Will did a double take. "Chloe—are you a lawyer, too?"

"No," she muttered, clearly not amused by Orin's boasting. "I only worked with our client's lawyer on the case. And we didn't win it before the Supreme Court. They merely refused to overrule a lower court decision in our favor."

"It set precedents," Orin asserted. "People refer to that case for guidance."

"People refer to their bookies for guidance, too," she said. "I don't know about Will, but I'd like a drink."

Will was too flabbergasted to even think about drinking. Chloe? This intense, passionate woman with the most alluring eyes he'd ever seen, and the sexiest rear end, and the legs he'd long ago run out of superlatives for—Chloe had prepared a case for argument before the Supreme Court?

"Trust me," she murmured, reading the astonishment in his expression, "it wasn't such a big deal."

It is so a big deal, he wanted to shout. He was proud of her. But before he could speak, she turned away, her expression sealed, informing him that she didn't wish to discuss her illustrious career.

Pinstripes and sensible shoes, he thought, unable to stop dwelling on Chloe's professional stature as he followed her into the kitchen. But the first picture that filled his mind was of her in her chic black above-the-knee dress and her delectable high heels—and the second picture was of her in his arms, in the throes of rapture.

"Chloe was the normal one in our family," Orin explained, yanking open the refrigerator and pulling out a couple of beers. "She was the levelheaded one. She kept us all grounded."

"Enough, Orin," Chloe briskly cut him off, although Will detected a quaver of uncertainty in her voice. "I didn't come here to discuss me. I came to discuss you." She sounded so businesslike Will got a mental image of her in sensible shoes. Yes, she could argue a Supreme Court case. Will was impressed, but also a little disappointed. How was he going to be her hero if she did everything herself?

"What about me?" Orin asked.

"What were you doing in Boston Friday night?"

"Friday?" Orin issued a fake smile. "Let me think...."

"Orin." Chloe's voice held a threat. "You know why I'm here. So stop—"

The back door of the kitchen suddenly burst open, admitting a man into the room. He was phenomenally tall, with black hair as thick as mink but long, slicked back from his face and held in a neat, chic ponytail at the nape of his neck. Bronze skin stretched smooth over a face that could have modeled for Roman coins. A physique Will could tell had been proportioned not by genes or exercise but by the hand of God Himself. The man's skintight shirt and jeans revealed the precise dimension of every rippling muscle, every bone and tendon. The V-shaped opening at the top of his shirt exposed a thick rug of black hair flourishing on his chest.

This was no mere man. This was Adonis.

And when his deep, dark gaze fell upon Chloe, his Greek-god face broke into a smile that bared teeth as white and even as polished ivory tiles. "Chloe," he growled, then spread his exquisitely muscled arms with the grace of an eagle spreading his wings, and swooped down upon her, lifting her out of her chair. She seemed to vanish within his embrace.

"That's Stephen," Orin announced, giving voice to Will's gravest fear.

This was bad, real bad. Her former boyfriend appeared to have stepped out of an advertisement for testosterone supplements—and he was hugging her, and she wasn't resisting. In fact, she was hugging him back.

"I've heard about Stephen," Will admitted in an absurdly blasé voice.

"I'll tell you," Orin commented, "they're meant for each other. Just look at them. You can feel it from across the room." Orin closed his eyes and smiled beatifically, basking in the invisible rays he sensed emanating from their euphoric embrace. Then he opened his eyes and grinned at Will. "Can you feel it?"

To his deep regret, he could. Chloe had her back to him, but he saw the way Stephen's arms fit around her, the way they held her. "Stephen," she mumbled, sounding as if someone had stuffed cotton balls in her mouth.

"Chloe," Stephen purred, making it sound like the most intimate pillow talk. "I can't believe it."

"Look, Stephen—"

"Can you begin to guess what having you here means to me?"

"Stephen…" Slowly—much too slowly for Will's peace of mind—she extricated herself from the smothering clinch. "Stephen, I'd like you to meet Will Turner."

He supposed he ought to be grateful she hadn't allowed the man she had made love with all morning to slip her mind. "How do you do?" he said politely, offering Stephen his hand.

Stephen's fingers were thicker than Will's by half, and his skin was tough and smooth—not just leather, but expertly tanned and buffed leather, the sort of leather one would use to make five-hundred-dollar après-ski boots for Aspen vacationers. Stephen's smile seemed genuine. "Nice meeting you. Are you a friend of Chloe's?"

"Yes." *More than a friend,* he wanted to shout. *She dumped you, remember? She and I are lovers. Don't you dare hug her like that again.*

"Welcome to the art colony. Glad you could come. Are you here to do art?"

"No."

"Will isn't an artist," Chloe said with a trace of defiance. "He writes children's books."

"Children's books? Hey, that's neat!" There was nothing condescending in Stephen's tone, which only made Will feel worse. Not only was Chloe the kind of accountant who dealt with the Supreme Court, but her last boyfriend was a he-man of untold potency. And to make matters worse, he was nice.

"Chloe," Stephen said in a husky baritone that struck Will as somehow phallic, "I wanted to surprise you, and instead you've surprised me."

"Well," she murmured, and then nothing.

Terrific. Stephen had rendered her speechless. This was bad—and getting worse.

"Ever since New Year's—"

"Stephen, I don't think this is the time or the place—"

"But I've been working on something for you. I've been working on it ever since New Year's, to show you my true feelings. I was going to unveil it as a surprise for you. I've designed it with my heart..." although he extended his manly hands as if to say the actual labor had come from them "...for you, Chloe. Inspired by you, created for you, dedicated to you. Only it's not finished yet."

"Oh."

Tell him to bug off, Will silently pleaded. He was beginning to fear that Mister Machismo had reduced Chloe to the mental capacity of a Barbie doll.

"But you're here," Stephen continued, "and I want to share it with you, even though it's not finished yet. I want you to know how I feel. Let me do that for you."

"Well...I don't know. We've been driving all weekend, and I've got some business to discuss with Orin and..."

"And I'm seeing you for the first time since this long, lonely year began. Please. Let me show you what you mean to me."

She sent Will an inscrutable look, then turned back to Stephen. "All right. Show me what you've got."

Aaargh! She was leaving the room with him. He was putting his arm around her shoulders and taking her away, and he was going to show her what he had—the specifics of which Will didn't even want to think about. He dropped onto the chair next to the one Chloe had been sitting on and took a long, woeful slug of beer.

"They're perfect together, aren't they," Orin declared happily.

Say that one more time, Will thought, *and I'll perform bare-handed surgery on your nose.* "Chloe told me they broke up last winter."

"A misunderstanding," Orin said. "I guess I shouldn't go into it with you. You're obviously a friend of hers, someone she's gotten to know since the big breakup.

Maybe it's hard for you to see her with Stephen. But trust me—they're a great couple. They're going to wind up married. They just have some minor details to work out."

Yeah. Like me, for one. The notion that he was nothing more than a minor detail made him livid.

"So, I mean...I know this must be hard for you, Will, but better to find out now than later, am I right?"

"Oh, sure," he said through gritted teeth.

"I mean, how long have you known her?"

"What's today, Monday?" He swigged some beer. "Three days."

"Three days. Okay, so it's no great loss, right?"

Wrong. It was the greatest loss Will could imagine.

If Orin was going to stand on the sidelines cheering for Mr. Mucho Macho, Will was going to take him down first, and then go after his true rival. "You stole her pebbles," he said.

Orin rolled his eyes toward the ceiling and inhaled through his nose, causing his nostrils to narrow into slits. "Her pebbles."

"Yeah. You know, her cuspidor."

"Humidor."

"Whatever."

"Yes," Orin conceded, leveling his eyes to Will's once more. "I stole them."

"That's why we're here."

"Great. As long as it gets Chloe and Stephen back together."

Something nipped at the back of Will's brain. He sat up straighter. "What do you mean?"

"I mean, I filched the humidor to get her to chase me here, so she could work out things with Stephen. That's what I mean."

Will almost lunged out of his chair. It took all his will-power to keep his hands wrapped around the neck of the beer bottle when what he wanted was to wrap them around Orin's neck. "You did what?"

"Hey, look, Will—I'm sorry. You're probably a nice guy, and it's too bad you got stuck in the middle of this. But Stephen's my best friend, you know? He and I go back a skillion years. And he and Chloe had a good thing going, and when she showed him the door it was bad news all around. He loves her. They've had their ups and downs, but he loves her. He came here to the artist's colony to create a masterpiece in her honor."

"And he told you to steal her pebbles to lure her out here?"

"No. That was my idea. He didn't want to show her the sculpture until it was finished. But he's been sulking for months, and I couldn't stand it anymore. So I flew to Boston, figuring I'd try to talk her into planning a trip to Hackett for when she was finished with the Mass Bank audit."

"The what?"

"The Mass Bank audit. It's one of the biggest financial overhauls in the history of New England. Chloe's firm was asked to help straighten out their teetering accounts. The feds specifically requested Chloe for the job. They've got a lot of respect for her."

"Do they?" Why hadn't Scott warned him? Why hadn't he told Will that Chloe was a heavy hitter, a superstar of the Boston financial community?

"Anyway," Orin went on, "I got to Chloe's apartment but she was out, and I figured, what the hey? I'll steal the humidor. That'll get her out here. I even left her a note, so she'd know where she had to come to get the thing."

Will grappled with his thoughts. "You have the humidor now?"

"Sure. A pile of crapola, if you ask me. I don't know why she's so attached to it."

"She's attached to it because it's the only possession your mother left her."

"Great. A pile of pebbles. If that were all our mother left me, I'd be so insulted I'd throw the mess out."

"I understand your mother left you her money," Will said dryly. "It sounds as if your mother was a smart woman. She left each of you the thing you value most highly."

"Hey, look—don't get heavy, pal, okay?" Orin protested. "I'm broke. Chloe's rich. What do you want from me?"

"I want her," he said fiercely, shoving himself to his feet. "I want Chloe."

Orin reached out and caught his arm. "Give them a chance, at least," he implored. "Let them work it out. Stephen's getting his act together. He's doing his best work. He's my best friend."

"He isn't *my* best friend," Will retorted. "I don't care what he's getting together—I love Chloe."

"You said you've only known her three days."

"That's all the time it took to figure it out. If your best friend couldn't figure it out in two years, he blew it."

"You can't begin to understand how it is with Veronas. We're temperamental—"

Will knew that.

"And we're tight-knit—"

Unglued was more like it.

"And no woman's ever dumped Stephen before."

Chloe was an original. All the more reason for Will to love her.

"So leave them be," Orin begged. "Give them a chance."

"I'm afraid I can't do that," Will said. Stephen had already had his chance.

Now it was Will's chance.

Apparently Orin detected his iron resolve. He reluctantly let go of Will's arm and shrugged. "You're fighting a losing battle."

"It's my battle," Will said, storming out the back door.

As he stalked across the newly budding grass that stretched between the house and the barn, he contemplated the fact that he had never entered into battle over a woman before. He'd loved Peggy—but not enough to fight for her once things between them began to collapse. He'd known other women since then, but never anyone he'd felt so strongly about.

This was different. This time Chloe was at stake. And his opponent was tall, dark and handsome, with hairy pectorals and Chloe's brother on his side.

Fold, a voice whispered inside him. *The betting's gone sky-high and you're holding a pair of deuces. You can't bluff your way out of this one.*

Ignoring the whisper, ignoring his common sense, he marched boldly over to the barn, ready to wager it all.

Chapter Thirteen

I want my pebbles, she thought, bristling at the light pressure of Stephen's arm around her shoulders.

And I want Will....

After traipsing halfway across the country she wanted to confront Orin. And she wanted Will by her side when she did it, helping her through the ordeal. She wanted to know she had a partner in this mess, someone she could trust.

But Stephen was so full of his own agenda, he wouldn't let her go. He had brought her to the barn to reveal, with undue pride, a monstrous metal construction occupying the front half of the cavernous room. It stood at least twelve feet high and resembled a pyre of steel girders—rather like a skyscraper after a close encounter with a wrecking ball.

"Well?" Stephen asked enthusiastically. "What do you think?"

You really don't want to know, she replied silently.

That wasn't fair. She could spare a few charitable thoughts for her erstwhile boyfriend. He was looking good. Heaven knew how he managed to stay in such splendid shape—Chloe had never seen him exercise anything besides his prerogatives. Maybe lifting steel girders into place was all the workout he needed. He did look terrific.

Unfortunately for him, she didn't care. There was only one man she wanted to be looking at right now, and he was currently sitting in the kitchen with Orin.

"I made this for you," Stephen proclaimed. He escorted her around the base of the sculpture so she could examine, from every angle, the grotesque arrangement of metal rods. "It's not finished yet, of course."

"Of course." As if she could tell one way or the other.

"The final stage is going to include two curved bars, one here and one here—" he pointed to a section already dense with girders "—which will represent your breasts."

"My what?"

"Chloe. I told you, this sculpture is about you. It captures the essence of my feelings for you."

Apparently, the essence of his feelings for her was that she was the Eiffel Tower after an earthquake. "It doesn't look anything like me!"

"It will after I add the breasts."

Before she could even think of a reply to that, he guided her toward a ladder to the loft. "Come on," he said, "let's admire it from above."

"I can admire it from down here. And if it's all right with you, Stephen, I'd rather admire it later. Right now I've got some business to take care of with Orin."

"What could be more important than this?" he asked.

She sighed. She needed a pebble. No, she needed Will, his hand in hers and his laughter warming her.

"Stephen, I'm going back to the house."

"No," he said. "Just look at it. It's my way of talking to you, Chloe. Just like I said last winter—we could be together. I can create these sculptures—"

"And I could traipse all over the place, watching you create them." She gave him a pensive smile. "No, Stephen. We tried, but I can't be the woman you want me to be."

"We could have such good times."

Maybe. But there was more to love than good times. What about stability? What about security?

What about Will? What if there was a chance she could have stability and security and him, as well? What if, after tonight he still wanted to be with her?

Stephen tugged her arm. "Just come up and take a look. Then you can decide."

She'd decided long ago, before she had even met Will.

She craned her neck to study the loft. It was appallingly high, and it had no railing. Going up there would be like flying without an airplane. "I don't want to climb up there," she said flatly.

Ignoring her statement, Stephen nudged her ahead of him in the direction of the stepladder. She tripped on an extension cord and stumbled backward. He instantly closed his arms around her, as reflexively as a Venus's-flytrap snapping shut around a doomed bug.

"Please, Stephen."

He bowed and nuzzled her neck, the sensitive spot right below her ear—the spot Will had kissed in his sleep that night in Ohio. Will had discovered it without even trying, and with one exquisite kiss he'd made it his. When Stephen kissed her there she felt nothing more than the tickling of his damp breath on her earlobe.

"Stephen," she muttered, moving her head to one side in order to free herself. "Okay, I admit it, it's a beautiful sculpture."

"Modeled on a beautiful woman." He curved his fingers around her chin and tilted her head to expose more of her neck, as if he were a vampire in search of a vein. His lips moved with precision on her throat.

If she were with Will, she'd be on fire by now. He didn't even have to kiss her to excite her. All he had to do was look at her, with his eyes as blue as the sky and as bright as the sun. But Stephen could nuzzle her neck with every ounce of passion in him, and her heart wouldn't miss a beat.

"Come on," he said, lifting his head and loosening his arms so he could propel her toward the ladder. "Let's view it from above. It's going to take your breath away."

That was exactly what she was afraid of. Where was Will? Why didn't he come and rescue her? She didn't want to go up into that loft. It was so... so *high*.

"I'm scared of heights," she confessed, mortified by the tremor in her voice.

She expected Stephen to be a gentleman and back off. Instead, he tightened his hands at her waist and lifted her onto the first rung. "Don't worry about a thing, Chloe—I'll be right there with you."

In front of her, the ladder rose. Behind her, Stephen stood. If she didn't climb, he would press into her back and possibly—God forbid—kiss her again. Climbing was preferable.

All right, she said, scaling the damned ladder. She would go up and look at his sculpture. She would tell him it was very nice, and then she would tell him that all the sculptures in the world couldn't change the truth.

Which was?

She loved Will.

She did. She really did. That they hadn't known each other long, that Will had indicated nothing about stability or security, nothing about making a commitment to her or even to Boston...

None of it mattered. She loved Will. And it was only her utter delight at acknowledging the truth that kept her from screaming when she reached the loft and saw how far below her the barn's floor was.

Stephen strode fearlessly to the edge, his expression radiating pride. "Look at it, Chloe. Isn't it something?"

It was something, all right.

"I hate it," she said.

He pivoted to face her. "You hate it?"

"It's ugly, Stephen. Maybe that's what you think of me—that I'm ugly, angular and cold and hard. I know I have unattractive elbows—I've never thought they looked like welded steel joints, but maybe they do to you. But that thing—" she waved at the sculpture "—as far as I can tell, it hasn't got a head. *I've* got a head."

"If you had a head," he retorted, "you'd stay with me. You'd admit that you still love me. We could be a team, Chloe."

"No." She shook her head emphatically, but that made her dizzy. Holding her head steady, she took deep, regular breaths. "No, Stephen. We can't be a team."

"Give me one good reason why not."

"I'm in love with Will."

"Would you mind speaking up?" a voice arose from the direction of the double doors at the front of the barn. "I didn't hear you."

Chloe risked a fleeting glance down and spotted Will standing in the doorway. As her gaze filled with the welcome sight of him, she automatically started forward, wanting only to race into his arms. A few paces from the edge of the loft, she realized how high she was. Without a barricade. Without anything to prevent her from falling.

Vertigo buffeted her. She started to quake and sway. She closed her eyes again and sank backward. If Stephen hadn't caught her, she would have collapsed.

"Are you all right?" Will called up to her, sounding miles away.

She swallowed. Her throat slammed shut on her. If she'd had anything to eat in the past few hours she would undoubtedly be throwing up right now.

"She's fine," Stephen shouted down. "What do you think of my sculpture, Will?"

"It's ugly," said Will. Even in her queasy state, Chloe couldn't resist a weak smile. "Chloe, come on down."

"I can't." She thought she was projecting, but her voice emerged in a feeble croak.

"What have you done to her?" Will questioned Stephen.

"All I did was ask her to view things from a different perspective."

The spinning sensation started to abate. She struggled against Stephen's hold, no longer feeling the need for it. "I want to go down, Stephen," she whispered, sounding braver than she felt.

"Are you sure that's what you want?"

"I want—" *Will*, she almost said. She had already admitted out loud that she loved him, but she had no idea how he felt about her. She didn't know where he stood.

Except that it was far away and down. A fresh wave of dizziness coiled through her and she tottered slightly.

Stephen wrapped his arms around her waist. "Lean against me," he murmured. "You're looking a little chartreuse."

"I'm plain green," she argued. "Don't get artistic on me now."

"She can't handle heights," Stephen explained to Will.

"I thought it was just airplanes."

"Same thing."

"Why did you take her up there if you knew she couldn't handle it?" Will challenged.

"I didn't know she was going to get like this. She always looks so strong and confident."

Chloe *had* been strong and confident. She still was. As long as there was a chance that Will might love her, she felt she could cope with just about anything.

Except heights.

Will addressed her quietly, soothingly. "I'm right here, Chloe. If you fall, I'll catch you."

If I fall... Just hearing the words made her gag.

"You're a big help," Stephen criticized. "She's about to pass out."

"Let her pass out. Then we'll carry her down."

"Nobody's going to carry me down," she mumbled. "I'll just stay here until I feel better."

"And when will that be?" Will asked. "Next Christmas, maybe?"

She moaned and rolled her head back against Stephen's shoulder. Her neck felt flimsy, her head burdened with extra weight.

"I've got a pulley contraption up here that I use for hoisting metal rods," said Stephen. "I could probably rig the sling under her arms—"

"I'm not going down in a pulley," she flared, shoving away from him and staggering toward the ladder. She ordered herself to relax. She'd driven into a ditch and survived, hadn't she? She'd climbed under a waterfall, right? She could get down from the loft without killing herself.

Dropping to her knees, she hazarded a peek at the stepladder. Will was climbing up. "I'm right here," he said. "Don't be scared. I'm right here."

"You think this is funny, don't you?" she muttered. "You're going to be throwing this back in my face forever."

"If I have the opportunity."

"What's that supposed to mean?"

"How long is forever?"

"If I fall and break my neck, not very long."

"Come on, Chloe." He gazed at her from his perch halfway up the ladder. "Come to me. I've got your pebbles."

"Where?" She peered past him to the barn door.

"Outside. Come down and I'll give them to you."

"Bring me one."

"You don't need a pebble. You've got me."

She crawled toward him, her gaze riveted to him. His eyes were bright, encouraging, more beautifully consoling than any pebble in the humidor. She heard Stephen's footsteps behind her, felt them in the vibrations of the floorboards, but Will held her full attention. The high-wattage light bulbs overhead ignited his auburn hair with licks of red. His slender, graceful fingers beckoned. His sensual lips enticed her with a smile.

The same smile he had given her the first time they had made love.

She wanted to hear him laugh again. She wanted to hear him laugh during sex. And if she didn't get down from this godforsaken loft, she never would.

Oh, Will, I love you, she thought. She swung her legs around and felt for the top rung with her toe.

In less than an instant, it seemed, she was standing on the floor. In Will's arms. Kissing him deeply, soundly, ferociously, desperately.

He was kissing her back.

"Survival is an aphrodisiac," Stephen pontificated, as he sprung down the ladder and sidled up behind Chloe.

Will grazed her cheeks and brow. He wove his fingers lovingly through her hair. "There's a lot to be said for aphrodisiacs," he murmured before covering her mouth with his again.

Stephen cleared his throat, prompting Will to draw back. "Okay, my friend. I'm willing to be a gentleman about this."

"What does that mean?" Will countered. "Pistols at dawn?"

Their voices skimmed back and forth past Chloe, as if she weren't even there. Not that she felt obligated to join in the conversation. She was happy just to be alive, standing on her own two feet, cuddling Will and waiting for the trembling in her knees to subside.

"Chloe and I go way back," Stephen said.

"If she has no objections, I expect she and I will go way forward."

"I have no objections," she murmured.

Will planted a light kiss on the rippling wisps of hair at the crown of her head, then leaned back to gaze at her. "Do you want to go to the house?" he asked her.

"Not if it means I have to let go of you."

"You're still a little shaky, huh."

"No," she said. "I just want to hold you."

That smile again, the smile that told her he was satisfied, happy in every cell of his body. Simply seeing it caused desire to bloom within her.

"Will?"

"Yes."

"Do you think I'm crazy?"

"Let's face it, you did lose your marbles. But now you're going to have them back, so you probably won't be as crazy as you were."

She lifted her head until her gaze met his. "I really am a very good accountant."

"I won't hold that against you."

"You like me crazy, don't you," she accused.

"Crazy the way you were this morning? Absolutely."

"Would you trust me to drive your van?"

"Hmm." He gave the question intense thought before answering. "I'd trust you with my heart. I'm not so sure about my van."

"Yeah? Well, I wouldn't trust you with my humidor," she retorted, her spirit returning to its usual feisty state. "Where is it?"

"I don't know. Your brother has it."

"You told me it was right outside the barn!"

"So I exaggerated a little. It's *somewhere* outside the barn. I'm just not sure where."

"You creep!" She shoved away from him, but she was laughing too hard to offer a convincing show of anger. Turning, she saw Stephen at the other side of the barn, gazing rapturously at his sculpture, apparently oblivious to her and Will.

She had to say something to him. She hadn't meant to break his heart last December, but perhaps she had. Perhaps she was breaking it again right now. The possibility saddened her. "Stephen?"

"You know what I think?" he said, studying the sculpture intently. "I think I'm going to paint it."

"Paint it?"

"Chartreuse. The pallor you had when you were in the loft. That shade of green captured a certain essence. It spoke of the precariousness of life. What do you think?"

"I think that's a brilliant idea," she said, grinning. So much for his being heartbroken.

"And instead of 'Chloe,'" he said, "I think I'll call it 'Fate.'"

"I would consider it a great honor if you did," Chloe said, slipping her hand into Will's. They shared a grin, and then she pulled him to the door. "Come on," she said. "Let's get my humidor."

HE WOULD HAVE PREFERRED a few more moments of holding her, comforting her, feeling her all weak and trembly against him. Of course he admired her strength and fortitude. But for a few seconds there, he'd felt almost as if he'd saved her life, and he'd liked it.

She had obviously made a complete recovery, though. In fact, her brush with terror seemed to energize her. Halfway to the house, she broke from Will and charged the back door, her hands furled into fists and her chin pitched high for combat.

"Orin? Give me my humidor! And while we're at it, you owe me forty-nine ninety-five! Right now. Pay up!"

Will hesitated outside the screen door, listening to Chloe's voice booming through the house. She hollered for her brother, roared that she wasn't going to let him take advantage of her ever again, warned that if he didn't produce her pebbles and some money really fast, she was going to tar and feather him for starters, and then maybe report him to her cousin's airline for mooching free tickets.

She doesn't need me, Will thought with a heavy heart.

But didn't she cling to him in the barn, long after her legs stopped quivering and her breathing had returned to normal? He remembered the way she'd kissed him even after she'd regained her equilibrium. He remembered the way her body molded to his, and her tongue parried his, and her soul and his seemed to twine together.

She *did* need him. Not to fight her battles for her—she could do that quite nicely for herself—but to do what she couldn't do for herself—hold her and kiss her and go forward with her.

She needed him.

Smiling, he followed her into the house.

Chapter Fourteen

She was petrified.

Just hours ago, as they were driving away from Hackett and wending their way toward the interstate, Will had suddenly said, "Let's not go back yet."

And like a fool, Chloe had smiled and said, "Let's not."

Under other circumstances she would blame her agitation on the fact that Will had gotten her to agree to such an illogical escapade. But she couldn't think about how terrifying that was when she was sitting in an airplane. Right now she had more immediate fears.

An airplane. What strange power did he wield over her that he could persuade her to board an airplane?

"Where's the humidor?" she moaned. "I need a pebble."

"Here." He bent down and pulled the tote bag out from under the seat in front of him. Inside, along with what was left of their snacks, was the carved mahogany box filled with pebbles and shells. He lifted the lid and let her choose one.

She selected a black marble chip and clutched it tightly in her palm, praying for her ragged nerves to smooth out like the polished surface of the stone.

The flight attendant stood in the aisle at the front of the cabin, demonstrating how the oxygen masks worked and pointing out the emergency exists. *This is supposed to make me feel safe?* Chloe thought, squeezing her pebble in one hand and Will's hand in the other. The warmth of his palm made her aware of how icy her fingers were. She was astounded by the flight attendant's solid stance as the plane lurched and jiggled over every pit and rut in the tarmac.

"Relax," Will whispered.

"Do we really have to go to Las Vegas?" she asked querulously.

He glanced past her at the control tower gliding by their window, the markers lining the runway and the wind socks puffing on their poles. "It's a little too late to get off now."

"We should have driven," she muttered as the plane continued to taxi.

"Once we take off, you can pretend we're driving on the clouds."

"We're going to go higher than the clouds?"

"That's usually the way it's done."

"I'm going to be sick."

"You're going to be fine."

"I mean it, Will. We should have driven. Do you think the van will be safe in the airport long-term parking lot?"

"It'll be safer there than it would have been with you at the wheel."

She didn't laugh. "Are you going to play poker the whole time we're there?"

"No. I'm going to make love to you the whole time we're there."

She felt marginally better. "We could have done that in Hackett," she said with a faint smile.

"We could not. Hackett is too quiet. Everybody would have heard us."

"You do like to laugh, don't you."

"Do you have a problem with that?"

"Oh my God," she groaned, suddenly conscious of the fact that the plane wasn't jiggling and lurching over potholes anymore. "We're in the air."

"And you're still alive."

"Just barely." She stared out the window, appalled. Below her, the ground was dropping away. Teeny-tiny cars zipped past itty-bitty houses along an eensy-weensy road. Unable to bear the sight, she slid down the window shade. "Why are we doing this, Will?"

"Because . . ." His smile was so dazzling, his eyes so bright. "Because it's going to be fun."

Gazing at him was fun. Making love with him would be even more fun. Going higher than the clouds, however, did not bear the dimmest resemblance to fun in her mind.

She turned back to the window. Timidly, one millimeter at a time, she edged the shade back up. "It's all white outside," she exclaimed. "We must be in heaven. We died and went to heaven."

"We're flying through the clouds, Chloe. We're going to be above them soon."

The plane broke through the foggy layer of moisture and into a sun-glazed paradise. Above, the sky was an unbroken blue. Below stretched a cottony carpet of white. "Wow," she whispered, stunned by the sight. "We *are* in heaven."

"But we aren't dead."

"It's beautiful."

He only smiled.

"How many hours 'til we get to Las Vegas?"

"Four and a half."

"Is that all?" She was unexpectedly disappointed.

"We'll be flying back again in a couple of days."

"I know, but still..." Her grip on the marble chip relented. She leaned across his lap and dropped it into the humidor on the floor in front of him. Straightening up, she caught him watching her, his expression brimming with amusement and something more, some emotion she couldn't decipher. "I don't know why I agreed to this."

"You agreed because you couldn't stand the thought of getting back in the van and driving back to Boston."

"I like Boston."

"So do I, but you weren't ready to go back yet. Neither was I."

"Because you don't know how to begin your next book. One of us happens to be gainfully employed, Will. I've got an audit to finish by the end of this month."

"Well, aren't you important? I'm glad one of us is such a fine, upstanding citizen. I'm glad one of us has the sort of respectable position that requires wearing high heels and stockings to work."

"You don't wear high heels and stockings to work, I take it."

"Never have, never will."

She smiled and leaned toward him, about to kiss him. The plane bumped and she screamed instead.

He clamped his hand over her mouth. "Don't start."

"Shta-wha?" she said through his muzzling fingers. Her heart fluttered inside her ribs like a trapped bird beating its wings against the bars of a cage. Her vision blurred. She was certain she heard a whistling sound in her ears—the screeching rush of air as the plane fell out of the sky and plunged to earth.

"Take deep breaths."

Her eyes wide, she nodded. He cautiously eased his hand off her mouth. The plane bumped again, and she jammed her own hand to her mouth to keep from wailing.

"It's called turbulence," he said, "and it's perfectly normal."

"Anyone who can sit so calmly in his seat while a plane is doing cartwheels is perfectly *ab*normal."

"We all have our faults."

She gave him a skeptical look. "Well, I'm glad you're letting me find out about yours before it's too late."

"It's already too late, Chloe."

He undoubtedly meant that it was too late for her to abandon the plane. But she found a deeper truth in his statement: it was too late to stop loving him. She was already so madly, deeply attached to him, even his tranquility while the plane barnstormed across the continent couldn't make her stop loving him.

"Close your eyes," he murmured, reaching across her to press the button that adjusted the back of her seat. He lowered his own seat back until it was level with hers, then guided her head down onto his shoulder. "Close your eyes and rest, Chloe. When you wake up, we'll be in Las Vegas."

"Or in heaven," she grumbled, nestling her head against him and closing her eyes.

"Or both."

HIS GAZE JOURNEYED across her serene face, her lips slightly parted, her hair a glorious mop of brown curls, her eyes closed. Her chest rose and fell in a steady rhythm as she dozed. Her left hand lay tucked within his right, and her right hand rested on his wrist, her opal ring catching a rainbow in the sunlight pouring through the window. A flight attendant paused and asked if he wanted a drink. He shook his head and waved her off.

He'd never had to fight for a woman before. He'd never wanted to. Until now. Until Chloe. He'd fought—and he'd won, and the thrill of victory was sweeter and more precious than he could have imagined.

They would arrive in Las Vegas at around six-thirty, mountain time. They would have all day there tomorrow, and then Thursday they'd fly back to Minnesota, pick up his van and make tracks back to Boston so she would have a shot at making a 9:00 a.m. appearance at her office the following Monday. Forty-eight hours in Las Vegas on a whim.

I overdosed on whimsy when I was a kid, she'd said that first night, as they'd begun their trip. And he'd said, *Whimsy isn't my thing, either.*

This wasn't whimsy. He felt as if they were starting all over again, starting something new. If this was a date, it wasn't a blind one. He was heading off into the unknown with his eyes open, his vision clear.

This must be love, he thought, wondering whether she had the same vision of it, same concept of where they were going. Las Vegas was their destination. What was their destiny?

At the very worst, they would have fun. They'd cruise the casinos, maybe take in a show, eat at an elegant restaurant, laugh at the city's gaudiness. Then they would fly back to Minnesota, drive east to Boston, and kiss goodbye.

No. He just couldn't do that. He couldn't kiss her goodbye.

So, it didn't make sense. So what? If they were sensible, they wouldn't have driven to Minnesota in the first place.

It might not be sensible, but it was right.

He only hoped Chloe saw it the same way.

"THIS IS LAS VEGAS?" she asked, surveying the garish baggage-claim area, with its array of slot machines along the wall.

"This is the airport."

"In other words, we're back on the ground."

"Yes, Chloe. We made it. Do you want to kiss the earth?"

"No. I'll kiss you, instead," she said, touching her lips to his cheek. She felt reborn—and incredibly lucky. The plane hadn't crashed; she was in one piece.

Will carried their suitcases, Chloe the tote bag, and they left the terminal. Outside, the air was uncomfortably hot and dry.

My God, she thought, *I'm in a desert.* She had let Will put her on a plane and fly her to a desert. Just because she loved him.

And what had he done for her? For him to take a plane trip didn't prove a thing. What measure did she have that he felt anything akin to what she felt?

He flagged down a cab and they got in. "Where to?" the cabbie asked.

"I don't know," Will said. "The strip, I guess." He settled back in the seat and looped his arm around her.

"What hotel are you folks staying at?" the driver asked.

"We haven't got a reservation," Will said. "Do you know of a place that's clean and moderately priced where we could get a room? It doesn't have to be fancy."

"Oh, sure, there's lots of motels. Not too glamorous, but the casinos are within walking distance."

Chloe stared out the window. The landscape was flat and barren, stressing a color scheme of brown and brown. Her father would have loved painting this scenery.

"Are you sure you aren't a high-stakes gambler?" she asked Will nervously.

He touched his lips to hers. "If you're talking about money, no."

She gazed into his blue eyes. "What about if I'm not talking about money?"

He contemplated his answer. "Accepting the opera tickets from Scott was the biggest gamble I ever took."

"It was a blind date, Will. Not a gamble."

He smiled enigmatically. "Don't be so literal, Chloe. Think big."

If she thought big she would probably scare herself. She had just stepped off an airplane. She didn't think she could handle anything bigger than that right now.

"So, this is a gamble, huh."

"What do you think?"

His question held a challenge. Not knowing how to answer it, she parried it with another question of her own: "Do you ever lose?"

Again that enigmatic smile, that mysterious light in his eyes. "Sometimes. But right now...I feel like a winner."

They passed subdivisions of houses, shops, mini-malls. Larger buildings. Casinos. Neon-encrusted buildings, flashing, electronically blazing facades. "Good God," she gasped. "Nevada must use more electricity than the whole rest of the country put together."

"Possibly," said Will.

"It's not even dark out yet, and every single light bulb in town is turned on."

"Did Boris want to marry you?"

The abrupt question made Chloe flinch. Suddenly she saw none of the frenetic gaudiness outside the cab's windows. All she saw was Will. "He didn't come right out and propose," she told him. "But he sort of sounded as if he might be heading in that direction."

"And you turned him down?"

"I broke up with him months ago. Why would I want to marry him now?"

"Why did you break up with him, Chloe? Because he was an artist?"

He sounded insecure. She couldn't believe that Will Turner could be insecure. Yet he was—and it made her love him even more. "I broke up with Stephen," she said, "because we were a lousy match."

"He's a good-looking guy."

"So?"

The driver turned off the strip and onto a side road, which was measurably less neon-lit. He passed two motels, then steered into the third. "This is a nice place," he told them. "My sister happens to be the manager."

"Have they got a bridal suite?" Will asked as he opened the door. "Chloe and I are used to bridal suites."

"Every suite here's a bridal suite," the driver assured them, motioning with his head toward a small white stucco building across the street, with a neon sign reading Dearly Beloved Matrimonial Center.

Chloe stared at the sign. Something rattled inside her—not her heart against her ribs this time, but something else. Something deeper. Something inside her soul.

Something so dangerous that flying in an airplane seemed like a cinch in comparison.

She closed herself to it, refused to acknowledge its existence.

The driver carried their bags into the motel's front office, gave the woman on duty a brotherly bear hug, and said, "Set these folks up in a good room. They're in love."

One of us is, anyway, Chloe sighed. Watching as Will filled out the registration card, she wondered about him. He was in a pensive mood, less talkative than usual, curiously somber.

She thought they'd come to Las Vegas because she'd never been there before and because Will liked to play cards, and because they simply weren't ready to go home and resume their old lives yet. She thought that once she had her humidor back she could face anything. When she'd said "Why not?" that morning, she'd been feeling brave.

She didn't feel so brave anymore. She felt nervous. Shakier than she'd felt at forty thousand feet.

So in love, it scared her.

She wished she knew what Will was thinking.

The room was fine—nondescript but clean. After setting down the bags beside the double bed, Will headed for the bathroom. He only peeked inside, though. "No heart-shaped tub," he reported with spurious dismay.

"Is there a shower?" she asked, then blushed. Then smiled when she saw the way Will was smiling.

She knew what he was thinking right now. Thinking the same thing, she glided into his open arms.

HE PULLED THE CURTAINS back and stared through the window. Nighttime in Las Vegas was almost as bright as daytime, with all the glaring lights reflecting against the sky, turning it a pale lavender.

He was looking at only one light, though, the one across the street. The one that said Dearly Beloved Matrimonial Center.

"Will?" she called from the bed.

He turned and let the curtain drop back into place. His eyes gradually adjusted to the room's darkness. He saw her shape against the white linens, the shadow of her hair curling across the pillow, the enticing slopes of her shoulders, the contours of her breasts under the top sheet.

"Why are you up?" she asked.

He crossed to the bed and slid under the sheet beside her. "Las Vegas never sleeps."

"If you want to go to a casino, Will—"

"I told you, I didn't come here to play cards."

"Do you want to play roulette?"

"I want to play with you," he said, tracing her collarbone with his fingertips, and then her breasts. The sound of her breath catching turned him on as much as the velvety texture of her skin, as her feminine fragrance, as the instantaneous stiffening of her nipple as he twirled his thumb over it.

She curved her hand around the back of his neck and drew him down for a kiss. Her lips were delectably, irresistibly sweet, but he didn't linger. "I take that back, Chloe. I don't want to play with you."

"Oh." She looked absurdly hurt.

"I love you." There. He'd said it to her. Actually spoken the words. In English. And meant them.

The ceiling didn't come crashing down on him. Chloe didn't laugh at him. She simply gazed up at him, her eyes dark and resonant and spellbinding.

"We could get married," he said. "Right now, if we wanted."

She continued to gaze at him. She said nothing.

Her silence shook him. This was the highest wager he'd ever made—and now he had to lie there, waiting for her to decide whether to see him or fold.

"Is that why you brought me here?"

"I don't know. Maybe. Subconsciously."

"You subconsciously want to marry me?"

"No. That part's conscious."

She studied his face, solemn despite her smile. "If we get married, we'll never have to go on blind dates again."

"That's a good enough reason for me."

"I always wanted a big wedding," she confessed. "With a fancy white gown like Barbie's in the dream-wedding collection."

"We could get married here, and then we could have a big wedding back in Boston. I have no objection to marrying you more than once."

"Is that legal?"

"Sure. This would be a civil ceremony. We can do a church ceremony later."

"With your parents and your brothers? And Orin and my cousins and my Aunt Mathilda?"

"You have an Aunt Mathilda? I can't marry someone with an Aunt Mathilda." She poked him in the ribs until he laughed. "Okay. I'll marry you, in spite of your Aunt Mathilda."

"She has lousy taste in perfume."

"Now it all comes out. Forget it. Let's just live in sin for the next fifty years."

"No," she said. "I want a long white dress, with lots of lace."

"And a plunging neckline?"

"And you'll wear a tux."

He sighed. "If it makes you happy."

"A big traditional wedding, with flowers and champagne and Adrienne and Scott as our matron of honor and best man..."

Oh, brother—was she on a roll or what? If he had known she was going to turn this thing into a big extravaganza straight out of the pages of *Bride* magazine, he wouldn't have asked.

Yes he would have. In an instant. She wanted a big wedding and a Barbie dress? Then that was what they'd do.

"I might have to have one of my brothers as best man," he said. "And while we're at it, we should probably let Orin be an usher. Which means we're going to wind up paying for his tuxedo."

"If I know Orin, we'll wind up paying for his wedding present to us, too."

"As long as it isn't a spray gun." He was smiling. His hand continued to move on her smooth, alluring skin, gliding down to her tummy, down between her legs. "We'll have one of those big weddings. Whatever you want."

With a helpless groan, she closed her eyes and arched against him for a moment. Then she curled her fingers around his wrist and drew his hand away. She waited until her breath was less erratic before she attempted to speak. "I love you, Will."

"What a relief. I wouldn't want to wear a tux for someone who didn't love me."

"You don't need to wear a tux," she said. Her eyes seemed to pierce the shadows, sending waves of emotion directly into him. "We can elope. We can get hitched right across the street. Right now, if you want."

"Not this minute," he whispered. "I don't think I could get my pants closed."

"Later, then. After breakfast."

"Before breakfast," he resolved, dipping his fingers into her and watching in delight as she gasped, as she moaned and twisted beneath him.

She sighed happily. "This is crazy."

"No, Chloe." He slid back the sheets and flicked his tongue over first one taut nipple and then the other. "This is sex."

"I mean, our getting married."

"Maybe a little," he allowed. "But so what? This is actually the start of the greatest adventure the world has ever known. Trust me."

"You know, every time you say that you wind up getting us in trouble."

"Am I getting you in trouble now?"

"The best kind," she sighed, clasping his head in her hands and guiding his lips to hers. "The best kind there is."

Smiling, he rose onto her. His body found hers and unlocked it, and he lost himself in the sheer pleasure of loving her. *She trusts me,* he thought. *She really does.*

He laughed, and so did she.

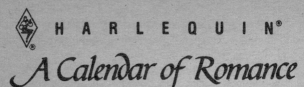

H A R L E Q U I N®

A Calendar of Romance

Be a part of American Romance's year-long celebration of love and the holidays of 1992. Celebrate those special times each month with your favorite authors.

Next month, it's an explosion of springtime flowers and new beginnings in

APRIL						
S	M	T	W	T	F	S
			1	2	3	4
5	6	7	8	9	10	11
12	13	14	15	16	17	18
19	20	21	22	23	24	25
	27	28	29	30		

#433 A MAN FOR EASTER
by Stella Cameron

Read all the books in *A Calendar of Romance,* coming to you one per month, all year, only in American Romance.

If you missed #421 HAPPY NEW YEAR, DARLING, #425 VALENTINE HEARTS AND FLOWERS, and #429 FLANNERY'S RAINBOW and would like to order them, send your name, address and zip or postal code along with a check or money order for $3.29 for #421 and #425 or $3.39 for #429 plus 75¢ postage and handling ($1.00 in Canada) *for each book ordered,* payable to Harlequin Reader Service, to:

In the U.S.
3010 Walden Avenue
P.O. Box 1325
Buffalo, NY 14269-1325

In Canada
P.O. Box 609
Fort Erie, Ontario
L2A 5X3

Please specify book title(s) with your order.
Canadian residents add applicable federal and provincial taxes.

COR4

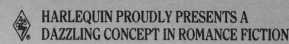

HARLEQUIN PROUDLY PRESENTS A
DAZZLING CONCEPT IN ROMANCE FICTION

One small town,
twelve terrific love stories

JOIN US FOR A YEAR IN THE FUTURE OF TYLER

Each book set in Tyler is a self-contained love story; together,
the twelve novels stitch the fabric of the community.

LOSE YOUR HEART TO TYLER!

Join us for the second TYLER book, BRIGHT HOPES, by
Pat Warren, available in April.

*Former Olympic track star Pam Casals arrives in Tyler to
coach the high school team. Phys ed instructor Patrick
Kelsey is first resentful, then delighted. And rumors fly about
the dead body discovered at the lodge.*

If you missed the first title, WHIRLWIND, and would like to order it, send your name, address, zip or postal code, along with a check or money order for $3.99 plus 75¢ postage and handling ($1.00 in Canada), payable to Harlequin Reader Service to:

In the U.S.
3010 Walden Avenue
P.O. Box 1325
Buffalo, NY 14269-1325

In Canada
P.O. Box 609
Fort Erie, Ontario
L2A 5X3

Please specify book title(s) with your order.
Canadian residents add applicable federal and provincial taxes.

TYLER-2

Following the success of **WITH THIS RING**, Harlequin cordially invites you to enjoy the romance of the wedding season with

BARBARA BRETTON
RITA CLAY ESTRADA
SANDRA JAMES
DEBBIE MACOMBER

A collection of romantic stories that celebrate the joy, excitement, and mishaps of planning that special day by these four award-winning Harlequin authors.

Available in April at your favorite Harlequin retail outlets.

THTH